CONSPIRACY OF SILENCE

When the lovely young Lizbeth Crawford walks into Joe Scintilla's office in late 1936, she tells him a curious story: she is convinced that her father, the wealthy industrialist James Allen Crawford, did not kill his brother Frank, even though Crawford confessed to the murder and is determined to serve out his sentence in Rahway State Prison. Is Crawford shielding someone? Why are both his mother and his wife happy to have him locked up in prison? And why did Frank's fiancée, Eva Dailey, commit suicide shortly after his death?

The case leads Scintilla to probe the baffling dynamics of the Crawford family of Pompton Lakes, New Jersey, and to investigate not only the circumstances of a decade-old murder, but also the mind of its self-confessed perpetrator—a man who feels honorbound to rot in prison for a murder he may not have committed.

CONSPIRACY OF SILENCE

A JOE SCINTILLA MYSTERY

S. T. JOSHI

THE BORGO PRESS
MMXI

CONSPIRACY OF SILENCE

CONSPIRACY OF SILENCE

CONTENTS

CHAPTER ONE

When that blonde bombshell walked into my office, the last thing I was thinking about was crime.

It was a crisp day in November. The year was 1936. My office had been empty for days, so I was just sitting back, feet on the desk, still chortling over FDR's crushing defeat of the hapless Alf Landon in the presidential election two days before. (Oh, yeah—there was also a third-party candidate, one William Lemke, a stooge of Father Coughlin and Francis E. "Share the Wealth" Townsend, but no one paid much attention to *him*.) I had half toyed with voting for Norman Thomas, but figured it would be a waste of effort. FDR had, in his first term, craftily steered a middle ground between the mossbacks of the Republican Party, all screaming that he was leading the country down the path to a socialist hell, and the firebrands on the left, like Townsend and the late and unlamented Huey Long. No one had expected the *extent* of FDR's victory: Landon couldn't even win his home state of Kansas, managing only to snag the conservative New England states of Maine and Vermont.

But back to the blonde bombshell.

Practically everyone who walks through my door seems shy and hesitant, and this broad was no different. After all, who needs a private investigator except someone wanting the dirt on a cheating spouse, or the dope on a missing relative, or some way he or she can skirt the law or get out of a jam? Add to that the fact that, once you open that door, you come face to face with me and not some kindly and smiling receptionist? The

New Deal had done some good, but not enough for me to hire back my Nellie. She had, I'm sure, long ago gone to greener pastures.

So here I was, face to face with a tall, slender, fur-covered dish (it was cold outside) whose large green eyes and spots of color on her cheeks made it clear she wanted to be anywhere but here. Before even speaking a word, she was breathing heavily.

Maybe I'm not the most reassuring guy in the world. I don't have what is called the avuncular manner. I just want to get down to business, whether it's with a slip of a girl like this (she couldn't be more than eighteen) or a hardened ex-con trying to escape one more trip to the hoosegow.

So I didn't do anything but look at her. She looked back at me—for a moment—then looked away.

Finally she spoke. "Are you . . . are you Mr. Scintilla?"

I took pity on her. In my gentlest voice I said, "Yeah, I'm Joe Scintilla. What can I do for you?"

That seemed harmless enough, but the babe reacted as if I'd electrocuted her. Her eyes got even bigger, her breathing even more stertorous, those bright spots on her cheek even more scarlet.

"Just sit down, ma'am, and relax," I said. "Take your coat off."

She did so. And it was my turn to turn bug-eyed.

This lady was built. No flat-chested flapper-style for this piece of work—that was so *passé*. She had a good figure and she knew it—knew also that the long black dress that hugged her form was just the thing to set men's hearts and minds aflame. If that fur coat hadn't told as much, that dress and the various trinkets of jewelry that ornamented her ears, neck, and wrists stated in no uncertain terms that she was no pauper. That might be good news for me, since it's hard to get money out of paupers.

Placing her fur over the back of the chair, she sat down. She still said nothing. I looked at her. She looked at me.

Finally: "I'm Lizbeth Crawford." She paused—as if expecting

me to recognize that name. When I made no response, she went on:

"My father was—er, is James Allen Crawford."

I looked up sharply. *Him* I'd heard of, although the details were now vague. A scandal of some kind a dozen or more years ago . . . a murder trial . . . something like that. Wealthy guy—family had made money in rubber, being one of the early suppliers for Henry Ford's motorcars. I didn't know whether the guy was dead or alive—and neither, it seemed, did his daughter.

She failed to meet my gaze when I looked at her. All she did was clutch her handbag and look down at her feet. At last she raised her head and said:

"He's in Rahway State Prison for the murder of his brother, my uncle Frank—Frank Crawford," she said in a small voice. Then, without warning, she cried:

"But he didn't do it!"

Those rosy blotches on her cheeks had now suffused her whole face. She looked at me almost truculently, as if daring me to deny her utterance.

But all I said was: "What makes you say that?"

I had spoken quietly, but it's as if I'd slapped her in the face. I thought she would break down and cry. I really don't like women crying in my office.

I was starting to remember more of the case. It had been a fairly big deal, not only because it came on the heels of the notorious Leopold and Loeb case, but because it had involved such a prominent and wealthy businessman. It had also ended the same way: although Crawford didn't have a Clarence Darrow to save him from the chair, he had pleaded guilty and gotten a stiff prison sentence. Unlike Leopold and Loeb, he hadn't killed merely for sport—it was believed to be a crime of passion of some kind. But at this point the details became hazy—for me, at any rate.

So, as a way of getting this dame to cough up what she knew—and, more importantly, what I could possibly do about it—I said, "Didn't Mr. Crawford confess, or something?"

She let out an immense sigh—the kind of sigh you give when a particularly dense schoolboy continually gives you the wrong answer to an easy question.

"Yes, he confessed," she said, "but that means nothing. I *know* he didn't do it!"

I said nothing but just raised my eyebrows a fraction of an inch. Even that mild expression of skepticism seemed to have the desired effect, for she finally spilled the beans.

"Look, Mr. Scintilla, I just turned eighteen last week. As a result of that, I've . . . I've come into some money from my trust fund. So I have as much money as you could possibly ask for to prove . . . to show that my father didn't commit this crime."

I replied coolly. "I don't doubt your ability to pay, Miss Crawford, but it's hard to prove a negative." I didn't study philosophy at Johns Hopkins for nothing. "If your father didn't kill your uncle, someone else did. And not only that—"

But she didn't let me finish. Seizing on my words, she reached into her handbag and slapped down on my desk a stiff sheet of paper, with some typewritten names on it. "There!" she cried, as if that proved her case.

I looked down quickly at the paper, then back at her. "What is this?"

"That's a list of people who were at a party when my uncle Frank died . . . was killed, on March 19, 1924. I was only about five and a half, but I got that list from my mother. One of them had to have done it!" She glared at me with those big green eyes of hers.

This was all getting a bit strange. In the first place, the idea of investigating a twelve-year-old murder didn't seem like the most profitable use of my time—except in the crude sense that I could bill this dame for a lot of legwork that would probably go nowhere. And in the second place . . . well, I couldn't put it more bluntly than I did.

"But Miss Crawford, *your father confessed to the murder.* Why would he do that? Why would he spend more than a decade—and, I imagine, the prospect of several more decades—

in the penitentiary for a crime he didn't commit? What's in it for him?"

Her eyes turned to glints of adamant.

"That's what I want you to find out."

CHAPTER TWO

Over dinner at Lüchow's—her choice, and her tab—I at last got a bit more out of Lizbeth.

"Since I was so young when . . . when all this happened," she said a little breathlessly, "I don't of course remember much. A lot of what I know I've learned from my mother, and my grandmother, and . . . and from visiting my father in prison."

She looked up at me between mouthfuls of a chef salad. Those pleading, little-lost-girl eyes could make many men believe just about anything she wanted.

"There really isn't a kinder, gentler, more loving person in the world than my father. There's just no way he could have committed this crime, even in the heat of passion." Her expression turned a little darker, even though I'd said nothing and, as far as I knew, my own countenance didn't change one iota. "I know what you're going to say . . . 'Mafia dons are kind to their children, too. And what evidence do you have? Where's the evidence?'"

She wasn't a bad mind-reader.

"OK, maybe I don't have much hard evidence, but I know what's in my heart, and I know what's in my father's heart. He's hiding something, protecting someone, covering up something. . . . Something's not right here. And my mother and grandmother are no help: it's as if they *want* him to stay in prison!"

Her outrage heightened her color again. I won't deny that, pale or flushed, she was nice to look at. The primal male in me wanted to do nothing but wrap her in my arms and defend her to the death . . . but the sensible businessman said, *Let's go slow here and see how this plays out. Maybe she's right, maybe she's wrong. But I need something to go on.*

She continued. "Our family is probably the best example anyone's ever come up with that money doesn't buy happiness." She let out another big sigh, but this one had a certain element of self-pity in it. After I'd heard her story, I concluded she had more than a little reason for self-pity. "We made lots of money in rubber, and my grandparents bought a nice tract of land in Pompton Lakes, New Jersey, not long after it was set up as a borough in 1895. They built a big house there—it's where I still live, although maybe that won't last much longer. . . ."

I didn't know what she meant by that: Was she about to get married? Or was her digging up this old matter of her father's murder case going to lead her family to ostracize her?

"My father had two brothers—Bill, two years older, and Frank, three years younger. Bill was killed in the war, in early 1918, several months before I was born. My grandmother was able to pull strings and get my father and Frank out of military service—my grandfather had had contacts with the Army and the National Guard and, and so Grandma was able to convince them that her two sons were needed to help with the family business, which in fact was providing rubber for Army planes and jeeps.

"After the war, my parents gave me the best possible upbringing." Possibly I had looked askance at that, for she burst forth with: "I don't mean money! Sure, we had money, but what they gave me was love and comfort. I never felt I was 'privileged'—just loved and cherished. I could tell you so many stories about how my father would come home from a hard day's work and seek me out—even before he greeted my mother—and take me on piggy-back rides all around the house, or bring me toys—nothing costly, just little things he'd picked up at a five-and-dime—or read me stories . . ."

She choked up a bit. "Sure, nothing special, nothing that any father wouldn't do for his daughter . . . but I *felt* special, and I got more love out of him than . . ."

She paused abruptly and didn't finish the thought.

"I'm trying to figure out what the relationship between my father and his brothers was. I have to believe—I'll tell you about that later" (she gave me a quick and rather nervous look and quickly turned away)—"that it's somehow connected with . . . with what happened. As I say, my uncle Bill was killed in the war, and my father was crushed—it took him years to recover, I'm told. He revered Bill, as the eldest brother and the future leader of the family. My father's always had the greatest respect for the family line, and he'll do anything to protect the family from shame and scandal . . ."

I didn't have to raise my eyebrow more than a fraction of an inch before she exploded:

"I know what you're going to say! But I'm *sure* this whole business is some kind of cover-up—as I said before, it's like he's shielding someone . . . or something. That's why you just *have* to find out what's behind it all. . . ."

The look she gave me was so appealing, almost frenzied, that I figured I'd best say something. I long ago became aware that in being a private investigator you have to be part detective and part psycho-analyst—and maybe part father confessor also.

"Listen, Lizbeth, I'll do everything in my power to help . . . to get behind this business. There seem to be some . . . peculiarities that need to be explored. But you gotta give me something more to go on."

"I know that." For a few moments she fished through her handbag, looking for something, then abruptly stopped.

"Listen, you have to understand what it was like with my father and Uncle Frank. I'm not sure *I* understand, but I've heard things. . . . It's hard to imagine two brothers being so different. With Uncle Bill dead, my father felt that the whole weight of the family—including the family business—fell on his shoulders. And he knew that Frank was a pretty thin reed as far as that went. As the youngest son, Frank was . . . well, a bit irresponsible. Just wanted to have a good time. Was very fond of the ladies, I hear—couldn't keep away from the skirts." She blushed and went on quickly. "And Frank couldn't care less about the rubber business—so long as it gave him enough money for him to do what he liked."

At this point Lizbeth slapped on the table—our dinner was long finished—that sheet of paper she had shown me at my office. It was a list of the people who had been in the house on the night of the murder (or, shall we say, the death) of Frank Crawford, and it looked uncannily like the cast of a play:

PEOPLE PRESENT AT THORNLEIGH HOUSE
MARCH 19, 1924

James Allen Crawford (my father)
Frank Crawford (my uncle)
Florence Bisland Crawford (my mother)
Helen Ward Crawford (my grandmother)
Eva Dailey (Frank's fiancée)
Daniel and Norma Bisland (my mother's brother and sister-in-law)
Dr. Nathan Granger (the family physician)

Lizbeth somewhat sheepishly mentioned that Thornleigh was the name the family had given to their house in Pompton Lakes. The look she gave me—and the look I must have given back—made it pretty evident what she left unspoken: "I know, not many Americans give names to their houses—only those who want to pretend they're some kind of aristocracy . . . ."

In any event, some items on the list were of immediate interest, not to mention one overriding query that had to be settled at the start.

"So why were all these people there at all at this time?" I asked.

"Well," said Lizbeth, "of course my father and mother, Uncle Frank, and Grandma lived there. Mama's brother and his wife were visiting—they'd been there a week or more, I think. It was just a dinner party—I think my father had arranged it."

I looked down at the list again.

"So Frank was engaged to be married?" I said.

For some reason Lizbeth colored a deep scarlet. "Well, I suppose. I'm not sure. . . . We all thought they would marry, but, as I just mentioned, Frank was a bit of a playboy . . . I guess he wasn't certain whether he wanted to be tied down so soon. I think"—her voice descended to a whisper—"I think he had some other . . . involvements also. I'm not sure whether Eva knew about them. Frank invited her, just to round out the party to make it an even eight."

"And what about this doctor guy? Is it customary to invite the family physician over for dinner?"

Lizbeth shrugged. "I don't know. He was a friend of the family—he'd been with us for years. He treated my grandfather in his final illness, a decade or so earlier."

It was my turn to let out a sigh.

"So you think one of these people—not your father, I mean— did the deed? Seems a bit risky to have done it with all these people about. Do you know any details of the . . . the death?"

She shrugged again—it was almost a shiver. "Not many. Remember, I was there too—even though I was only about five and a half. I just remember some commotion in the downstairs study, and Dad coming out of the room with this strange, frozen look on his face and saying that he'd just killed his brother. Said his brother had been making advances toward . . . toward my mother." She looked down at her lap.

Gently I said: "Is that true?"

She looked up quickly, eyes blazing. "How do I know? I was five! They won't tell me anything . . ." Suddenly she seemed like a little girl, resentful of being excluded from adult affairs that didn't concern her.

"What does your mother say?"

"Well, of course she denies it—says it was all in my father's head . . ."

"Don't you believe her?" This too was spoken gently.

In a small voice Lizbeth said: "I don't know what to believe . . . anymore."

I leaned back in my chair. There were a few glints of light, and perhaps a few avenues of exploration, but I was still fumbling largely in the dark.

"So, Lizbeth, what do you want me to do? Would it do any good to talk to your father?"

She gave me an exasperated frown. "I doubt it. He just sticks to his story. 'I killed Frank, I killed Frank.' He's just been stuck in that prison for twelve years, and he looks terrible now . . . doesn't even seem to be my father anymore." Her eyes were glistening. "I'm the only one who ever visits him. My mother and grandmother never go—*never*. And even I am finding it a bit hard . . . he's so unhappy, and he's hiding something . . . carrying some horrible weight on his shoulders." The tears were falling now. "If we can just find out what it is, maybe he can get better."

"Maybe." I patted her hand gently. Then:

"What about this Eva Dailey? Maybe I could talk to her. She must know something."

Lizbeth's face froze, and she turned away from me.

"Well, that might be difficult. . . . You see, Eva killed herself about three months after Uncle Frank died."

CHAPTER THREE

Now I had something to go on.

If what Lizbeth had told me was even roughly accurate, then one obvious scenario became immediately evident: Eva had killed Frank Crawford (somehow), perhaps out of jealousy (maybe Frank had in fact been fooling around with his own sister-in-law), perhaps merely out of his apparent disinclination to commit himself to her; then, out of remorse, she had taken her own life.

Problems with this scenario still abounded. It seemed incredibly risky to have done the deed at a time when so many other people were at Thornleigh. In any case, if James Crawford had actually set up the party and Eva was just a last-minute addition on Frank's part, she would have to have worked pretty fast to seize the opportunity to knock off her hoped-for fiancé.

And then there was the overriding matter of why James—I got the impression nobody ever called him Jim or Jimmy—had decided to take the rap for her. He too had acted quickly, wasting no time in telling the cops he was responsible. What could have possessed him to do that? Was that his bizarre way of protecting the family name? How was it any less scandalous to admit to killing your own brother—and spending much of the rest of your life in prison—than to allow his resentful sweetheart to serve time for the act?

Well, some of these points were queries for another day. Right now I had some fairly concrete leads to follow, and the best place to start was the police station in Pompton Lakes, New

Jersey.

As I headed out in my well-used Chevy roadster, across the George Washington Bridge into the wilds of New Jersey, I felt I was heading back into a past that had already come to seem ancient. This case would take me into an era that, after seven years of a depression, already seemed as remote as Thebes or Babylon. In 1924 I was barely out of Johns Hopkins, looking out upon a world that seemed to have endless possibilities. I didn't waste any sympathy on the sudden and unexpected death of our sainted president, Warren G. Harding, the year before—it turned out he had the good luck to die before the Teapot Dome scandal dragged him into its clutches. My pal Henry Mencken was riding high, lambasting all and sundry with cheerful vitriol—nothing like the dour, furiously anti-FDR curmudgeon he had now become. Sinclair Lewis was still basking in the glory of his best-selling novels, *Main Street* and *Babbitt.* Fitzgerald had yet to publish *The Great Gatsby,* Dreiser hadn't come out with that behemoth called *An American Tragedy* (who ever heard of a two-volume novel?), the world had never heard of John Thomas Scopes, flat-chested flappers were everywhere . . . and so were jobs.

Casting my mind back to that spring of 1924, I remembered that Doug Fairbanks Jr. was working on that Oriental extravaganza called *The Thief of Baghdad*—and (as Mencken told me) had to hire the poet George Sterling to write captions, for of course there were no talkies. Valentino was still alive and causing ladies to swoon, Chaplin was riding high, even though trouble was looming with his ill-advised fling with the sixteen-year-old Lita Grey; and everyone was singing "Everybody Loves My Baby" and "Riverboat Shuffle."

Not everything was a song and dance, of course. After five years, people were already beginning to have second thoughts about Prohibition. It wasn't merely the fact that the Mob had quickly taken over the bootlegging business; it was that corruption on every level—from federal judges to state legislatures to police officers to Prohibition enforcement agents—was turning just about everyone into overt and unashamed lawbreakers. More and more people were coming around to thinking that that high-pressure arm-twisting group, the Anti-Saloon League, was as bad as the Mafia. Even though evading the Volstead Act had become a kind of game for many, the 18th Amendment had turned the country into something not far from a police state.

As for me, I kicked around New York City for a couple of years before deciding that I didn't like any boss except myself—and sometimes I didn't like him either. Silent Cal Coolidge was about to come up with that priceless gem of homespun wisdom—"The chief business of the American people is business"—but he also would thank his stars he got off this planet before he and his successor, Let 'Em Starve Hoover, reaped the harvest of their "rugged individualism" and let the country and the world into the worst depression in history. Wall Street had been given a license to engage in legalized gambling, and that's just what it did—but no one seemed to mind so long as the money kept rolling in.

Well, there was no use being bitter. I may not have my secretary anymore, but I still had a job, which was more than I could say for those luckless guys selling apples on the street. In 1924 nobody thought it would ever come to that; and the Crawfords of the Crawford Tire and Rubber Company had no reason to think that their palatial life at Thornleigh wouldn't go on forever.

Pompton Lakes proved to be a town—maybe even a village—not far from Wayne. If it had more than three thousand people, I'd be surprised. Thornleigh was well north of the town proper, on a slight acclivity overlooking the body of water that gave the town its name; but I wasn't interested in the house just yet. The town itself seemed a mix of *nouveau riche* and down-and-out. I suspected that any recent population growth had occurred in the latter.

The police station lay conveniently in the center of town, and I had little difficulty finding it. I had no idea how the police chief would react to my request to examine police records of a decade or more ago, but I figured there was no harm in asking.

The sergeant, after learning what I wanted, led me blandly into the chief's office. The door to his office announced him as one Frederick Taber.

Taber looked at my card, then met my gaze with the blankest expression I've ever seen. "What's your interest in this case, Scintilla?"

I said: "I'm working on behalf of Miss Lizbeth Crawford. She thinks she has some evidence to exonerate her father, James Allen Crawford." This was a bit of a stretch, but it made my case for examining the files a bit more compelling.

"The matter was pretty well settled, I thought," Taber offered.

"Miss Crawford doesn't seem to think so."

Again that blank look from Taber.

I went on: "Do you remember anything of the case?"

For the first time, Taber's face showed something that could be called an emotion. What was it?—nervousness? fear? doubt? suspicion? Whatever it was, it took him a while to say: "Well, can't say as I do."

"You don't remember a murder case involving the most prominent family in town?" I said incredulously.

That made him angry. "No, I don't remember, mac. I wasn't here!"

Quietly I said: "Where were you?"

Maybe that remark sounded sarcastic, although it wasn't meant to be. Taber got even madder when he said: "I wasn't the police chief at the time! I wasn't even in the area. I transferred here from Connecticut five years ago. It wasn't my call!"

I needed to calm the guy down. "OK, OK, Mr. Taber. I'm not blaming you for anything. I just want to see the records. There's no harm in that, is there?"

Taber seemed embarrassed by his outburst, and he looked a bit sheepish. "Sure, there's no harm. Go ahead."

I told him I'd like to see the records both for the death of Frank Crawford and the apparent suicide of Eva Dailey. He shrugged and pointed to a file cabinet where, he said, all that I could want would be filed under each name.

The Crawford file seemed awfully thin. The police had been called to Thornleigh on the evening of March 19, 1924, about 10:30 P.M., when a telephone call—it was not clear from whom—had come to report the death of Frank Crawford. The family physician, Dr. Granger, who was conveniently at hand, had declared that Crawford had died about an hour before. James Allen Crawford had immediately stepped forward to claim that he had strangled his brother to death.

There was a statement by James, taken down the next day. It was short and to the point, and read as follows:

"I, James Allen Crawford, being of sound mind and without coercion from any party, declare that I willfully and deliberately killed my brother, Frank Crawford, on the evening of March 19, 1924. I had learned that he had been making advances toward my wife, Florence Bisland Crawford, and was so enraged by his behavior that I came to believe his death would be the only means to cleanse the family of this taint. I am remorseful for what I have done, but I believe I have protected the honor of my wife and of my family. I am prepared to face whatever criminal penalties may fittingly be imposed upon me for my actions."

This didn't tell me much that I didn't know already; but it seemed a bit odd that whoever had examined the body—if there had in fact been anyone aside from Dr. Granger himself—had made no mention of any marks or bruises around Frank's neck. And there were other things in the record that struck me as more than a little curious. Or maybe I should say things that were *not* in the record.

I looked up to Taber, who had been hovering nearby like a mother hen.

"I don't see any autopsy on Frank Crawford. Surely the medical examiner performed one?"

Taber shrugged. "I told you, Scintilla, I wasn't here. I had nothing to do with the case."

I looked down at the papers again. "I see that the police chief was one Myron Franklin. Your predecessor?"

Taber nodded.

"Where he is? Can I talk to him?"

Taber got that fearful-nervous look on his face again. "I guess you can. He's retired now."

"Still in the area?" I asked.

"Yeah, he lives right in town."

"Got his address?"

Taber sighed and trudged back to his office. "Yeah, I'll get it for you."

In the meantime I decided to look quickly at the record for Eva Dailey. It too seemed to shed little light on the matter. She had been found dead in her apartment here in town on June 6, 1924. An autopsy *had* been performed on her body, and an overdose of sleeping pills was found in her stomach. No note, but suicide was the obvious assumption.

But there *was* one bit of new information:

Eva Dailey had been five months pregnant.

It seemed likely enough that she had been carrying Frank's child. Did he know? Had she told him? She had probably known of her condition back in March, and it was hard to believe she wouldn't have used that bit of information to pressure Frank to do the decent thing and marry her. But if so, why the hell had she killed him (if she had)? Had he simply refused to take responsibility for her and her child, and had she killed him in a rage? How, exactly, could she have done that? In the absence of an autopsy on Frank Crawford, the *cause* of his death remained a mystery. James had said he had strangled his brother, but given the incredibly cursory examination that the body had undergone, there was no particularly compelling reason to think that was the case. Women tend to resort to pills and poison rather than guns or knives—or their hands. Could Eva have somehow poisoned Frank and then taken her own life by similar means less than three months later?

I jotted down various points in both reports, then waited for Taber to come back—which he did grudgingly—with that address I wanted.

"Thanks," I said, taking it out of his hands.

"Don't mention it," Taber replied. And that remark *was* sarcastic.

Myron Franklin definitely lived in the down-and-out part of town. The house, as I pulled up in front of it, would have been more fitting in the Ozarks of Arkansas. To note that it needed a lick of paint and a new roof was the kindest thing one could say about it. Not that its neighbors were much better. It was hard to believe that someone who had been a police chief, even of a postage-stamp-sized village like Pompton Lakes, would have to spend his final years in a place like this. It was exactly people like him that the Social Security Act that FDR had signed last year were designed to help, though they would still have to wait a couple of years for the benefits to kick in. And yet, I had to laugh a bit ruefully when I saw the Packard 426 Roadster in the driveway. Whatever pathetic remnants of cash Franklin had had on hand must have gone into this expensive toy, although even this gewgaw seemed a bit the worse for wear.

I thought it would be best not to announce myself ahead of time, so I just went up to the door and knocked.

It took a while for Franklin to answer. I gathered he wasn't used to guests.

The cold, hard look he gave me convinced me I was right. Myron Franklin was short, paunchy, and, I'm sorry to say, apparently not accustomed to taking baths. Either he hadn't shaved in days or didn't even bother anymore, leaving a perpetual salt-and-pepper stubble unevenly covering his cheeks, chin, and neck. His jowls sagged, he had bags under his watery eyes, and his slack-jawed expression was at once pathetic and vaguely menacing.

"What d'ya want?" he said truculently.

I felt it best to be both polite and official-sounding. "Mr. Franklin, I'm Joe Scintilla, a private investigator." I offered him my card, but he did no more than glance at it and refused to take it. "I've been hired by Lizbeth Crawford to investigate the death of her uncle, Frank Crawford, back in 1924. She believes her father isn't guilty of the crime."

Did I detect an undercurrent of fear worming its way into Franklin's gruff countenance? He said nothing for several moments, then burst out:

"What's that to do with me? The guy confessed!"

"I know that," I said quietly. "But it's possible that he was shielding someone. There are some oddities in the case that we need to get to the bottom of."

I suspect it was that "we" that made him curl his lip in disdain.

"What's that to do with me? The case is long over. What possible new evidence could turn up now?"

"Mr. Franklin, may I come in and just discuss the matter with you for a few minutes?"

He again stood there, saying nothing. His hand was on the doorknob, and I could sense that he was on the verge of slamming the door in my face. But the poor sometimes have an innate respect—or fear—of their social and financial betters, and I think Franklin also knew that I wouldn't drop the case no matter how much he tried to stonewall me. So, with a crestfallen look that instantly earned my pity, he backed away and let me walk in.

He vaguely waved me to a Morris chair that, like everything else in the place, had seen better days. It took some effort to sit in such a way that the coils weren't poking into my back or posterior. Franklin sat in a couch across the room—about as far away from me as he could manage. The place was ill-lit, so he was virtually swathed in gloom.

I figured there was no reason to waste time on inessentials, so I got right to the point.

"Mr. Franklin, why was there no autopsy performed on Frank Crawford?"

I thought Franklin was about to erupt out of his seat and come over and throttle me—but he had neither the physical nor the emotional energy for that. After tensing up for a second in both rage and fear, he almost collapsed into himself and said in little more than a whisper:

"Scintilla, you don't understand. . . . Do you know what it was like dealing with those Crawfords?" He passed a hand over his face, as if to wipe imaginary sweat off his brow. "They were the biggest, wealthiest, most powerful family in town. And me . . . well, even though I was police chief, I came from the wrong side of the tracks, and"—his hand swept the room with a gesture of self-contempt—"as you can see, I've gone back there. There was no way I could have stood up to them.

"Anyway, that brother of his, James Crawford, confessed right on the spot. Just came right up to me and offered me his wrists as if I was supposed to slap the handcuffs on him then and there." Franklin smirked bitterly at the memory. "I didn't, of course. There was no need. He wasn't going anywhere."

Franklin leaned toward me, and even at a distance of twenty feet it seemed as if his fat, untidy face was inches from my own.

"Scintilla, *he confessed*. My work was done. Why the hell should I make extra trouble for them . . . and myself?"

"Where was the medical examiner?" I asked.

"He didn't come," Franklin said shortly. "The family already told me there was a doctor on the scene, and remember—I had to handle this whole matter with kid gloves. I was shaking in my boots, Scintilla! . . . I just think they were trying as hard as they could to avoid scandal. Keep it out of the papers. Sure, I had to take James Crawford into custody, but his trial was just a formality . . . it was over in five minutes. Even yellow journals like Hearst's *New York American* couldn't milk much out of the story. We didn't even take the body to the morgue—just let the family turn it right over to their undertaker."

I stared at him. "Isn't that . . . highly irregular?"

"Of course it is!" Franklin exploded. "But so what? Who was going to report us to the authorities? We *were* the authorities! If a family like the Crawfords, with the kind of pull they had, didn't want strangers handling the precious corpse of one of their own, who were we to complain? If I'd tried to do anything, I'd probably have found myself demoted to a flatfoot pounding the beat in Paterson. No thanks, guy!"

I mulled things over for a bit. Things were getting stranger and stranger. OK, I didn't usually hobhob with American royalty of the Crawfords' sort, but it struck me as incredible that such sloppy and careless police work could have passed muster. On the other hand, I had to admit, from my years of dealing—usually in an adversarial role—with the cops, that they'll take the easy way out whenever they can. I couldn't blame Franklin for not making waves in the case, especially when he had a culprit fall into his hands with no effort expended on his part. If James Allen Crawford wanted to rot in jail for a crime he may or may not have committed, who was Franklin to stand in his way?

I tried another tack. "What about this business of Frank 'making advances' to Florence Crawford, his sister-in-law? You put any stock in that?"

Franklin shrugged quickly. "How the hell do I know? I knew nothing about that family. I wasn't exactly in their social register." That sneer again. "I wouldn't put anything past people like that. They think they can do anything. If Frank wanted to squeeze his brother's wife, that was his lookout."

"And what's the deal with Eva Dailey?" I said.

Franklin's face screwed up in a puzzled frown. "Who?"

"That was Frank's real squeeze . . . or one of them. You must remember that, surely."

"Maybe," he said . . . doubtfully.

"She killed herself a couple of months later. Right here in town. Does that ring any bells?"

His face cleared somewhat, but then lapsed into bland indifference. "Yeah, OK, it's coming back. Straight suicide. Nothin' much there."

"She was pregnant, if you'll recall."

Franklin shrugged again. "Yeah, so what? Dames like her get knocked up all the time. Maybe it was Frank's kid, maybe someone else's. And maybe she was so cut up about losing the father of her baby that she offed herself. Nothin' much there either."

I got up heavily and thanked Franklin for his time and information. I guess I really hadn't hoped to get much out of him. But I had another lead.

The police report on Eva Dailey said that her body had been claimed by a sister, Maureen. A quick check of the Pompton Lakes city directory at the public library gave me her address. It was time to see whether I could figure out how—or whether—Eva fit into this whole business.

CHAPTER FOUR

"Are you Maureen Dailey?"

The blowsy woman who stood in the doorway of the cramped apartment on Van Ness Avenue struck me as a pretty tough nut to crack. A big-boned, not especially attractive redhead, with glinting green eyes that immediately narrowed as she caught sight of me and heard my question, she stood like a rock and looked me full in the face, her big breasts and thick legs making her seem like a particularly intimidating figurehead on a ship. If a heavily armed tanker could have a figurehead, this would be it.

"Yeah. . . . Who wants to know?"

Whether or not she'd ever had trouble with the police, I got the impression she may have had difficulties with other enforcement authorities—like bill collectors.

"Joe Scintilla. Private investigator." I held out my card, but Maureen looked at it about as briefly and uninterestedly as Myron Franklin had. "I wonder if I could talk to you about your late sister, Eva."

At the mention of her name Maureen's green eyes blazed bright for a moment, then subsided into doubt and suspicion again.

"What's this about? Who are you? What do you want from me?"

It was impossible to answer all those questions at once, so I just said: "I'm investigating the death of Frank Crawford. I believe Eva was . . . involved with him."

That might have been the wrong thing to say. Maybe Maureen mistook my meaning, for she lashed out at me:

"Whaddya mean, 'involved'? You blamin' her for knocking him off? Where do you get off sayin' somethin' like that? *He* knocked *Eva* off . . . or he might as well have done, even though he was dead. His brother did him in, mister, and that's all I know."

She started to slam the door in my face, but I stuck a hand out and stopped it in mid-path.

Without raising my voice, I said, "Miss Dailey, please let's talk about this. I'd like to get to know what was behind it all. I'm aware that your sister . . . took her own life, and I know that she was probably carrying Frank's child. . . . I'm sorry about all that; I know it must have been very tough for you."

It's as if all the air had been let out of a balloon. Maureen Dailey almost collapsed in front of me. She clung to the edge of the door with both hands, tears began to flow at once from those piercing green eyes, and she almost fell to her knees.

"Oh, God, copper"—I didn't bother to correct her mistake as to my profession—"it's been so hard. . . . Little Eva was the world to me. She was all I had! Parents long dead . . . and then my little sister snuffs herself out!" She looked up at me, with the most plangent expression of pain and bitterness I'd ever seen. "Do you know what it's been like these last twelve years, mister?"

"I can imagine, ma'am. It must have been tough."

Eventually she backed away from the door, letting it open fractionally. I figured that was my cue to enter.

Maureen Dailey's apartment was in what might be called the fair to middling part of Pompton Lakes. Not the haven of derelict shacks like that ex-police chief's, but many steps down from the grandeur of Thornleigh, a brief glimpse of which I had caught along the drive to this place. The apartment itself was little more than a one-room affair with a kitchen alcove. It was clean enough, but had more stuff in it than a place twice its size ought to have had. Maybe Maureen had had to gather up her late sister's effects—and couldn't bear to part with them.

I sat down on a couch that had only one space for human occupancy, the rest taken up with boxes, knick-knacks, and other paraphernalia. Maureen made to sit in a wing-backed overstuffed chair nearby, but almost immediately got up and began foraging in an open cardboard box on the floor.

She fished out a couple of photographs and handed one to me. "Wanna see her?"

I nodded and took the snapshot. It showed a surprisingly delicate countenance, nothing like Maureen's brassy face. Here was a girl who looked shyly, almost fearfully into the camera—one of those people who look perpetually timid, as if apologizing for their very existence. I couldn't quite tell the color of the hair, but it looked auburn, and framed the face flawlessly. The features were, as I say, delicate—heavy-lidded eyes, smallish nose, lips slightly parted, somewhat pointed chin. There was a fairy-like quality to the overall expression, as if she were a sprite who had unwittingly flitted into the world of men and was looking for a way out again.

I don't doubt that a man so keen on female company as Frank Crawford was reputed to be would have fallen for a face like that.

"That's her," Maureen said unnecessarily. Then, less irrelevantly: "Just about a year before she . . . died."

She swallowed hard and handed me another photograph.

This was a shot of Eva and a man—"I took that one," Maureen piped—that had to be Frank. He certainly looked like the fun-loving, devil-may-care playboy type: a huge grin on his face, twinkling eyes, cowlick of dark hair falling down across his forehead and almost into his eyes. It was just a head shot of the two of them, but you could tell that he had his arm around Eva, and his cheek snuggled against hers. She still looked a bit shy and embarrassed—perhaps because of this public display of intimacy—but there was a twinkle in her eyes.

"So this is Frank?" This was my unnecessary comment.

"Yeah," Maureen almost snarled. "That low-down two-timer!

. . . What am I saying, two-timer? He probably had a bevy of squeezes holed up on every street in this burg!" She continued to fume as she looked down at the picture.

"So you knew Frank?" I said.

"Sure, I knew him," she replied. "Met him lots of times. Eva *was* my baby sister, after all. I tried to warn her about him, but by the time I figured out what kind of a guy he was, it was too late. She was hooked . . . star-struck. It was as if Valentino had dropped down from a cloud and said, 'Be my baby, Eva!'

She finally sat down heavily in that wing-backed chair and, after a pause, went on: "Get a load of this, shamus. They met at a restaurant where Eva was a waitress—*and Frank was with another girl at the time!* Can you imagine a fellow flirting with the waitress while his current tomato is sitting right there next to him? Well, that's the kinda guy Frank was." She wrinkled her face to think and remember, almost as if she was doing a problem in differential equations. "And yet, it was as if Frank was a kind of overgrown kid, just playing with everything life had to offer. And, for someone like him, what it had to offer was a lot of women.

"Money?" she went on, talking almost to herself. "He had lots of money, but didn't really seem to care. It was just there— no need to waste what little brainpower he had over where to get it and what to do with it. He was lucky to be born into a wealthy family, because he probably hadn't the faintest idea how to make a living. Just a big kid."

"When did they meet?" I asked.

Maureen shrugged. "Oh, I don't know . . . maybe a year before . . . maybe in 1923. Eva was barely twenty-two, Frank not much more, I gather. He already had a reputation as a skirt-chaser, but that didn't matter to Eva. After that first meeting in the restaurant, he came back the next day and asked the manager about her—and, I figure, probably greased his palm to give out Eva's address. She lived not far from here."

She sighed heavily before going on. "Oh, I suppose Frank cared for her in his own frothy way—he wasn't just trying to get a good lay, if you'll pardon my coarseness, copper." I couldn't figure out why Maureen kept misconstruing my occupation: maybe to her a copper and a shamus were pretty much the same thing. "He could get that wherever he wanted. Those Crawfords are like kings around here—and Frank was like a crown prince coming down amongst the common people. All he had to do was curl his finger and any number of dames would gladly jump into his bed—and I'm sure they did.

"But I'll give him this much credit: he treated Eva well enough, until . . . right at the end. Took her to places she'd never been, gave her lots of presents, sweet-talked her like you'd never believe—it was pretty nauseating sometimes." She stuck out her tongue to clinch the point. "But it wasn't an act—I could tell. He really was sweet on her. And of course Eva fell for him like a ton of bricks. I mean, who in her place wouldn't have?"

She looked at me with narrowed eyes. "You gotta understand something, Scintilla. My family don't hang around with people like the Crawfords—except to be their maids and bootblacks." Her tone had descended to bleak self-pity. "Our parents came from Ireland, and we were poor *there*. They were lucky even to get through Ellis Island before the immigration laws cracked down on people like us. They lived in Hell's Kitchen in Manhattan for a decade before they had the sense to get outta there into a place where you can at least breathe. Not that they, or we, could do much better here. Eva got that waitress job just because of her pretty face and figure—I could see how that lowlife manager looked at her out of the corner of his eye. She was a little wisp of a thing—Frank Crawford could probably have picked her up with one hand, and probably did—but she had a heart bigger than his or any of that high-falutin' family of his."

She bent toward me, eyes shining and nostrils flaring. "You know the real culprit here, copper? It was that witch of a mother . . . what the hell was her name?"

I could help her out. "You mean Helen Ward Crawford? The mother of Frank and James Allen Crawford?"

A sneer marred her face. "Yeah, that's her. Helen Ward Crawford." She pronounced her name as if she held it against the woman that she had three names. "You know the type: *Nothing and no one is good enough for my sons.* She only allowed James to marry because his wife came from a well-to-do clan in upstate New York—nothing like the millionaire Crawfords, but close enough to their league to be acceptable. That dame was a piece of work, too, let me tell you . . . but that's another story."

I was surprised at how well Maureen Dailey seemed to know the inner workings of the Crawford clan, but didn't make a point of the matter. I began to suspect that this was a case where I'd learn the most just by letting people talk. What they said, how they said it, and most importantly what they *didn't* say could make all the difference.

Maureen went on: "Well, you can predict what happened. As soon as Helen Ward Crawford, Mrs. High-and-Mighty, learned that her precious youngest son had hooked up with a lower-class Irish waitress down in the village, she blew her top. Demanded that Frank stop wrapping his arms around his savory piece of flesh." I couldn't believe Maureen would speak of her own sister like that, even sarcastically. "And, again to give just a smidgen of credit to Frank, he stood up to his battle-axe of a mother . . . even went to the extent of saying he was gonna marry Eva, and dared his mama to cut him off without a penny, or whatever it is that rich people do in cases like that."

"He said that?" I said sharply. "He said he was going to marry Eva?"

"Yeah, sure, he said it," Maureen said. "At least, that's what he *told* Eva and me he'd said. But who knows what that meant? Maybe he was just being an unruly kid—just teasing his mother to see how far he could push her." She shook her head so hard that her flaming locks fluttered around her face. "I don't think he meant it—or at least, I don't think he ever planned to go through with it. For one thing, Frank had other . . . action going on. Get my drift, copper? I think he was seeing at least two other women at the time, although maybe they were just bedmates. I mean, Eva was a bedmate too—he seemed to get a kick out of spending nights over at her postage-stamp of an apartment, kinda like a king going out in disguise and shacking up with the peasantry—but she was more than that. I could tell."

"So," I said gently, "that baby . . . was Frank's?"

Maureen almost exploded: "Of course it was! Whose else? You think *my* sister slept around? No way, pal! OK, she wasn't the best Catholic in the world, but she did draw the line some-where! She'd put all her eggs in one basket—it was Frank or no one. I don't know if she really expected Frank to marry her, but she at least expected him to provide for her, and her child, in some way. When it became obvious that wasn't going to happen, she"—Maureen choked up suddenly—"she took the only course she thought was open to her. . . ."

I said nothing for a few moments; then: "Didn't . . . didn't Eva try to get the Crawford family to provide . . .?"

Once again Maureen blazed with anger. "Oh, she tried—but I told you, Eva was just a scared little girl. How does a girl like that stand up to a clan as powerful as the Crawfords? That mother—and James Allen Crawford too, for that matter—looked at Eva as if she was some kind of pest that had to be eliminated. There was no way they were going to yield an inch—or a penny. I think one of them even gave her the name of their family doctor . . . and you can guess what for."

Maureen sighed loudly, then put her hand up to her face. I could tell there were tears there. Again I kept quiet for a time. Then I said:

"Miss Dailey, do you really think James Allen Crawford killed his brother Frank? And if so, why? James claimed that Frank was fooling around with his wife, Florence. Do you know anything about that?"

Once more, rage got the better of her sorrow. "How the hell do I know? I wouldn't put anything past Frank . . . or that whole family. I wouldn't put it past that James guy to have knocked his own brother off just to get him out of his involvement with my sister." I started, not having thought of that angle at all. "That

Florence broad wasn't much of a looker, but to someone like Frank that didn't matter. Anything in a skirt would do for him." She paused a bit to get a grip on herself. "But, for what it's worth, I think that's barking up the wrong tree. I can't say as I knew the ins and outs of that goddamn clan, but Frank had enough action on the outside without risking getting his butt kicked going after his own sister-in-law."

She had a point there. "But then," I said, "why would James say something like that? Do you really think he even killed his own brother?"

Maureen shrugged, as if she'd lost all interest in the matter. "I wouldn't be surprised at anything he did. He was an odd one, that James. It was like he felt the weight of the world was on him. The guy never laughed, or even smiled. With the eldest brother gone, it was as if he thought of himself as the linchpin of the whole family—without him, it would just collapse. He knew Frank was a light reed—couldn't be relied on for anything. And he was right about that! But . . ."—and here again she paused as if puzzling over some inscrutable conundrum—"it doesn't make much sense for him to knock off his own brother. I mean, what's the point? And this thing about Frank making a move on James's wife—I don't buy that, and I don't buy that James would *kill* over something like that. He was a guy who really held his emotions in check—he had the bearing of a military man, and I think he wished he was one. No way he could have committed a crime of passion like that."

Everything Maureen Dailey had said struck me as pretty sensible in its hardscrabble way. She may have been embittered at how the Crawford family treated her sister, but she saw things clearly and even sharply—she was a good psychologist. Her tale held together.

If she was lying about anything, she did it with a flair.

I thanked her and left.

So where was I? The most troubling part of the case was the sloppiness of the police investigation—and yet, what Myron Franklin had said about the kid-gloves treatment that a family like the Crawfords would expect to receive in a town like this made a certain sense. As for what Maureen had said, if her tale was even partly accurate, then it seemed fabulously unlikely that Eva Dailey had somehow taken it into her heart to kill the man she had obviously become enamored with; she had held out the forlorn hope that he would do the decent thing and marry her, and held on to that hope until his death had canceled it in no uncertain terms. Unable to stand up to the united front the Crawfords had apparently put up, she had done what *she* thought was the decent thing and taken her own life, so that the world would have one less unwed mother—not to mention a bastard child—to worry about.

The whole matter seemed to revolve around the precise state of mind of James Allen Crawford, and perhaps the rest of his family. Even though I was working for Lizbeth Crawford, I had to admit that her doubts about her father's guilt might be misplaced. There was still every reason to believe that he had in fact committed the crime—even if the *motive* he had given to the police was a cover for something even more bizarre. I began to sense that this was a case that would be less about the accumulation of physical evidence than about the analysis of character.

I called Lizbeth and gave her some idea of the progress I made. She claimed to be encouraged, but still sounded tentative.

"So what happens now, Mr. Scintilla?"

"Well," I said, "I need to get a better angle on certain things... and I think the place to start would be to talk to your mother and grandmother.

"I'll want you to take me to Thornleigh."

CHAPTER FIVE

There was something surreal in the drive through Pompton Lakes to Thornleigh. It was as if we were simultaneously passing through both time and space—leaving the workaday world of depression-era America and entering an ersatz Edwardian England where the ugliness of war and poverty was a kind of social embarrassment. One didn't talk about such things. I proceeded north in my Chevy, Lizbeth at my side, leaving the town well behind and entering upon a rolling hillside so reminiscent of the British Isles that I momentarily thought I should be driving on the other side of the road.

The architect of Thornleigh clearly had English manorial houses in mind when he built this pile. The style was chiefly Georgian, with its rich brick façade and elegant symmetry—a kind of squared U-shape, with wings on either side reaching back almost to the woods that surrounded the house on three sides. Farther back one could see the aqueous formation called Pompton Lakes (I never figured out what the plural signified, since it seemed a single, albeit quite long and narrow, body of water), whose shore was so close to the east wing of the house that the lake could be regarded as a kind of private swimming pool.

During the inevitably long drive to the front door I began to wonder what kind of reception we—and, in particular, I—would receive. Lizbeth had hinted that her investigation of the circumstances behind the death of her uncle were unwelcome to the rest of the family, but she had been reluctant to elaborate. I was frankly prepared for resistance on the part of both her mother and her grandmother—although why either of them would oppose or impede efforts to find James Allen Crawford innocent of the crime he claimed to have committed was not apparent to me.

The butler who opened the door was not quite the caricature I had expected, although his penguin suit was not encouraging. The warm smile he gave to Lizbeth when he saw her made me think he might be an ally down the road. His name, it transpired, was Joseph—his last name I never learned. I was suddenly glad that I never used my full given name in public or private.

We were apparently expected, for I saw two ladies, one middle-aged and one elderly, seated a bit stiffly in what I assumed was the parlor, where we were led. I was about to meet James Allen Crawford's wife, Florence Bisland Crawford, and his mother, Helen Ward Crawford.

I had to disagree with Maureen Dailey that Margaret was unattractive. True, she didn't have the spectacular looks of her daughter, and she didn't have the wistful beauty of Eva Dailey; but her austere elegance would have been appealing to many. Possibly her blonde hair was pulled back a bit too tightly in a bun behind her head; possibly her attire was a little on the severe side; but her finely chiseled features—aided, to be sure, by cosmetics and a professional's careful touch—were striking and impressive, if not actually beautiful. And yet, it is not a paradox to say that the hint of perpetual sadness that hovered around her eyes enhanced her loveliness rather than detracted from it.

Helen Ward Crawford was something else again. She had not aged well. I took her to be no more than seventy, and yet she easily looked a decade older. The harshness of her sharp, angular features was augmented by a kind of repressed rage or torment that flashed sporadically from her bright green eyes. I got the impression that her anger did not stem merely from my unwelcome arrival: she had lived so long with the effort of bottling up some sort of volcano of shame or horror or disgrace that she seemed ready to snap at any moment.

My clothes were not exactly what one would wear to a formal dinner party, so I was not unprepared for the hesitancy with which both women rose to greet me and the disapproving gaze they gave me as they looked me over. I shook their hands as Lizbeth, with a faint tremor in her voice, introduced us. We sat.

No one spoke for a moment.

I decided to break the ice by saying: "Ladies, I'm sure you know that, at the request of Miss Crawford here"—I nodded quickly in her direction—"I'm investigating the death of Frank Crawford. There seem to be some irregularities that need to be explored."

The two women continued to give me a blank and vaguely hostile look. Then Florence spoke up. "I'm sure *you* must know, Mr. Scintilla, that both my mother-in-law and I do not care for this line of inquiry." She said it with the implication that no possible rebuttal could be offered.

At that moment I had to decide quickly what sort of response to give. If I came back with something that she would regard as hostile or insulting, I might never get any information out of her, let alone her husband's mother. But if I attempted to be diplomatic, she might regard me as weak and force Lizbeth to give up the hunt. I didn't know Lizbeth well enough to be certain of her ability to persevere in the face of family pressure. On the other hand, hostility sometimes causes you to burst out with exactly the sort of dope you want to hide.

I decided to be forceful and hope—perhaps against hope—that Florence would resist the temptation to feel offended. In the cases of many successful businessmen and their families, bluntness and firmness induce respect, even if they don't engender fondness.

"Ma'am," I said, "I'm working for your daughter, Lizbeth Crawford. She's paying my bills, and she has the money to pay them for a long time. If Lizbeth wants me to pursue this matter, I'll pursue it wherever it leads. I hope you'll help, as I think it may be in your interest to do so."

At this point Helen almost exploded: "What do you know what's in our interest? What do you know about our family? Who do you think you are, anyway?"

I had lately discovered the impossibility of answering several distinct questions at once, so I didn't try. Instead, I threw a question back at her, but without raising my voice.

"Ma'am, don't you want your son to be exonerated of the crime of killing his own brother?"

Helen's eyes almost bugged out of their sockets.

"Listen, you . . ." I don't think she could find a term of abuse sufficiently vile to cover me—or at least none that she would soil her lips in enunciating. "Two of my sons are dead and the third is in jail. How much more suffering do you want to put me through?"

All of a sudden the faintest trace of a crushing sadness burst through her hostile exterior. For a brief moment I didn't have the heart to take up arms against this old battle-axe. She and her family had been through hell already.

"Ma'am," I said in the gentlest voice I could, "I want to help. That's all I want to do."

In the silence that followed, Lizbeth almost jumped up from her seat and went over to her grandmother. "Granny, let's leave Joe to talk things over with mama by themselves. It'll be better that way."

Helen looked up at Lizbeth, who was standing over her. For a time she seemed to consider resisting, telling her granddaughter not to order her about; but after a few moments she almost collapsed inwardly, nodded briefly, and got up.

Lizbeth led her away to some other region of this capacious abode. With a backward look she all but ordered me to get as much out of her mother as I could.

I had my doubts how much that would be, but I figured it was worth a try.

"Mrs. Crawford," I said, "could I ask you some questions regarding the . . . incident?"

Florence, left by herself, suddenly seemed to shrink. It was as if she felt exposed, unprotected, defenseless. In spite of the forcefulness of her outward personality, I began to suspect that she might be one of those women who expected to be protected by a man, and who therefore could ill resist when a man confronted them.

"If you like," she said in a small voice.

"May I ask what was the occasion of this dinner party on March 19, 1924?"

"No particular occasion," Margaret said flatly. "My husband set it up. Maybe he wanted to make my brother and sister-in-law feel more at home."

I had taken out the list of guests that Lizbeth had prepared for me, and I now looked down at it.

"That would be Daniel and Norma Bisland?"

"Yes."

"They had been your houseguests for some time?"

"Not long. Maybe a week. They were down from upstate New York, where they lived . . . still live. After I married, I didn't get to see them very often, or any other members of my family. Sometimes I felt a bit lonely, since James was so busy running the company, and Frank . . . well, Frank was off doing whatever he was doing." She lowered her voice a bit, even though no one seemed to be within earshot. "I'm not entirely sure how well my mother-in-law has welcomed me into this family." By the time she had finished, she was looking into her hands.

I was a bit surprised how forthcoming she was with information. So I decided to play all my cards.

"Mrs. Crawford, do you think your husband killed your brother?"

She looked up quickly. There were both fear and tears in her eyes.

"I really don't know." Her voice was trembling so much that she could hardly get the words out. "It was all so . . . strange."

"How so?"

She shrugged, almost shivered. "Why would he . . . do it just at that time? It makes no sense. So many people about . . . But after dinner, he and Frank went into the library, and after about half an hour we heard a big thump, and then James came out with a kind of frozen expression on his face and said, 'Frank is dead. Better call the police.'"

"Then what happened?"

"Well, Dr. Granger . . . our family doctor, you know . . . rushed into the library, looked down at Frank, and pronounced him dead. At that point it seemed so cut and dried, although I'm sure I wasn't the only one who wondered how a young, healthy man like Frank could have just keeled over and died.

"But things got even odder when the police arrived. It was just then that James marched up to that boor of a police chief and announced that he had killed Frank. And it was then that I remember Dr. Granger giving James the strangest look I've ever seen on a man's face."

"Strange how?"

Her fear had turned to frowning puzzlement. "I don't know... Incomprehension, incredulity, wonderment . . . ."

"Well, James had apparently killed his own brother. Surely that was cause for wonderment."

"Yes, I suppose." She didn't sound convinced. "But that didn't seem to be the problem." She shook herself almost violently. "Oh, I don't know."

I knew I was treading on thin ice, so I said quietly: "You know, James maintained—and apparently still maintains—that Frank was . . . interested in you."

I expected her to be angry, hostile, fearful, resentful. The last thing I expected was a hearty laugh.

"Oh, but that's ridiculous! Frank's . . . um, fiancée, Eva Something-or-other, was right there! She was a little wisp of a thing, but Frank really loved her. He never made a pass at me... never. I wouldn't have allowed it. Anyway, I don't think Frank considered me particularly . . . desirable." She blushed quickly and intensely.

"Could James have *thought* there was something going on between you two, even if there wasn't?"

Florence shrugged. "I suppose. . . . James was a bit . . . protective. Jealous, I suppose. Didn't want to let me out of his grasp. Not that he was the most affectionate husband in the world. . . ."

She looked up at me with a scared look on her face, as if she'd let out a secret that should have been kept hidden.

"So then what happened?"

"Well, the police had came over, Dr. Granger pronounced Frank dead, and then they left."

"Just like that?"

"What do you mean?" She seemed genuinely puzzled.

"Ordinarily," I said, as if explaining some elementary problem in arithmetic to a child, "the police will take the body away, put it in the morgue, and perform an autopsy. None of that was done."

Her eyes goggled in horror. "Oh, no, we couldn't allow that! It was Frank, part of our family! We took him right to our personal undertaker . . ."

"Ma'am, that's highly irregular, even illegal. It's not how things are done. It defies every code of police procedure ever drawn up."

She looked blankly at me. "But, Mr. Scintilla, we're the Crawfords. I know it sounds terribly snobbish and elitist, but we *own* this town. We couldn't have let them take Frank away."

I shrugged. The rich have their prerogatives, and nothing can stand in the way. They just don't understand how things can be otherwise.

"What about Eva Dailey? Do you know her story?"

"How do you mean?" Margaret seemed to have lost all interest.

"You know that Eva committed suicide about three months after Frank's death. And she was carrying Frank's child, in all probability."

She raised a languid eyebrow. "Is that so? Well, I'm sorry to hear that." She suddenly turned unwontedly vicious. "But she was just a little golddigger . . . poor as a churchmouse . . . trying to cling to Frank to take her out of the ghetto she was born in

. . . little Irish minx . . . Expected Frank to marry her!—as if someone of his stature could link his fortunes to a little nobody like that! The idea!"

I was not prepared for this kind of hostility against someone who was dead and seemingly harmless. But I let it pass.

"Can you tell me how you and James met?"

Without warning, a pall of fear came over her eyes. "Why... why do you want to know that?"

I looked at her closely for a time before saying, "No reason. Just trying to get the background."

She seemed to answer very carefully. "My family had known the Crawfords for a long time. They liked to come up to the Finger Lakes to sail their yachts." She looked at me almost defiantly, as if daring me to express resentment of my social and financial betters. "We weren't as wealthy as the Crawfords . . . our money was in wine-growing in Cayuga and Seneca counties . . . but we were part of their social circle. Had been for years."

A point suddenly occurred to me. "Who's running the company now? . . . now that James is . . . incarcerated?"

She answered quickly. "Oh, the plants—we have two of them, one here in Pompton Lakes and the other in Wayne—have excellent managers. They handle the day-to-day operations. And my mother-in-law is a very capable overseer of the whole enterprise. I do my part also."

"And Dr. Granger . . . what about him?"

"What about him?"

"Was it customary for him to be invited over for dinner?"

She shrugged again. "Oh, he came over from time to time... he'd been the family doctor for years, after all. A very friendly man—everyone got along with him."

"Could I talk to him?" I asked.

"I don't see why not. He's still in Pompton Lakes. All you have to do is ask."

I said I'd do that.

Lizbeth came back a short time later, after she realized that I had finished my conversation with her mother. She didn't dare pump me for information while Florence was present, so on the pretext of ushering me out she followed me all the way outside to my car.

"So what did she say?" she asked breathlessly.

"Oh, she said quite a bit," I said. "But I have a feeling it's what she didn't say that will give us the ammo we need."

Her face screwed up in puzzlement. "What do you mean? What sort of ammo are we going to need?"

"Never mind," I said carelessly. Then: "You know, at some point I think I'm going to have to go to the source."

"The source?"

"Yes, the source. Your father, James Allen Crawford. He's going to have to tell me what he knows."

CHAPTER SIX

Before I left Thornleigh, I asked Lizbeth to take me to the gravesite of her uncle. This turned out to be on a remote corner of the estate—a relatively small patch of land in a clearing in the woods well to the west of the house, surrounded by a low stone wall and dominated by a mausoleum built chiefly for the patriarch of the clan, Patrick Henry Crawford, Lizbeth's grandfather. This edifice was inaccessible to us, as a locked wrought-iron gate barred our entrance; but I could see, on the left side of the interior, the impressive sarcophagus that housed the deceased, and on the right an empty shelf that was no doubt designed to bear the mortal remains of his wife, Helen Ward Crawford.

It appeared that other members of the family were not to be interred in this imposing structure but would have to content themselves with the area around it, as if they themselves were serfs in perpetual attendance on their lord and master. An obelisk some twenty-five yards away from the mausoleum was the focal point of a cluster of graves. It did not take me long to find not one but two headstones of interest:

WILLIAM ALLEN CRAWFORD
1892–1918

FRANK WARD CRAWFORD
1897–1924

There was, in fact, a third headstone that read:

JAMES ALLEN CRAWFORD
1894–

It always unnerved me to come upon the gravesite of a living person—as if that final date was in some kind of hurry to be filled in.

This raw and overcast November day did not make the site any more cheerful. The maples, oaks, and elms that enclosed the little tiny graveyard on all sides, looming over it like stone-faced sentinels, had scattered their dead leaves all over the area, so that each step produced a distinct crunch like the cracking of innumerable tiny bones. We stood there silently, both of us envisioning the ill luck—the mischance of a world war and of some nameless crime of passion, whoever its ultimate perpetrator may have been—that had felled an entire generation of an illustrious family, two by death and one by incarceration. Lizbeth could not have known her elder uncle, but I don't doubt that she had abundant memories of Uncle Frank—and however much of a rogue or a scamp or a wastrel he may have been, I suspected that it was exactly those qualities that had endeared him to her. Lizbeth's tortured expression as she peered at his grave said as much.

We entered the house again, for another thought had occurred to me. In this cavernous dwelling, where the servants far outnumbered the nominal occupants, it was not entirely clear what I could find that would be of any use; but I did inquire about any possible papers left by either James or Frank. Lizbeth told me that James's study, located upstairs in the east wing, was locked at his own request and had never been entered, so far as she knew, by anyone since his imprisonment. I raised an eyebrow at that, but felt this was not the time to pursue the matter.

As I was leaving, I did get collared by Helen Ward Crawford, who seemingly glided out of nowhere to bear down on me.

Lizbeth was still hovering nearby, and in spite of a stern glance from her grandmother she held her ground.

"Mr. Scintilla"—I felt she used the title grudgingly, since she clearly regarded me as no better than one of her servants, and perhaps quite a bit worse—"may I have a word?"

I stopped at the doorway but said nothing.

Possibly my lack of deference threw her a bit, for she herself stood by in an awkward silence before continuing: "I would like to know how far you intend to go with your . . . inquiries."

I looked at her closely. There was some kind of alarm, even terror, behind those hard, shiny eyes and taut jaw. I made a quick decision. Turning to her granddaughter, I said:

"Lizbeth, may I speak to your grandmother in private for a moment?"

She looked at me with a flash of apprehension, then dropped her eyes and retreated out of earshot.

"Now, ma'am," I said, turning back to Helen, "I want to make certain things clear if I haven't already. I told you I'm working for Lizbeth, not you or anyone else. She has asked me to pursue this matter, and I will pursue it—wherever it leads. Right now I don't know where it will lead. Lizbeth seems convinced that her father is innocent of the murder of his brother Frank."

"And you believe that too?" she said sharply, almost accusingly.

"I didn't say that. In fact, I have no evidence to that effect, and I don't even know what evidence, if any, Lizbeth herself has to make her feel as she does. But there are curiosities in this case that warrant investigation."

Helen looked at me intently for what seemed a full minute before replying. When she did so, her tone was surprisingly subdued.

"Mr. Scintilla, our family has been through more troubles than most. My husband was a pioneer in his field and worked hard to give us the enjoyment of this house and our estate; it is a small comfort to me that he did not live to see how his own sons . . ." For the first time, I saw her choke up as if with an overriding melancholy. ". . . his sons failed to fulfill their promise.

"Perhaps you don't think the wealthy suffer like other people. But we do suffer, Mr. Scintilla. I've suffered more than you could possibly imagine. My dreams have been shattered, and I am now a lonely old woman just waiting for death."

I didn't know what to make of their hyperbolic, theatrical utterance. Was this an act, or did Helen Ward Crawford really speak this way to everyone? I didn't doubt that the core of her statement was sound—her ashen face said as much—but I also had little doubt that she was wielding as much emotional pressure as she could to compel me to drop my investigation.

"Ma'am," I said softly, "maybe I don't know what you've been through. I don't know what it is to have my children die on me. But I have a job to do. Whatever you may think of me, I'm not a heartless man. I'll do my best to spare you pain and trouble, but I'll follow this case wherever it takes me."

She almost collapsed in front of me, as if deflated by the failure of her mission to deter me. With scarcely a second glance, she turned on her heel and said over her shoulder:

"Then I wish you good luck, Mr. Scintilla."

My next task was to track down this doctor, Nathan Granger. His office was not difficult to find, as it was smack in the center of the better part of Pompton Lakes. I didn't have an appointment, as I felt it best not to tip him off. So I marched right into his office, placed my card in front of his secretary, and asked to speak to him.

As she looked at the card, her eyes enlarged a bit and she looked up at me with a trace of apprehension.

"I don't think he's available right now," she said nervously.

"Then I'll wait," I said, making myself comfortable in one of the many chairs—all empty—in the anteroom.

The secretary quickly got up, my card in hand, and retreated into an inner office.

Within a few minutes, a tall, slim, but large-headed man with a shock of gray hair framing his face stalked out to meet me. He was a bit younger than I had expected: he couldn't have been much older than fifty, meaning that he would have been quite a young man to have tended to the elder Crawford during the latter's final illness, whatever that was. Crawford had died just before the war.

Granger scarcely allowed me to stand up before extending an arm jerkily for a firm handshake.

"I'm Nathan Granger. How may I assist you, Mr. Scintilla?"

I wasted no time in small-talk. "I'm investigating the apparent murder of Frank Crawford by his brother, James Allen Crawford, in 1924. I believe you were present at the incident."

I was certainly not mistaken in thinking that a wave of nervousness and fear clouded Granger's face the moment my words were out. But he put on a brave front. Eyes narrowing, he said tartly:

"On whose behalf are you conducting this investigation?"

"On behalf of James's daughter, Lizbeth, who has hired me."

Granger continued to peer into my face as if that alone could have unlocked the secret of my presence and my mission. He was thinking furiously—that much was obvious. Quickly turning around, he said, "Come with me, Mr. Scintilla. Let's talk in private."

I followed him into his office, where he not only closed but locked the door.

I sat down at a chair in front of his desk, while he took his seat in the chair behind it. This room did not have any medical apparatus in it—that was apparently reserved for another room leading off a private door to the left—but contained only the records of his patients, along with many hundreds of medical works, ranging from textbooks to periodicals. As Granger sat down carefully, I could tell that he was attempting to gain the upper hand by situating me in his domain. But it would take more than that to intimidate me.

For a time we simply sat there, staring at each other across the desk. We were like two prizefighters, sizing each other up.

Finally he said: "What exactly can I do for you, Mr. Scintilla?"

"Just some information, Dr. Granger." I took out a small

steno pad, as if I were a reporter. "You were indeed present at the death of Frank Crawford on March 19, 1924?"

"Yes," he said shortly.

"And you pronounced him dead?"

"Yes."

"And you were present when James Allen Crawford confessed to killing him?"

"Y-yes."

Granger's hesitancy made me look up sharply at him. "James confessed on the spot, didn't he?"

"Only when the police showed up." He seemed to cough up that remark a bit reluctantly.

"Is that so? What did he do before that?"

Granger took his time answering. "Mr. Scintilla, that whole evening was . . . curious. I don't really know what I was doing there. I was not exactly an intimate member of the family, even though I'd been the family doctor for years, perhaps a decade or more. I don't know how much you know about the dynamics of the Crawford family . . . ."

"I know plenty," I said shortly.

He paused abruptly at that, and once again a pall of fear passed quickly over his face. "Well, then, you know that James's wife, Florence, had some relatives visiting her . . ."

"Yeah, her brother, Daniel, and his wife Norma."

"Yes, exactly. Perhaps she wished me to make them feel at home."

"Did they visit Thornleigh often?"

"Not that I know of." Granger exhibited little interest in them. "And then, of course, there was Frank's . . . er, girlfriend, or maybe fiancée, Eva."

"What do you know about her?" I said quickly.

He shrugged. "Nothing. I'm not sure I ever met her before, and I never met her again."

"You know she took her own life a few months later."

"Yes, I know that." Once again, Granger's interest could not have been any less. "But she was an unsuitable mate for Frank.

He needed someone of his own . . . rank."

"You mean someone who wasn't poor as a churchmouse and had a long pedigree." I don't doubt there was bitterness in my voice.

Granger looked at me almost with a certain pity, and I regretted that I had given him an opportunity to feel superior to me.

"Mr. Scintilla, I don't think you quite understand. The Crawford family has a certain standing to maintain. It has to be careful whom it lets into its charmed circle. That may be offensive to true-blue Americans like yourself, but I fear it is a necessity to people in the Crawfords' position. They have too much to lose by letting just anyone into the family."

I had to turn the tables on him, and quickly.

"You know, Dr. Granger, I've read the police report on the death. James Allen Crawford claims he strangled his brother. But there were no marks or bruises of any kind on Frank's neck or throat."

This wasn't the opening I had hoped for, as Granger replied loftily: "That means nothing. Many cases of strangulation leave no marks. All I know is that Frank was dead, and that his brother confessed to the crime. It was an open and shut case."

"It certainly seems to have been," I said. "The police certainly did no investigation."

"Why should they have? They had their man. It would have been just a waste of effort."

"No autopsy was performed," I pursued.

Once more Granger shrugged. "What of it? It would simply have caused additional pain to the family, and in their situation they certainly didn't need that."

"So you don't think," I pursued, "that there's any chance that James confessed to a crime he didn't commit?—that he was taking the rap for someone else?"

Granger's face was suddenly transformed into a mix of puzzlement, anger, and fear. "What sort of nonsense is that? Who was he 'taking the rap' for?"

"That's what I'm asking you."

"Rubbish. It's all rubbish."

"You don't think, for example, that Frank might have been poisoned?"

"Poisoned?" Granger almost exploded. "How? By whom?"

"Well, an autopsy might have told us something."

To this Granger merely barked a gruff laugh.

"Could somebody have slipped him something in his food?" I said. "Given him a hypodermic injection?"

Again Granger looked at me with a certain condescending pity in his eyes. "Mr. Scintilla, you've been reading too many detective stories. Things like that don't happen. How could there have been any opportunity to do such a thing with all these people about? There must have been eight or nine or us, not to mention the servants."

"I'm aware of that." I sighed heavily. "There was never a time when anyone was alone with Frank that evening?"

Granger gave me an expression of mild incredulity. "I have no idea, Mr. Scintilla. It was twelve years ago. I can't remember many of the details at this point in time."

"But it could have happened?"

"Well," Granger said grudgingly, "anything *could* have happened. But I doubt that it did."

It was clear I wasn't going to get anything from this fellow— not without more information. But I began to suspect there was information out there to get—and once I had it, I might be able to shake something out of this dapper physician.

This case was beginning to smell worse and worse. Too many people were trying to prevent me from coming to grips with what had actually happened on that night of March 19, 1924. Too many people seemed to have something to hide.

And the person who had the most to hide was languishing in Rahway State Prison. So that's where I was headed.

CHAPTER SEVEN

Getting to Rahway from Pompton Lakes was not in any sense direct, and for a hardened Manhattanite like myself it seemed at times as if I were lost in the backwoods of Arkansas or South Carolina. It always comes as a shock to city dwellers how much of our immense nation is still rural—not suburban, but actually rural. Farmers tending plots large and small, their dilapidated red barns in such alarming states of disrepair that a puff of wind would seem enough to bring them tumbling down; sheep farms, pig farms, cattle farms, dairy farms—even here in New Jersey they were all doing their bit as the breadbasket of the country, a thankless task that these stoic tenders of the land performed year after cheerless year as their fathers and grandfathers had done before them.

After leaving the dismal penumbra of Paterson, I skirted the prosperous towns of Montclair and Bloomfield—the haven of the state's social aristocracy, just as Princeton farther south made up its intellectual aristocracy—and passed through the Oranges (East, West, and South—no North), Irvington, Union City, and Roselle Park, finally reaching Rahway after a several-hours' trip that seemed as many days. The prison was in fact well to the south of the city—it had been built on a plot of state property called Edgar Farm. It had been opened about thirty-five years ago, and only in the last year or two did it accept inmates above the age of thirty. One of those was James Allen Crawford.

I had made this trip alone: at this juncture I didn't think it wise to have Lizbeth with me. Her emotional involvement in the case, and in her father's fate, would be more a distraction than a help. It was quite possible that Crawford would refuse to see me—I wasn't clear whether Lizbeth had even informed him of my work. But that was a chance I had to take.

My first order of business was to speak to the prison shrink. I had called ahead and been told he would be available. He was a Dr. Solomon Klass, a psycho-analyst who never let you forget that he had sucked at the teat of Dr. Freud in Vienna. I had no interest in whether he swung with Freud or Jung or the new behaviorist guy Watson; all I wanted was the straight dope on Crawford. What made him tick? What was he doing here? How had he dealt with being incarcerated for the last dozen years?

Klass was a short, balding, ineffectual-looking man, but he knew his stuff. He had taken a particular interest in Crawford precisely because he felt that this was a guy who shouldn't be here. What Klass told me was, in substance, this:

When Crawford arrived here in the late summer of 1924, he was at once deeply depressed and somehow content with himself. When I asked him how that could be, Klass chose his words carefully. It seemed, in the doctor's opinion, that there was some cloud hanging over Crawford—one that had hung over him for years. He was a man of incredible tenacity of purpose, the highest moral fiber, and with the greatest possible devotion to his family. He *wanted* to be in prison, because he felt that he had righted some dreadful wrong. The course he had taken was, in Crawford's judgment, the only course he could have taken to cleanse the family of some hideous and appalling taint.

When the doctor told me this, my spirits tumbled. Everything Klass said pointed to Crawford's guilt in the murder of his brother. The story he told—that Frank had been "making advances" (whether accepted or not) toward his wife, and that the only remedy to this contemptible action was death—now hung together. The ignominy of a philandering brother—especially one who, in addition to flirting with his own sister-in-law, was about to make a horrible *mésalliance* with the social nonentity known as Eva Dailey—could well be, in Crawford's judgment, much worse than the scandal of a murder. In his lights, Frank's death would indeed be a kind of cleansing agent that would render the family as pure as circumstances would allow.

I was not at all clear on how much Klass knew of the details of the case, but that didn't seem to matter much. I went on to ask him what Crawford's current state of mind was.

"Pretty much the same as it was when he got here," Klass replied blandly. "I have never seen a person with less *affect*—that means an observable emotional response, Mr. Scintilla—than James Allen Crawford. The man is a kind of automaton. An ideal prisoner, in his way—never makes trouble, does exactly what he is told to do, even helps to restrain others when they are unruly. It's as if Crawford is fulfilling some perverse kind of *duty* in being here."

"Well," I said, "he did admit to killing his brother."

"I know that," Klass said quickly. When he hesitated, I went on:

"Don't you believe him?"

It took Klass some time to respond. "It's not that I don't believe him . . . it's that I think there's more to it than that. There is something that goes much deeper, but I've never been able to ascertain what it is. To say he is an enigma would be putting it mildly, Mr. Scintilla."

I was about to say *Yeah, you're telling me,* but merely said:

"Do you think he'll see me?"

Klass shrugged. "All you can do is ask."

I did so. A bit surprisingly, when the message was relayed to Crawford, he apparently agreed with some alacrity. I was led down a long corridor to a small interrogation room, where I waited for a prison official to bring Crawford in.

When the door opened, I caught my first glimpse of the man I was attempting, in spite of himself, to get out of jail.

James Allen Crawford had clearly been grievously wounded psychologically; whether it was self-inflicted or not was part of what I had to find out. A man of medium height, dark hair, and chiseled features, he impressed me at the outset as one who kept a tight check on his emotions, his desires, and his dreams. The deep-set eyes were clouded with a nameless sorrow, the hair was gray and receding with age and worry; and when I saw his tight-lipped mouth, I felt that his own mind was a far worse prison than the one he occupied—a prison that would bar the least flicker of self-revelation.

He would be a tough nut to crack.

Rahway was a minimum-security prison; murderers—or those convicted of murder, like Crawford—were a rarity. The guard was content to wait outside the interrogation room, making clear to me that I only had to call or gesture to bring him in if the prisoner caused any trouble.

Crawford sat down in the chair across the table from me, and looked at me with understandable wariness as he glanced down at my card in his hand and said:

"How may I help you, Mr. Scintilla?"

"Mr. Crawford," I began, "I don't know if your daughter Lizbeth has told you what she has done . . . but she has hired me to look into the circumstances of the death of your brother."

From a man so seemingly in control of himself, I did not expect the response I got.

He partially rose from his seat, his eyes bugged out of their sockets, and he almost screamed:

"What right do you have to do that! How *dare* you probe into my family's affairs!"

He was actually huffing with anger and alarm.

I looked at him blandly and, I hope, not unsympathetically. "Sir"—I wondered when was the last time anyone had called him that—"I'm only doing what your daughter has asked me to do. I gather she hasn't informed you of her actions."

"Of course not!" he exploded. "I would never have permitted it!"

"Well," I said, "she's paying me, and so I figure I have a job to do."

Crawford was quickly overcoming his initial burst of rage.

He was no idiot: he realized that he had been put at a disadvantage by being kept ignorant of his daughter's plans, but he had been in big business long enough to know that a level head wins a lot more battles than insensate anger. He calmed down rapidly, seating himself slowly and gingerly in the chair as if it might have been electrified.

"So it would seem," he said at last. "But I fear you're barking up the wrong tree. I killed my brother, and that's the end of it."

"Why?" I asked simply.

My blunt question seemed to take him by surprise. He almost blubbered: "Well . . . he . . . he was trying to corrupt my wife. The scoundrel! If you know anything about him, you'll know that no skirt was safe with him. And my own wife! Can you imagine what that means, Mr. Scintilla?"

"And it was worth killing him over something like that?"

He looked at me with incomprehension, as if I had denied the truth of the multiplication table. "Of course it was! The shame and dishonor to our family if something that ever got out! It would have been intolerable."

"I'm sure you know that your wife denies that Frank made any overtures toward her."

He glanced up at me quickly and appraisingly. "Oh, so you've talked to her, have you?" The tone of disdain he expressed in referring to his wife puzzled me. "Well, she can deny all she wants to, but there was something going on, let me tell you."

"So you think she's lying?" I said, deliberately attempting to provoke him.

"Of course she's lying! Don't let that ice-queen exterior fool you, Scintilla. Florence will spread her legs for any man she thinks is a better lay than her husband."

The coarseness of the statement almost flabbergasted me. How a man could speak of his own wife in this way, even one whom he accused of carrying on an adulterous affair with his own brother, was beyond my understanding. I recalled Lizbeth's bitter admission that her mother had never visited Crawford in prison, not even once—so perhaps his hostility was not entirely surprising. But I also recalled the derisive laugh that Florence had given when I had asked her about Frank's advances toward her. To her, the idea was so preposterous that it was hardly worth rebutting.

Something wasn't adding up here.

I tried another tack. "It would seem, Mr. Crawford, that your incarceration has cast a cloud over the long-term future of your family business. Doesn't that worry you?"

He shrugged, as if the matter didn't deserve a moment's notice. "We have good managers at our plants—they keep things running well. Anyway, I'll be out of here in ten or fifteen years. I won't be an old man—I'll take over the reins again. It's true I had to give my wife power of attorney to handle financial matters, but my mother is there to keep her in line."

"Is there some reason why neither your wife nor your mother ever visit you?" Once again I was being deliberately provocative, but Crawford didn't rise to the bait.

"Look, Scintilla, what my family does is my affair. If they don't want to visit, that's their choice. I'd be mortified to see my mother in a place like this. It's not her custom to hang around with thieves and murderers."

Crawford said this with a sneer, but it seemed incredible he wasn't aware that, by his own admission, he was one of the murderers whom his mother shouldn't be fraternizing with.

"But your daughter does visit," I said.

The mere mention of Lizabeth seemed to have some kind of transformative effect on him. All of a sudden his face lost much of its tensity—its baffling fusion of fear, anger, depression, and resentment. I became aware that James Allen Crawford was both an accomplished and a handsome man—a worthy leader of a community if only he could get out of jail.

"Lizbeth is a dear . . . she's all I have, Scintilla," Crawford said with a break in his voice. "She's been so loyal to me . . . as no one else has," he added with a faint trace of bitterness.

"She thinks you're innocent, you know," I said quietly.

"Yes, I know she does," Crawford said with a kind of puzzled resignation. "I know she does. But she's wrong, Scintilla. She loves me so much that she can't stand to think badly of me—can't stand to think I've done anything wrong. But I have, and I deserve to be here."

For that moment, at least, I believed him.

CHAPTER EIGHT

Something Crawford had said opened up a new avenue of investigation for me. So I made my way to the office of the *New York Herald Tribune.*

A couple of years ago I'd struck up an acquaintance with a woman named Marge Schaeffer. She worked as a society reporter for the *Herald Tribune,* and she'd helped me on a case. We'd become friends, colleagues, pals. In fact, we'd become bedmates. Once I'd made her give up sticking a huge wad of chewing gum in her mouth, everything was fine. Well, not quite everything. We enjoyed each other's company—and on top of that, I was no monk, and she was no nun. So what about marriage? Well, here's the thing: Since Marge had to hobnob with the upper crust, she couldn't exactly tag along with a shamus whose suits were all bought for $11.95 at one of the discount stores on 14th Street; and she didn't exactly fit into my world of cheating spouses and bail bondsmen either. So we were an "item," but that's about all: whether we'd ever shack up and tie the knot was a big question that neither of us was anxious to answer anytime soon.

But this isn't about me. What I'd found was that Marge was an incredible source of information on people who were generally out of my league. She knew everyone worth knowing and kept files on everyone whether they were worth knowing or not. She and her colleague, Gene Merriwether, had done me lots of good turns over the years.

So when I sauntered up to their office on West 40th Street,

it was not entirely a surprise. They were always glad to see me, and they liked feeling useful. Maybe, too, they liked vicariously slumming in my world.

I got right down to business. When I told them I was poking around in the James Allen Crawford case, they were mildly interested. They of course had heard of the business, but it was almost ancient history to them; and, not knowing the details of the case, they wondered what there was to investigate. But they knew the Crawfords well enough, even if the social and financial aristocracy of New Jersey doesn't cast much of a shadow on New York's Four Hundred.

But what I wanted to know was not anything about the Crawfords; it was about Daniel and Norma Bisland, Florence Crawford's brother and sister-in-law.

They remained the wild cards in this case. What, really, were they doing at Thornleigh in March of 1924? By what coincidence were they on the scene when the death of Frank Crawford had taken place? Maybe there was nothing suspicious, maybe there was. But it was an angle I had to follow up.

The Bislands were only a little less of an enigma to Marge and Gene than the Crawfords. I'd recalled Lizbeth saying that they lived upstate, but for New Yorkers upstate begins north of Westchester county, and the farther you get from Manhattan the less interesting you become; and by the time you get up to Ithaca, you might as well be in Indiana.

But Marge dutifully looked in her files for anything about the Bislands. There wasn't much, but what there was proved pretty compelling. They owned plenty of land up in the Finger Lakes area and had extensive interests in wine making and some dairy farming. But what piqued my curiosity particularly were two tiny bits of information:

In late 1923 the Bislands had declared bankruptcy.

In the summer of 1924 they threw a lavish party at their home to commemorate their return to prosperity.

It became clear that a trip upstate was on my agenda.

Once again, the trip out of Manhattan proved a study in

contrasts. The moment you left the city and entered Westchester, a new world dawned. The county was still largely rural, with scattered homes buried in the woods, and towns like Yonkers and Bronxville trying to maintain their suburban innocence while they served as bedroom communities to New York. The Hudson River, as you passed through Dobbs Ferry and Tarrytown, widened out to the dimensions of a small lake, and I couldn't criticize our Chief Executive for wanting to spend as much time at his estate at Hyde Park as he could. It was only one of the many noble edifices you come upon as you head up to Newburgh and Poughkeepsie.

Heading west and skirting the lower fringe of the Catskills, I made my way past Binghamton and Elmira, then headed north. The Bislands lived in a place called Moravia, a tiny village about twenty miles northeast of Ithaca. As I drove into the town, I saw that it was little more than a main street with a number of streets branching off of it, situated a few miles south of Cayuga Lake. And yet, it was a surprisingly bustling and prosperous place: I even saw an opera house there, and recalled that Caruso had performed there a few decades before.

The Bislands lived in a house called the Jewett Mansion. For a mansion, it was on the smallish side, but its brick façade and several towers were imposing, not to mention the acre or more of land that encompassed it. Once again, I'd decided to come unannounced, but I was prepared to stay until I got something out of these folks.

My knock was answered, of course, by a butler, and when I announced my business and handed him my card, he looked down at it—and up at me—as if I were some kind of derelict who had come here by mistake. But my gaze made it pretty clear I wasn't going anywhere, so he grudgingly let me in.

In a short period of time, a middle-aged woman came down the curving stairs to greet me hesitantly.

"Mister . . . er, Scintilla," she said, peering down at my card, which the butler must have given to her, "I'm Norma Bisland. I'm not sure how I can help you . . . ."

I came to the point. "I understand you were present at Thornleigh when Frank Crawford met his death."

At that, she flushed a deep crimson. Norma Bisland was a would-be aristocrat who didn't quite have the bearing and the manner to pull it off. She was short, dumpy, and not particularly attractive. Her gray hair and coarse features were an ill match to the expensive elegance of the dress she was wearing. She would have been more appealing if she'd made fewer attempts to conceal the middle-class housewife that she obviously was.

"I . . . I don't know what there is to investigate," she said blunderingly.

"I'm pursuing several angles. I wonder—"

She interrupted me: "May I ask on whose behalf you're making these . . . these inquiries?"

"On behalf of Lizbeth Crawford, the daughter of James Allen Crawford."

"Little Lizbeth!" she exclaimed. "But she's only a child!"

"Not anymore," I said bluntly. "She's eighteen, and she has the money to pay me."

"Eighteen! My, how the time goes . . . ," she trailed off.

"Mrs. Bisland, I wonder if I may speak to you and your husband on this matter. Is Mr. Bisland available?"

Once again she flushed. "Well, I don't know . . . I think he's out . . . ."

"You *think?* Don't you know?"

She attempted to give me an imperious stare, as if it was not my place to speak to her like that; but she only managed to look scared and outraged.

"If he's not around," I pursued, "I'll be happy to wait."

Mrs. Bisland was getting so flustered that I wondered if she would faint on the spot. But her butler, whatever his name was, came to her rescue. Appearing as if out of nowhere, he sidled up to her and said: "Madam, shall I call the master?"

She looked at him as if he were a kind of lifeline and said: "Yes, please do . . . ."

A bit ineffectually, she directed me into a sitting room. We both sat down, I in a fancily upholstered wing-back chair and she on a sort of divan. I looked at her stonily, saying nothing. She tried to look everywhere but at my face.

After an excruciating several moments, a large, stocky man entered the room. Daniel Bisland, too, seemed not quite suited for the role of landowner and squire of the manor. He had the build of a prizefighter, and the bearing of one. The dark suit he wore seemed to hug his frame so tightly that it seemed he would burst out of it at any moment. His features, too, like his wife's, were a bit on the coarse side; and his pencil moustache made him look like a villain out of a Charlie Chaplin movie.

"Daniel Bisland," he announced abruptly, extending a hand and scarcely allowing me to stand up to shake it. "May I ask your business here, Mr. Scintilla?"

I repeated much of what I'd said to his wife, and I could see that, with each passing sentence, his temperature was rising. His face was becoming simultaneously flushed and livid, and it seemed he could scarcely control his rage and apprehension. When I suggested we sit down and talk the matter over, he almost exploded:

"What is there to talk over? What do you want from us?"

Once again, that bad habit of asking more questions than anyone can answer at once.

I didn't want to antagonize the Bislands even before I started, so I said quietly:

"Sir, I'm just trying to get to the bottom of certain . . . irregularities in this case. I think your testimony will be very valuable."

Bisland peered at me keenly.

"How do you think I . . . we can help?"

"I'd just like to know what you remember of that night of March 19, 1924. I'm still not clear on the details."

This had the effect, oddly, of calming him down a bit, and he sat down abruptly on the divan next to his wife, even though there was scarcely room for the two of them there.

"Scintilla," he began, "that was one of the strangest days of my life." His wife nodded vigorously as he continued: "I don't even know what that whole dinner party was about. We'd been there a week already, and we really weren't particularly keen on socializing. It certainly wasn't for *our* benefit . . . ."

"May I ask what was the reason for your visit?"

At once Bisland became a bit nervous. "Just a social call... hadn't seen my sister Florence for a while. It may not seem like a long way, but we didn't visit often . . . and they certainly couldn't trouble themselves to leave that palace of theirs and come up here."

I ignored the bitterness of the remark and said: "So can you tell me what exactly happened that day . . . or evening?"

Daniel Bisland seized upon my words. "I'll never forget it in a million years. . . . There was so much tension there, it was like a torture chamber. First of all, that high-and-mighty matriarch of theirs, Helen Ward Crawford, couldn't help looking at us as if we were some kind of poor relations . . . and I guess we were, as far as that went. I won't deny we were struggling just then.... And then there was that doctor . . . what was his name?"

"Nathan Granger," I supplied.

"Oh, yeah, Granger. . . . Odd fish. I never heard of anyone inviting the family doctor to a formal dinner. And as for that little minx that Frank was squeezing—" Norma Bisland clucked at her husband's indelicacy, but he forged ahead—"she was as out of place as a wine-soaked derelict would have been. Granted, she was nice to look at, and she barely said a word during the whole proceedings, but what she was doing there I'll never know."

"So nothing unusual happened over dinner?" I said.

"Not particularly . . . unless you think that the incredible number of awkward pauses and silences was unusual. Frank, oddly enough, was the only one who seemed to be having a good time—in fact, now that I remember it, he was in the best of spirits. As if he didn't have a care in the world. Do you remember that, Norma?"

"Yes," she said in a small voice.

"But it was after dinner that things began to get strange," Bisland continued. "We all filed away into the parlor for coffee and after-dinner drinks. Mercifully, the grand old dame didn't insist on separating the men from the women, so we all just hung around, not saying much and pretending to take an interest in what little anyone had to say.

"Then"—and here Bisland bent forward and looked at me intensely—"James and Frank suddenly shuffled off . . . said they had things to discuss in the library. That was pretty far down the hall from the parlor, so we wouldn't have been able to hear them, whatever they were doing there. So the rest of us continued to stand around like idiots. And after about half an hour James calmly walks back into the parlor and says his brother is dead."

"Just like that?" I said.

"Yeah, just like that. I mean . . . he had *no expression on his face*. Blank as a newly washed blackboard. No color in his face, no nothing. Isn't that right, Norma?"

She just nodded quickly.

"Let me be clear," I said. "James Allen Crawford just said, 'My brother's dead,' or something like that?"

"That's exactly what he said."

"He didn't say, 'I killed my brother'?"

"No, absolutely not."

"So then what happened?"

"It gets even stranger," Bisland went on. "Naturally, we were all flabbergasted . . . or, should I say, *some of us* were. That old bat, Helen, scarcely blinked an eye. Maybe she felt it was unseemly to express any violent emotion, even at a time when your own son has just been killed, but she just stood there like a stone. Shock? Maybe, but it didn't strike me that way.

"Anyway, we all rushed over to the library. There was such a crowd of people at the entrance to the room that I couldn't see much, but I did see Frank Crawford lying flat on his back on the floor, right in the middle of the room. Didn't seem to have any marks on him—there was certainly no blood or anything like that.

"But listen to this, Scintilla." Again Bisland leaned over at me, even though I was yards away from him. "That doctor took out a hypodermic and inserted it into Frank's arm. He tried to do it secretly so no one would notice, but I saw it. And I spoke up.

"'What're you doing there, doc?' I said, or something like that.

"And he looked up at me with this nervous expression on his face and said, 'It's just a solution to try to get the heart action going again.' That's all he would say; after that he just went on tending to the body, making what struck me as pretty feeble gestures to revive Frank. But of course it was useless.

"Meanwhile, someone—maybe that butler of theirs—had called the police, and they showed up eventually. I remember that fat police chief . . . what's his name? . . ."

"Myron Franklin," I said.

"Yeah, Franklin. . . . Didn't really seem to know what he was doing, or maybe I should say he didn't seem as if he wanted to be there at all. I guess he was scared of the Crawfords, as they were the big fish in his little pond. But Scintilla, *it was only then that James Crawford suddenly announced that he had killed his brother.*"

Bisland stopped, as if he had finished a difficult aria in a grand opera and was expecting the crowd to explode in applause.

"And what do you make of that?" I said.

"Scintilla, you don't understand. It was only then that everyone was really shocked. Both that mother, Helen, and the doctor seemed ready to faint . . . their eyes bugged out as if they'd been electrocuted. I think Florence really did start teetering for a while, and it was lucky that Norma was there to help her. Weren't you, dear?"

"Yes," she said. I began to wonder if she could ever utter anything else in her husband's presence.

"So then what happened?" I asked.

"Well, there was a bit of turmoil for a while, especially

since James stuck out his hands as if daring the police chief to handcuff him. They didn't dare do that, of course, but they did cart him off to the station. Meanwhile, the rest of us were just standing there dumbstruck. I think we eventually filed back into the parlor, just to get away from the . . . the scene."

"But there's something very odd here, Mr. Bisland. Why didn't the police take the body away to the morgue?"

His eyes narrowed. "Yeah, why didn't they?" He leaned back a bit and said out of the side of his mouth: "I'll tell you why. Both Helen and that doctor bearded that cowering police chief and told him they'd handle it—said they'd take the body right over to their undertaker the next morning. *Then they just closed the library door and locked it, and that was the last we saw of Frank.*"

"You mean they left the body in the room all night?"

"So it would seem."

We both paused in a stunned silence. I'd never heard anything like this before.

"May I ask you something, Mr. Bisland? Do you think that doctor poisoned Frank Crawford?"

Bisland looked at me a bit warily before replying. "I don't know, Scintilla. I just don't know. Maybe he was telling the truth . . . had some kind of drug that could induce the heart to start up again. He did say that Frank had died of heart failure... although"—he smirked cynically—"I guess everyone dies of heart failure, right? I'm no medic, I know nothing about these things . . . and I'm not going to accuse anyone."

"But it smells bad to you?"

"Sure it smells bad."

"Let's just say, for the sake of argument, that the doctor did somehow knock off Frank. Why would he have done that? And why would James have taken the blame for it?"

Bisland shook his head in bafflement. "You got me, shamus. That's the biggest mystery of all, isn't it?"

I shifted gears a bit. "Is there any chance that anyone else could have poisoned Frank . . . earlier, maybe, during dinner?

Slipped something in his food?"

Bisland's face screwed up with thought. "I don't think so. In fact, I could say with near certainty that nothing like that was possible. No one got up during dinner, and we were all served by various serving-maids. I don't see how it could have been done."

"But wait a minute," I said. "Frank was present at least for a while in the parlor after dinner, wasn't he? Did he have a drink then? Coffee, anything?"

Again Bisland's face frowned with the effort of recollection. "Maybe . . ." He looked over at his wife. "Do you remember anything, Norma?"

She quickly shook her head—although I didn't know if that meant she couldn't remember or that she was denying Frank had taken a drink in the parlor.

"I'll be honest with you, Scintilla," Bisland went on. "I don't recall, and I guess it's possible he had had a drink. Whether someone could have slipped something in that drink . . . I just don't know."

I looked over at both of them. "Well, Mr. and Mrs. Bisland, you've been very helpful. This clears up a lot." I paused. "But there is one thing I'm obliged to ask. . . . Is it not the case that you'd declared bankruptcy some months before your visit to Thornleigh?"

Bisland's eyes narrowed. "I figured you'd bring that up, Scintilla. Yes, we were struggling, as I said. We'd had several years of bad weather up here . . . no rain, almost drought conditions. Sure, nothing like the dust bowl that those poor Okies are going through, but it was pretty bad up here. Year after year our grape crops suffered. We're not made of money, Scintilla. There wasn't much we could do."

"But you managed to recover pretty quickly," I said quietly.

"Look," Bisland said bluntly, "I know what you're fishing for. And it's true: We got a big . . . loan from Florence some months later. Why not? That's what families are for. You gotta help each other. We're doing OK now, but we're still not exactly in the

Crawford league—never will be. So, yes, we got a big handout. So what? Surely you don't think . . .?"

"I don't think anything, Mr. Bisland. I just wanted to know."

"Well, now you know."

And that seemed to be the end of the conversation.

* * * * * *

It is not my policy to keep important information from my clients—they are, after all, the ones paying me—but I was in serious doubt as to what, and how much, I should tell Lizbeth about what I had found so far. When we met at a coffee shop in Pompton Lakes after my long drive back to New Jersey, I think she could tell that I wasn't being entirely up-front with her. She was, to begin with, startled that I'd gone ahead and seen her father without letting her know about it, but I managed to convince her that her presence might have worked against his opening up to me. As for Granger's actions during the fateful night of Frank's death, I kept mum on that also, just saying that he needed to be grilled some more about possible misstatements he had made to me—and to the police.

When she heard that, her eyes widened in alarm. "You don't think he . . .?"

"I don't think anything yet," I replied quickly and a little sharply. "And I won't until I have some evidence."

My tone made her look down at her hands in her lap.

"Lizbeth," I said, a little more gently, "I wish you'd tell me what you really know about this whole business." I smiled wryly to myself at my veiled accusation that *she* wasn't being forthcoming to *me*. "Do you have any hard evidence of your father's innocence?—something beyond your gut feeling?"

That made her look up at me. Her eyes were shining, and she reached over and took my hand.

"Joe," she said—and something about her use of my given name jolted me—"I wish I could put it into words . . . but there's nothing I can point to. I've lived with this horror and tragedy for twelve years—my whole life, Joe!—without being able to say why I feel the way I do. Something's being kept from me...I feel that everyone's lying to me—my father, my mother, my grandmother . . . and now, it seems, even Doctor Granger.

"What could they be hiding, Joe?" she said, gripping my hand more tightly.

"I don't know, Lizbeth," I said grimly, almost reluctant to look her in the face, "but I'm gonna find out."

CHAPTER NINE

One avenue of investigation had become plain.

It was just possible that the hypodermic injection Dr. Granger had given to Frank Crawford was what he said it was—an attempt to bring him out of cardiac arrest. Then again, if Daniel Bisland was right—and I could see no reason for him to lie—that Granger's act had been covert, something much more sinister might be involved. I was still beset with the difficulty of *motive:* what possible purpose would be served by Granger's killing of Crawford? Was it some kind of unfathomable pact that he and James Allen Crawford had made to get the brother out of the way for some reason? Why would James condemn himself to decades in prison to take responsibility for someone else's crime? I had to admit that this new revelation only darkened the mystery, but at least it gave me something to go on.

That was why I was planning to dig up Frank Crawford's grave.

I am not accustomed to breaking the law. Usually it's very bad for business, even worse than getting emotionally involved with a client—which, I was beginning to realize with a sinking feeling, was also happening. But it was plain to me that Granger had been the chief culprit in the highly irregular and possibly illegal failure to conduct an autopsy on the body of Frank Crawford. Somebody had something to hide, and Granger was the most obvious suspect. I had little doubt that James Allen Crawford was neck-deep in this aspect of the matter also, for clearly it was his money that greased the wheels somewhere along the way. I couldn't help but think of ex-police chief Myron Franklin's once-shiny and expensive Packard—a vehicle he had probably used well in the past decade or more.

The process of exhuming a body is not the easiest thing in the world to do. Even if it can be done secretly, it requires an immense amount of sheer labor . . . and in mid-November, digging up a twelve-year-old grave would be beyond the abilities of a solitary individual. I needed help. There was no way I could ask Lizbeth to join me—there was no way I could even tell her what I was going to do—and Marge was similarly out of the question. So it was her luckless colleague Gene Merriwether or no one.

I'd gotten to know Gene on a former case, and as Marge's fellow-worker at the *Herald Tribune* he was part of our social circle. I'll be honest with you: a man of muscles he was not. I wouldn't call him a 98-pound weakling, but he'd have a long way to go to challenge Houdini or Sandow in the brawn department.

And for some strange reason he too had a certain disinclination to break the law and dig up bodies.

I remember the bug-eyed expression he gave me when I revealed my little plan. I believe he actually started to blubber. But Marge, loyal to the core, worked her magic on him, and eventually he caved. Ever the one for some novel horseplay, Marge herself wanted to tag along, but I put my foot down at that. Old-fashioned I may not be, but this was no work for a woman.

The fact that Frank was buried in a private cemetery was immensely in our favor. What was against us was the weather, and the relative proximity of Thornleigh to the gravesite. I'd say the distance was no more than a thousand yards, and that was just a bit too close for comfort. But I didn't see that I had much of a choice.

I'd scouted out the terrain ahead of time and knew that we'd have to approach the grave from the opposite direction from where the house was situated. This meant bypassing the private road that led to the house's main entrance and traversing the thick forest that extended a considerable distance to the west of the estate. I wasn't even certain we'd be able to find our way to the cemetery, as it was in a quite small clearing in the midst of that copse of maples, oaks, and elms.

It was well past two A.M. when we left my car on a little-traveled side road and plunged into the depths of the forest, Gene carrying a kerosene lantern that offered a smoky and flickering illumination as we trudged through the pathless grove in what I hoped was the right direction. It had been a particularly raw and cold day, and the descent of night had rendered this tenantless region so pitch-dark that we could scarcely see our hands in front of our faces. The lantern, carried in Gene's not entirely stable hand, cast odd shadows as we walked, making us repeatedly flinch at the prospect of animal predators lurking in the distance.

At one point, when the trees thinned slightly, I caught a quick glimpse of the monumental pile of Thornleigh, squatting darkly like a tiger in the dark waiting to pounce on its hapless prey. The sight helped to orient me, as I realized we had gone a little too far to the south; indeed, we had almost emerged out of the copse. That was not good; for no matter how unnerving it was to be plunged in the thick of these looming trees, it would be much worse to risk detection and capture by coming out into the open.

I urged Gene toward a roughly northeastward direction, furiously attempting to recall the exact location of that gravesite. In my one glimpse of it I had of course come to it from the opposite direction, and in the daylight—even if it was the brooding daylight of a dour November afternoon—and my bearings were not entirely sound. The trees at this juncture were in particularly close juxtaposition, and progress through their low-lying branches and dead vegetation underfoot was neither swift nor easy.

I was already beginning to have doubts about the wisdom of the entire enterprise. Whatever solution Dr. Granger had injected into the arm of Frank Crawford, I had to believe that some traces would remain even at this late date; but of course that would mean that we would not only have to dig up the corpse, but take it away with us. How exactly that was to be done through this nearly impenetrable forest was something I had not sufficiently thought through. But I could see no other option: I was being stonewalled on all sides by a conspiracy of silence and deceit, and my only way to break through was to come up with hard evidence that things were not as they seemed.

Almost without warning we came to the clearing where the cemetery lay. At this point Gene wanted to extinguish the lantern, but I felt that the surrounding trees provided enough cover so that we could keep it lit at least for a time. We certainly needed the illumination to find the right headstone, and we had to hope that the coffin was in fact directly beneath it—not always a sound assumption, if past experience was any guide.

But we had no choice. So we started digging.

The chill of that mid-November night had already penetrated to our bones, and we quickly realized that it had penetrated the earth as well, for our initial attempts at excavation were about as successful as the attempt to chip off flecks of marble with a kitchen knife. I was not prepared for the frozen solidity of that earth, and the almost despairing look—tinged with fear and a certain shame—that Gene gave me very nearly led me to give up the whole misguided undertaking. But with a renewed burst of energy I began making some headway, and Gene, taking heart at my progress, followed suit.

Six feet of earth is more square footage than most people can comprehend. We had already erected an impressive mound of dirt when an anomalous interruption burst in on our labors.

A shotgun blast sent a bullet yards above my head, to lodge firmly in a tree behind me.

Gene almost screamed with terror and dropped his shovel, almost plunging into the newly dug hole in a crazy attempt to hide before disgust and apprehension caused him to jerk to a halt. I was a little calmer, but only a little. I heard, then saw a large figure running in our direction from the house, and I could see a shotgun in his hand. My quick inventory of the occupants of Thornleigh led me to suspect that this defender of the family plot was Joseph the butler.

I thought fast. Urging Gene to stay put in spite of his protests, I plunged over the low stone wall that surrounded the gravesite.

In less time than I could have imagined, Joseph stalked up to Gene and shouted:

"What are you doing there? What's your business here?"

I had to give credit to Joseph for his bravery: he couldn't possibly have had any idea of how many graverobbers he would have to confront, and he could easily have been outnumbered. Perhaps the stereotype of the loyal servant wasn't so far off the mark.

All Gene could say was: "Don't shoot! I'm not armed!" In good cops-and-robbers fashion, he had raised his hands high over his head.

Peering cautiously over the wall, I could tell that Joseph had quickly taken an inventory of the scene; I don't doubt that he saw *two* shovels on the scene, and perhaps assumed that the other culprit had run off. Taking up the lantern in one hand and holding the shotgun rather loosely with the other, he barked at Gene:

"You're coming with me. We'll see what the police have to say about this."

It was when the two of them began marching back in the direction of the house that I made my move. Leaping nimbly over the wall and striving as best I could to avoid the crunch of the dead leaves scattered all around, I approached Joseph from behind.

In a few seconds he felt an automatic at his back.

"I'm sorry, Joseph," I said, "but we're not going anywhere."

He knew instantly who I was; he probably suspected I was behind this caper. Almost collapsing in defeat, he dropped his shotgun and stood still.

Picking up his weapon, I motioned them to return to the

grave. We had to finish our work.

I felt a trifle guilty ordering Joseph to take my place with the shovel, but he had left me no alternative. He gave me a look of mingled resentment, outrage, and self-pity that came close to wrenching my heart. But I said nothing, and with a gesture suggested that it would be in his best interest to do his work quickly and quietly.

The coffin was finally reached, but additional work was required to clear the dirt around it so that it could be lifted out of its cavity. Once again Joseph looked up at me, this time saying plangently:

"Mr. Scintilla, please . . . this is a desecration. You mustn't . . ."

"Joseph," I said, "you know this is something I have to do."

Dropping his head, he resumed his toil. He and Gene managed to position themselves on opposite sides of the coffin, lengthwise; clutching the handles affixed there, they gave a mighty tug.

At this point I had to help them, but suspected that Joseph no longer had any inclination to be rebellious. Placing both his shotgun and my own automatic at some distance from the site, I gave them a hand. In due course we had the coffin on the level ground next to the grave, where it landed heavily with crunch over the underlying leaves and twigs.

For a time we all stood there looking at the thing. There is something about the tokens of death that evokes a kind of primal fear in all human beings. Countless millennia of horror and loathing have warned us to give the widest possible berth to death and its appurtenances, and just as many millennia of myth and superstition have instilled in even the hardest of heads the faint hints of a suspicion that maybe the dead do not always stay dead, and that it's best not to approach too closely in a foolhardy attempt to find out.

But I was not to be deterred. Taking my shovel, I sought to pry the lid off.

Once again Joseph tried to intervene.

"Sir, you mustn't!" he cried out in the darkness. "This is evil! You're endangering your immortal soul!"

"That's a risk I'll have to take, Joseph," I said, continuing my work.

And yet, I was vaguely prepared for what I saw—or, rather, didn't see. The coffin was empty.

The three of us stood there like idiots, jaws open in wonderment. It could have been minutes before any of us moved or spoke. That coffin, lined with white linen so bright that it almost shone in the pitch-darkness of this bleak night, was so pristine that it could have been pressed into service on the morrow. We had no suspicions that body-snatchers had somehow preceded us in our grim task: this coffin had never been used for the purpose for which it had been designed.

I turned silently to Joseph, as if he could provide some clue to the mystery.

But that elderly manservant, quaking in his boots, jaw working spasmodically, was manifestly as stunned as any of us. All he did was peer back at me with incomprehension and not a little terror, as if some violation of natural law had taken place.

We were all so preoccupied with the bizarrerie of that empty coffin that we didn't hear the quick patter of footsteps behind us until their owner was almost directly upon us.

Then, quickly turning around, I saw Lizbeth clutching a nightgown draped hastily over her lithe figure.

She took in the scene quickly and efficiently. Open-mouthed, she glanced from the empty coffin to our dirty shovels to the three of us standing there in frozen wonderment. None of us spoke or moved until I made a tentative effort to keep her away from the scene.

"Lizbeth, you'd better . . . ," I started.

But she cut me off.

"I knew it!" she cried in ecstatic triumph. "My father's innocent! He didn't kill Uncle Frank! What do you think of that, Mr. Detective?"

For once, I had no answer.

CHAPTER TEN

"Now don't jump to conclusions, Lizbeth," I said.

We were sitting at the A1 Pancake House on Colfax Avenue in Pompton Lakes. Gene and I had crashed at a nameless flophouse for what little remained of that night, and now we were doing our best to wake up our brains and bodies for what promised to be even more difficult work in the coming days.

Lizbeth, I suspect, hadn't gotten a wink of sleep, but her energy was irrepressible. And she looked more tempting than ever. Maybe there ought to be a law against beautiful eighteen-year-old girls.

"C'mon, Joe," she chided me. "I was right all along, wasn't I?" She gave me an impish smile, as if she'd beaten me in a game of checkers.

"Lizbeth," I said, pouring more coffee into me than was good for me, "I don't want to put a damper on things . . . but the fact that Frank's coffin is empty doesn't mean that he's alive. He could still be dead."

I didn't want to add, "And your father could still have killed him," but I think the unspoken thought flashed through Lizbeth's mind, for her face clouded over for a moment—but only for a moment.

"Oh, Joe," she scoffed, "you don't really believe that."

"I don't know what to believe," I said.

And I meant it. This turn of affairs had complicated, not simplified, the situation. All it indicated was that some shenanigans had gone on both during that fateful dinner of March 19,

1924, and its immediate aftermath. The conspiracy of silence and deceit that I had encountered in my investigation had now turned into a conspiracy of some other kind—exactly what, I didn't have enough evidence to say. But it was clear that it was the work of multiple hands.

Let's assume that Lizbeth was right and that her Uncle Frank was still alive. What did that mean? It meant that he and his brother James had staged his death—and, at a minimum, that Dr. Granger was involved. Could we extend the conspiracy any further? To Frank's mother, Helen Ward Crawford? To James's wife, Margaret? I had my doubts. In a case like this, the fewer people who were in the know, the better. Joseph the butler's nearly apoplectic reaction to the empty coffin made it clear he was not in the loop—and why should he have been? Even that police chief, Myron Franklin, was probably just bought off with a wad of dough: there was no reason for him to know what the plan was, or where it was heading.

And that was my difficulty, too. *What was the plan?* First of all, why stage Frank's death at all? Merely to have him escape the clutches of Eva Dailey, who expected him to marry her? A powerful family like the Crawfords could easily have thrown money at her to skedaddle to parts unknown, taking her bastard child in tow—or to have Frank do so. Someone like Eva simply didn't have the power and influence to create any kind of scandal for Frank Crawford or anyone else.

And, overriding this perplexity, was an even greater one: *Why did James Allen Crawford confess to a murder he didn't commit?* This, really, was the crux of the whole affair. If Frank's death had been staged, then why did James willingly inflict decades of incarceration upon himself for no discernible reason? What could possibly have been his motivation? From what I knew about Crawford, he didn't strike me as some kind of masochist, willing to throw the best years of his life away for a murder that didn't even happen.

This whole puzzling scenario was based on the premise that Frank Crawford was actually alive. But I had no evidence of that. Frank may not have been in his grave, but there was still not the slightest indication that he was still on this earth; and if he was in fact no longer in the land of the living, there was still a substantial amount of evidence that James, at a minimum, was complicit in his death. Twelve years had passed, and no one had caught the faintest glimpse of him.

I hadn't let Lizbeth know the full upshot of my talk with her father in prison . . . especially his chillingly despairing indictment of himself—"I deserve to be here." Those words carried conviction to me, even if I couldn't penetrate to their full meaning.

So I wasn't yet ready to give James Allen Crawford a free pass.

Lizbeth was thirsting to confront all and sundry—her mother, her grandmother, even her father—about what we had unearthed. I cautioned her against that, and with difficulty convinced her to let me handle the case as I saw fit. I had to remind her that I was the professional and that she had hired me to do a job. I told her that knowledge was our only weapon here—and that, in fact, we didn't have as much knowledge as she may have thought. We were still playing with a weak hand—and the only way to strengthen that hand was to gather more information.

"I need to go through your father's effects," I said. "I recall someone saying he had a study in the house that's kept locked. I need to get in there."

She brightened at the prospect. "That's easy, I can arrange that. Joseph has the key. I can get it from him . . . he'll do anything for me."

We had all made it clear to Joseph that he'd better keep his mouth shut about what he saw at the gravesite if he knew what was good for him. It didn't take much persuading, and I could tell that his almost fatherly devotion to the youngest of the Crawford clan would seal his lips better than any threats we could make.

"OK," I said, "get that key. I think I'll be back for another session at Thornleigh tonight."

This was a solo job, and I wanted even Lizbeth to stay out of my way as much as possible.

She had gotten the key from Joseph almost immediately upon returning to the house, and she had handed it to me as I waited in the long gravel driveway after our late breakfast. There was nothing more to do here until the dead of night, and after dropping Gene off at the *Herald Tribune* building I went back to my own place for a little shut-eye.

Nightfall came early at this time of year, and, even though Lizbeth said her family all tended to retire early, I knew I would have to give the entire household plenty of time to drift off to sleep before invading their domain. Luckily, James's study was in the east wing of the house, where no one slept, so there was a good chance I could do my work undisturbed.

At one A.M. I was let in a side door by Lizbeth . . . and I tried not looking too intently at her nightgown, as she had neglected to wear a wrap. Gliding like a ghost, she almost ran up the stairs to the second floor of the east wing, stopping me in front of a solid oak door in the middle of an immense corridor.

"Here it is," she whispered.

I inserted the key, and the door opened easily. Lizbeth made motions to follow me in, but I barred her with an upraised hand.

"You'll have to stay out here, Lizbeth," I said. "I need to do this alone."

She almost exploded with outrage. "I want to know what you find!" she hissed at me in a loud whisper.

"No." I said the word as forcefully as it is possible to say in a whisper. "This is my job. Let me handle this."

We stared at each other for what seemed like minutes. At last, with a hint of tears, she yielded without a word, stepping back into the hallway.

I closed the door and locked it from the inside.

The room was spacious but sparsely furnished. Aside from book-filled shelves lining the walls and a file cabinet or two, the only prominent object in the room was a large rolltop desk, its cover shut tight. I was afraid that it was locked, but it proved not to be. Although well-swept, the room had a deserted air to it. It seemed inconceivable that this was where the operations of the Crawford family business were run. And if this study really had been shut up since James's incarceration, it was not clear what usable evidence it would contain.

Quite frankly, I didn't know what I was looking for. What could I find that would verify either the death or the continued existence of Frank Crawford? I was beginning to doubt that that was even the central issue in this whole case—it was starting to seem like some kind of obfuscating sideshow. But if I could at least ascertain that Frank was still alive after March 19, 1924, that would be something.

But there was nothing—at least, nothing that seemed to be of any real value. All the papers and files contained material only prior to that fateful day. There was virtually no correspondence here—certainly no personal letters of any kind. James Allen Crawford must have had some kind of mania for tidiness and organization, for nothing seemed out of place. Files relating to Crawford Rubber and Tire were indeed present, but all predating 1924; and I was not enough of a businessman to make head or tail of the receipts, ledgers, and other paraphernalia that cluttered the cabinets. The desk contained almost nothing of personal interest. Unless a cache of material lay elsewhere, this investigation was leading nowhere.

After an hour or so, I cautiously opened the door. On the wall facing the room, Lizbeth had slumped to the floor, disheveled and half-asleep. But as I quietly approached her she quickly snapped awake and stared at me wide-eyed.

"What did you find?" she asked breathlessly.

"Nothing," I conceded. "Nothing at all."

She bowed her head, crestfallen.

Neither of us spoke for a time. Then I said: "Is there any other place where personal records—letters, diaries, anything of that sort—might be found? There's almost nothing of recent vintage in that room. What about the family's current business papers? Where would they be?"

She looked up at me with a sense of despair. "You'll never be able to get a look at those," she said. "My mother and grandmother guard them like hawks. Even the servants aren't allowed near them without a family member present."

"Is there any kind of storage room that might have old files or papers?"

She screwed up her face in thought. "Well, there might be something like that . . . but honestly, Joe, I've never been there. It's also kept locked. Grandma has the only key."

"And there's no way you can get it from her?"

"Not a chance."

"Where is this room?" I asked.

"It's on the third floor of this wing, toward the back."

I did some quick thinking. "Is there a window in the room?"

"Well, I think so," Lizbeth said uncertainly. "I think there must be—you can see it from the outside. But how . . .?"

"Never mind that. Tell me something else: Is there a way to get on the roof?"

"The roof?" She almost spoke the words aloud. "What are you thinking . . .?"

"Just tell me. Is there a way to get on the roof?"

"Yes . . ." hesitantly. "I think so. You go up to the third floor, and there's a ladder at the very back of the wing built into the wall, and that takes you to a trap-door onto the roof."

"Good. I'm going there . . . tomorrow night."

"Why tomorrow?" she asked.

"I'll need some . . . equipment."

CHAPTER ELEVEN

I was beginning to think I was getting too old for this kind of work.

I was standing on the flat roof of the east wing of Thornleigh, looking down over the edge to the flat brick façade. My target was a window at the very back corner of the wing, only six feet below the roof. Lizbeth had let me in, in a reprise of the night before, at around 1 A.M., and we had little difficulty finding the ladder leading to the trap-door opening onto the roof. As I left her peering apprehensively up at me through the trap-door, I shut it and realized that the hard part was ahead of me.

In addition to other paraphernalia, I had brought with me four large suction-cups that I proceeded to attach to my feet and hands. It had been years since I had engaged in this kind of gymnastics, and I was not at all sure how well they would hold up. And if I took a tumble down the walls of Thornleigh, I'd probably be fit for Frank Crawford's empty grave.

A three-story structure—especially with the high ceilings that dominated Thornleigh—is higher than it looks; or maybe it just seemed that way when looked at from above. But I didn't have much choice in the matter.

So I began crawling over the edge of the roof and down the wall.

I went feet first, affixing my feet to the wall first, then my hands. After that, I was careful to move only one limb at a time. The suction-cups worked well enough, although occasionally some grime or other impedimenta caused a slight slippage that made me freeze abruptly until I was certain that all four cups were secure. I felt vaguely like Count Dracula climbing down the wall of his castle in Transylvania while Jonathan Harker looked on in horror—although, from my recollection of both the book and the recent Bela Lugosi film, the count had gone down head first, something I wasn't quite so foolish as to try.

The six feet from the roof to the window seemed like sixty at the pace I was going. I managed to pull my body parallel with the entire window-frame, positioning myself to its left, and felt comfortable conducting the next phase of the operation.

This involved withdrawing a contraption of my own construction, made up of a small suction-cup attached to a foot-long metal rod; from the rod itself extended a string, to which a glass-cutter was affixed. Fastening the suction-cup to the center of the lower windowpane directly under the window-latch (which was, of course, placed on the inside, hence at the moment out of my reach), I proceeded to cut this section of the pane—about ten inches by twelve—out of its wooden frame. Having completed this operation, I put the faintest bit of pressure on the suction-cup and was rewarded with a virtually inaudible crackling sound indicating that the pane had been severed. I carefully removed the suction-cup from the pane and placed both items in a carryall slung over my shoulder. I performed this entire task while my two feet and one hand were affixed to the wall of the house by their suction-cups.

It was when I reached inside to flick the latch to open the window that disaster struck.

In my haste, or carelessness, I moved too fast—and felt both suction-cups on my feet to be slipping. In a panic, I grabbed whatever I could—and that proved to be nothing more than the very narrow windowsill at the bottom edge of the window. I was now hanging precariously, three stories from the hard, frozen ground, my fingers clinging spasmodically to about two inches of wood.

For a time my feet swung wildly beneath me. In spite of the cold, I felt sweat pouring from my face and, worse, from my palms. My hands were quickly losing their grip. Forcing myself to calm down, I affixed first one of my feet's suction-cups, then the other, to the wall below the window. This lent me enough stability to pull my left forearm up to the windowsill, which restored my balance to some degree.

I had, unfortunately, failed to flick that latch to open the window, so I was not in much better position than before. It would require a full three-foot extension to reach that latch: I attempted to touch it with my right arm fully extended, and found that I was still several inches shy. My only option would be to raise myself bodily to a higher level.

Bracing both my arms on the narrow windowsill, I first pried off my left foot off the wall. Making sure it was now fastened at least half a foot above its former position, I did the same with the right. This had the result of allowing me to extend my arms at full length on the windowsill, as if I were doing some kind of push-up. But I was able to reach the latch, and I flicked it with a certain harried impatience.

I wasn't out of the woods yet. The bottom half of the window had clearly not been opened for years, and it stuck fast. I again forced myself to pause—not only to calm myself, but to gather my strength. It was impossible to use both hands simultaneously to open the window, so all I could do was to use the palm of one hand, then the other, to nudge the window upward.

But it was no go, so I had to proceed to Plan B—to bring the upper part of the window down so that I could clamber in from above. The wooden frame around each of the six windowpanes afforded less than an inch of play, and the sweat on my fingers wasn't helping matters. Nevertheless, after what seemed like an hour, I managed to get the upper window to descend in such a way as to allow my body to go through it.

Almost before I was aware of it, I had stumbled into the room, falling heavily—but, I hoped, more or less silently—onto the floor.

I hoped to heaven that that cut windowpane had survived intact in my bag, for I was intent on reattaching it when I left.

But that was a secondary concern right now. I was in, and I had to make the most of my time.

I felt it was safe enough to turn on the light-switch, which I could dimly make out near the one door in the room. What faced me when the light flooded in was a room piled high and in a certain disarray with trunks, papers, files, ledgers, and other miscellany whose function was not immediately apparent. From the dust encumbering virtually every corner of the room, it was clear that this was not a repository for any kind of current personal or business records. But if there was anything here after 1924, it might afford a clue.

I do not have a head for business, so I was not able to make much of the immense ledgers that lay stacked in a far corner of the room. These ledgers did indeed date to the mid-1920s up to about 1930, but they seemed to contain nothing untoward. Their neat, feminine handwriting was, I gathered, that of James Allen Crawford's mother, who was clearly running the show in his absence.

What I was looking for were *personal* documents, rather than business records. Correspondence, diaries, anything that might shed light on what exactly had happened on—and subsequent to—that fateful night of March 19, 1924.

My canvassing of the room finally focused on a large trunk that lay in another corner, beneath mounds of papers that didn't seem of any interest. The lid of the trunk was locked, but that proved a minimal impediment. A lock-pick that I habitually carried with me made short work of that large and clumsy lock.

What met my gaze seemed indeed to be a gold-mine, although in some senses it was an embarrassment of riches. The trunk was full of an immense mass of correspondence, all addressed to Helen Ward Crawford and extending back many years. It would take hours to go through this cache, so I did my best to sort through it by its apparent relevance. Many items could be put aside quickly—invitations to parties and weddings, idle chatter from fellow bluebloods, even some very old letters from Helen's husband, dating from before the war. I was about to give up—or, rather, to conclude that this ocean of documents needed to be examined more carefully in a less compromising situation—when I came, near the bottom of the trunk, upon a series of letters, still in their envelopes, that had been neatly fastened with two rubber bands.

Every one of the letters was postmarked from Ojinaga, Mexico. The addresses varied, and the postmarks ranged from the summer of 1924 to the winter of 1930.

All were written by one Félix Calderón.

All were, without question, requests—or demands—for money.

Once again, I felt I had something—but I didn't know *what* I had.

Who was this Calderón? Why was he asking for money? Blackmail was the obvious answer—and the fact that this batch of letters dated to no earlier than the summer of 1924, a few months after the "death" of Frank Crawford, did not escape my notice.

I quickly returned to the business ledgers. I found no record of any such payments to a Félix Calderón. And the payments would not have been insignificant: ordinarily he asked for about $20,000 every six months. This may still have been peanuts to a clan as well off as the Crawfords, but us ordinary folks it was a fortune.

I pocketed the letters and closed the trunk, restoring the papers over it as best I could.

I'll not trouble you with my escape from this increasingly claustrophobic third-story room. My exit out the window; my closing the window and flicking back the latch; my reaffixing of the glass pane I had cut, with glue I had packed with me; and my ascent to the roof by means of my suction-cups—all went without a hitch. I descended through the trap-door and clambered down the ladder.

Once again I found Lizbeth crumpled up on the floor, fast asleep in her gauzy nightgown.

She awoke with a gasp when I touched her shoulder; I

almost covered her mouth to make sure she didn't cry out, but she gained control of herself quickly. She gazed at me with a poignant mixture of hope and apprehension; all she could say was:

"Did you find anything?"

"I may have," I said. "I think I need to take a trip to Mexico."

CHAPTER TWELVE

On the plane ride from Floyd Bennett Field to El Paso, I paused to consider where we stood.

Without letting her know of my discovery of the letters, I asked Lizbeth whether she recognized the name Félix Calderón.

She peered at me quizzically, as if I myself were some kind of suspect. She didn't like being kept in the dark.

"No . . . why should I?"

"No reason," I said blandly. "Could he have been some kind of footman"—I wasn't even sure what a footman was, but I figured the Crawfords could have employed such a person—"or maybe a gardener, or chauffeur, or something like that?"

Her eyes narrowed even further. "What do you mean? Who do you think this person is? What possible connection could he—"

"That's exactly what I'm trying to find out, Lizbeth," I said, a little more tartly than I had intended.

"You mean he could have been involved . . .?"

"I didn't say that. And I know you were only five years old when all this happened, but I'd really like to know who this guy was. If you don't know, maybe someone else does. How about Joseph?"

She shook her head vigorously. "I doubt that."

At my silent look of surprise and skepticism, she went on: "He doesn't have anything to do with the other servants—it's not like he's their boss, or anything like that."

"Who is?" I said bluntly.

"Grandma," Lizbeth said.

"That's no good," I said, discouraged. There wasn't a chance than Helen Ward Crawford would spill the beans about this Calderón fellow under any circumstances, even if he had nothing to do with the "death" of Frank Crawford. And I had to believe that he *did* have something to do with the whole affair: the timing was too convenient. He must have bolted out of here within weeks, perhaps days, of the incident.

Exactly what Calderón knew—and how he could have known it—were the things I had to settle. The large sums of money Helen was secretly paying out over more than a decade—I was confident the payments had continued beyond 1930, when the latest of the letters I had found was dated, and probably continued to this day—were some kind of hush money. Maybe Helen herself had contrived to repatriate him: if he was a Mexican, it was best for her sake that he get out of this country and go back where he came from. His liberal allowance would ensure that he kept his mouth shut.

It was faintly troubing to me that Calderón was exacting such a *large* sum of money. After all, what had presumably happened was that a murder had been *faked,* not that a murder had actually been committed. This made me wonder whether my assumptions on this point were even sound. Perhaps I was so keen on proving Lizbeth right that her father was innocent of murder that I was overlooking the plain fact that Frank Crawford's continued existence had not been proven, or even rendered likely. What if Crawford had somehow been killed later, for reasons unknown, and that this Calderón fellow had found out? *That* would justify the large amounts of cash that were being shoveled in his direction.

So I began to realize that Lizbeth—and James Allen Crawford—weren't out of the woods just yet.

The flight to El Paso was uneventful, but it was only the beginning of what would no doubt prove a long and tedious journey. For I now had to rent a car and travel a good two hundred miles to Ojinaga. I could have crossed the border right at El Paso, going across to Ciudad Juárez, but I decided to stick to American soil as long as possible. My only option was to take the long, winding road that hugged the Rio Grande, flanked as it was by a succession of rugged mountain ranges—Finlay, Guitman, Sierra Vieja, and Chinati—that loomed imposingly on my left.

I finally learned what Shakespeare meant when he talked about "the way to dusty death." I'd never been this far south and west before, and was stunned by the parched, inhospitable terrain, which could as easily have been the surface of the moon. I was well south of the Dust Bowl, and recalled reading of the dismal "Black Sunday" of April of last year, when an immense dust storm had blanketed cars, livestock, and even whole farmhouses; things like that made you wonder whether Nature harbored some kind of innate hostility to human existence.

My car—a boxy Ford Model A of about 1930—was already well used, and the pounding it took on this problematical road seemed to add years to its life in a matter of hours. About halfway on my journey I had to stop for sheer respite, soothing my parched throat with a tolerably cold beer and wolfing down a sandwich of indeterminate contents at a ramshackle roadside bar that seemed on the verge of collapse. At that hour of mid-afternoon, I was the only occupant of the place aside from the grizzled owner. He could tell I was a foreigner—for him, anyone not from his immediate part of Texas was a foreigner—so he couldn't be bothered to exchange more than the barest minimum of words with me.

I hit the road again, finally reaching the small town of Presidio, just on this side of the border from Ojinaga, by mid-evening. There seemed no point in crossing over now, so I found what seemed like the only hotel in the town—an establishment that was probably decrepit when Texas still belonged to Mexico—and crashed in a room there. In a nearby eatery, a bowl of chili and crackers was enough for me, and it was all I risked ordering from the surly waitress.

The next morning found me in Ojinaga.

Nobody paid much attention to me at the border crossing; the guards were more concerned about who and what was coming from the other direction. Ojinaga itself was a surprisingly spruce little town that was doing its best to get through the worldwide depression. I was surprised to find that it had originally been a Pueblo settlement dating to as early as the thirteenth century; the Spaniards had arrived around 1535. It had been the site of several battles during the Mexican Civil War in early 1914, and a sad little cemetery just outside of town marked the victims of that conflict.

My goal, however, was the Palacio Municipal, on the corner of Zaragoza and Trasviña y Retes. I had no idea what kind of hoops I would have to go through to ascertain the current whereabouts of one Félix Calderón, especially given my rudimentary Spanish, but I wasn't confident that a little town like this would have an up-to-date phone book or city directory.

The thin, wiry, bespectacled young man who met me at what I took to be the tax office looked at me with skepticism when I finally managed to make my purpose known. I made no attempt to maintain that I was here in any official capacity, even though I could have pulled out any one of several quasi-legal deputy sheriff's badges I had garnered over a chequered career. Instead, it became clear to me that this fellow's tongue would loosen by more direct means, so I casually fished out of my pocket a wad of American bills that Lizbeth had pressed on me for the trip.

His eyes fixated on the tight green ball, and a few bills of medium currency did the trick.

To my surprise, I found three Félix Calderóns listed in the tax records. But two of them had been here for many years— had apparently been born here.

The third Félix Calderón had arrived on April 2, 1924.

He had moved several times in the past decade or so, and it appeared that he now lived in the far southwestern corner of town, in the Francisco Villa district, well south of the road that would take you to Chihuahua. It was the work of a less than fifteen minutes for me to leave the Palacio Municipal, get back into my vehicle, and pull up in front of what was presumably Félix Calderón's house.

It was a humble residence, but well kept. A well-used Ford was parked around to the left, and I could hear the cluck of chickens in a fenced-off area in the back. For some reason the place had been given a wide berth by its neighbors, and the nearest house was more than an acre away.

I marched up to the door and knocked.

I heard an odd scuttling inside whose purport I couldn't ascertain. After several minutes, the door opened.

The man who stood in the doorway, looking with ill-concealed suspicion and hostility at me, was tall, bronzed, and muscular. Something in his manner led me to think he was not alone.

But I knew at once that I'd seen this man before.

He was in a photograph that Maureen Dailey had shown me.

So all I could say was: "Frank Crawford, I presume?"

The response was like nothing I could have predicted. Leaping *backwards* in a manner I'd never seen before, Crawford almost crashed into a nearby table before falling down on hands and knees and scrabbling for a small wooden box on the floor. Out of it he pulled two revolvers, firing both of them wildly at me through the open door.

His aim was very bad, and the shots came nowhere near hitting me. Paying no attention to the woman's scream from the house's interior, I myself came close to doing a backwards somersault to get out of the firing line of this madman. My car was my only defense, for not only would it afford me a certain cover from more gunshots, but my own automatic was lying on the passenger seat, ready for just such an eventuality. I quickly opened the passenger door and retrieved the weapon.

I didn't return fire immediately: in the first place, my supply of ammunition was not unlimited, and in the second place, it was vital that I capture Frank Crawford alive. He would be worse than useless to me dead. But Crawford seemed in no mood to go quietly. Continuing to fire almost randomly in my approximate direction, he bolted out of the house and plunged almost head-first into his Ford, starting the car instantly and skidding off his property with a grinding of gears and a cloud of suffocating dust.

I had to waste several seconds circling my own vehicle to get into the driver's seat and head off after him. Crawford had headed due south, as I suspected he would have. There was no likelihood he would want to go north toward the U.S. border, for no matter how perfunctory the customs inspection might be, the inevitable delay would allow me to come close to seizing him. I didn't doubt that he knew the Mexican terrain a lot better than I did, and I suspected he would do his damnedest to give me the slip.

While following Crawford on the main road out of town, which quickly turned into a dusty and ill-kept road whose bumps and gulleys shook both our vehicles brutally, I did my best to penetrate the overriding purpose of his actions over the past twelve years. What led him to this obscure little town? Why here, of all the places in and out of the United States one could have chosen for a quiet getaway where no one knew or cared who you were or where you came from?

And, most puzzling of all, *why go through the bother of staging your own death when you could just leave the country without all these bizarre shenanigans?*

Whether I would ever get answers to these questions depended on hunting down this frantic prodigal son. And he showed no signs that he wanted to be caught.

Crawford was driving as fast as his somewhat antiquated machine would take him, recklessly passing slower cars along the way and raising clouds of dust as he sometimes skidded off onto the shoulder. It quickly became apparent to me that he was heading toward the steep hills—tantamount to a low mountain range—that guarded the southern side of Ojinaga like some immense, looming crescent. What was beyond those hills I couldn't say, and how Crawford expected to evade me on this flat, barren desert road was beyond my powers of imagination. Now and then he reached his right hand over his left shoulder and fired his revolver crazily in my general direction, but the shots were far off the mark.

I followed tightly behind him, realizing that a bolder challenge could spell disaster for both of us. I wanted him alive, but I wanted myself alive even more. I was not so foolhardy as to risk aiming my own pistol anywhere in his direction; at the speed he was reaching in his mad desperation, even a gunshot to a tire might cause a crash that would instantly snuff his life out. Frankly, I was not interested in preserving his life—a life he had clearly wasted almost as thoroughly as his brother rotting in jail—except insofar as he could help me get to the bottom of this inscrutable case.

As we headed up the narrow, winding dirt road up into the hills, I saw that trouble was brewing. Crawford was still going at such a hectic pace that he was increasingly unable to control his vehicle, and more than a few parts of this road teetered on the edge of precipitous cliffs that could easily send one plunging to a fiery death. Crawford's frenetic pace caused him to skid almost out of control several times, but somehow he managed to retain control.

Then something odd happened. Just as he was coming to the summit of the hill, his car slowed down, emitting barking coughs and puffs of smoke from its exhaust pipe. Then there was a massive shake, and the car came to a standstill.

It was out of gas.

But Crawford wasn't. Leaping out like a crazed gymnast, he plunged down the steep, gravelly bank of the hill in what seemed an entirely random direction. Stopping my own car, I jumped out and followed. What exactly did Crawford expect to do now? Lose me by hiding in some hillside cave? I'm no athlete, but it was child's play to follow him as he ran, stumbled, crawled, and almost rolled along the declivity. We were the only human beings in sight—there was no house, no road, no trace of human habitation anywhere in sight.

The inevitable happened. At one point he stumbled, apparently over his own feet, and fell tumbling head over heels without the faintest ability to stop his downward plunge. His hands grabbed furiously for any kind of purchase, but all they came up with was loose sand and rock. Without warning his body glanced off of a withered tree clinging to the hillside; a grunt of pain and shock was forced out of him, and he came to a slow stop.

I rushed to him to assess the damage. His eyes were closed, either from unconsciousness or exhaustion, and there was a thin trickle of blood dripping from the back of his head. His mouth hung open slackly, his tongue lolled out, and a thin stream of saliva coursed down his chin.

I shook him gently, then slapped his face.

"Crawford! Crawford . . . are you all right?"

In a few minutes he opened his eyes.

"What do you want with me, copper?"

Odd that he would use the same expression that Maureen Dailey constantly threw out at me.

"Crawford, I'm not a cop. I'm a private investigator. I just want to talk with you."

"Some other time," he said, dropping off into oblivion.

CHAPTER THIRTEEN

That other time came the next day.

I won't bother you with the tiresome details of the laborious task of dragging Frank Crawford back to my own car and driving him back to the one hospital in Ojinaga. His head wound was slight, but he had apparently suffered a concussion, so I wasn't able to speak to him that day. Even the next morning, as I was on tenterhooks to see him, the doctors advised that I not trouble him unduly. I didn't know if that was possible, but I figured the best way to manage it was to let him talk while I listened.

I did my best to explain my mission and what I'd found out so far—neglecting to mention my digging up of his empty grave. His only response, at the outset, was:

"So Little Lizbeth is eighteen! . . . Yes, I guess she must be. Cute kid . . . I always liked her."

I said nothing, just looking at him in a way that he quickly understood.

"Yeah, OK, Scintilla, I know what you want. I got some explaining to do, right? Well, this is kind of a long story, and my head ain't so good, so you may not get this all at once."

"Fine," I said. "Just spill the beans in your own way."

"Yeah, I'll do that." He took a deep breath and said:

"Scintilla, you gotta understand something about my family. They're not like me, and I'm not like them. For my whole life they've made that quite clear to me. . . ."

As he lapsed into brooding melancholy, I said:

"Who's made that clear?"

"Everyone," he said, rather bitterly. "My mother, both my brothers—Bill and James—even my sister-in-law's relatives, those Bislands from upstate New York. They all thought of me as a playboy, a wastrel, a do-nothing, know-nothing scoundrel. Well, after a while, I thought: If that's what they think of me, then I'll do my damnedest to *be* exactly that!"

He looked at me defiantly, as if daring me to mimic the moral condemnation of his relatives. But I said nothing and looked at him blankly—perhaps with a bit of wearied impatience.

"OK, maybe you don't wanna hear all this, but it has a lot to do with . . . what happened. And I'll tell you how.

"Ever since I was a boy, all my family ever wanted to do was make money and be respectable. My father ground himself into an early grave by starting this rubber company—that was his whole world. And once she married into this pile of dough, all my mother ever wanted to do was to throw that money around in a way that showed everyone she was the queen of her little domain. Why do you think we stuck ourselves in the wilds of New Jersey? Because we knew that we didn't have quite the money or the class or the blood to make it in the cut-throat world of New York high society! But, by God, we could be kings of Pompton Lakes! That seemed good enough for us.

"Some of us, anyway. As for me, all I wanted was a good time. I'm no dummy, Scintilla: I went to Groton and Princeton, and I knew that it takes more than money to become a real aristocrat. You can buy all the *objets d'art* you want, but if you don't have *breeding,* you just can't cut it. *No one* in America knows what breeding is; just read some Henry James and you'll find that out.

"It was made clear to me right from the start that I was on the bottom rung of the totem pole. My sainted brother Bill was a war hero of hallowed memory; and when he died, I was told in no uncertain terms that I was a member of the Crawford family only by sufferance, and that all the hopes of continuing the line and the business rested with James. And that was fine with me—I wanted to have nothing to do with the business; it could go hang for all I cared. As long as it brought in the dough, that's all I cared about.

"I know what you're thinking: *Privileged rich bastard, not caring about anyone but himself.* But, listen, Scintilla, I wasn't asked to be born into this family. Hell, I think I might have been happier working as a stevedore at the Port of Newark! If you knew how every moment of my life at Thornleigh was one humiliation after another—a constant assumption that I'd amount to nothing—you wouldn't be in such a hurry to condemn me."

I wasn't aware that I'd done that, but I saw clearly that Crawford had a lot to get off his chest.

"Being the youngest of three sons isn't such a ball of wax, Scintilla. Mother and Dad had groomed Bill to run the business after them, and it was a real shock to Mother—Dad had already passed away by then—when he died. Family was in turmoil for months, maybe years. Anyway, then James was the next in line, and all hopes got pinned on him. If you've met him, you'll know what a humorless cuss he is—it's like he has a board up his spine. I can't tell you the number of times he looked at me as if I was some kind of insect—as if I was somehow not a real Crawford, not worthy to lick his boots. But by God, what is life for but to have a little fun? All work and no play . . .

"Yeah, sure, I liked the ladies. Why not? I could show them a good time, and they could return the favor. Money helps there, you know? Buy them little gewgaws, and they'll do anything you want! Just make sure not to promise them too much! And before you write me off as a *roué*, just look deep in yourself and say to me honestly you wouldn't do the same in my position."

All I could say was: "What about Eva Dailey?"

"What about her?" he shot back. "She was a nice squeeze, and I showed her as good a time as any man could. Look, Scintilla, I felt something for her—she was different. Sure, she was as far from the upper crust as you could get, but what did that matter? I don't know that I ever thought of marrying her, but she was a good bedmate, and lots more besides."

A sinking feeling came over me.

"Frank, are you telling me you don't know what happened to her?"

"What do you mean?" he snapped. "Of course I know. I got her knocked up. She told me that, and she was pressing me to marry her. But there was no way I could do that—you better believe Mama Crawford wouldn't have allowed that before hell froze over. That's why I had to . . . you know. I figure they dealt with the kid somehow."

"No one has told you what happened?"

"No. . . . It's not as if anyone writes to me very often," he said petulantly.

"Eva Dailey killed herself about three months after you bolted. She took her unborn child with her."

Frank Crawford's face crumpled with pain and horror. It was twelve years ago, but I'll give him credit for still having feelings for her. Maybe he wasn't a total wretch.

"Scintilla," he said haltingly, "you gotta believe me . . . I didn't know . . . I didn't know, I tell you!" he repeated in a louder tone of voice—so loud that an orderly came in to see what was going on.

I raised my hand in front of Crawford's face. "Keep it down, man. I believe you."

He had lapsed into brooding again. "Poor kid . . . Scintilla, I did care for her. I'm sorry for what I just said—she was more than a good lay. She was sweet and kind . . . thought the world of me . . . Gawd knows why . . . I coulda done a lot worse marrying her. . . ."

Then, after a pause, he blazed in anger again.

"It was all Mother's doing! That witch. . . . She couldn't risk letting even her wastrel son marry a down-and-out waitress with no money and no prospects. And then, when it came out that Eva was pregnant, well, then Mother really hit the roof. A bastard child of the Crawfords! How could they ever live down the shame? So that was when . . ."

He stopped abruptly, face screwed in puzzlement.

"But there's something that doesn't click here," he went on. "Why didn't they just buy Eva off? They could easily have paid her a wad of dough to have the child and send it for adoption. No one would have been the wiser. Why go through this whole charade? . . ."

"That's exactly what I want to know," I said.

"Scintilla, you gotta understand . . . *it was not my idea.* If they really wanted me out of the scene, as a prodigal who would never reform his skirt-chasing ways, all they had to do was let me go off wherever I wanted and I'd have been happy to live out my life in peaceful anonymity . . . which is exactly what I've done these past dozen years. . . ."

"So whose idea was it to fake your death?"

"James's," he said promptly. "He managed to persuade both Mother and me that it was the only way to get Eva Dailey entirely out of the picture. In all honesty, it didn't make a lot of sense to me, and it still doesn't. But somehow he made it sound right. I think the idea was that Eva would be so distraught at my death that she would just crawl away in defeat and wouldn't make any fuss. I don't think anyone thought that she would actually . . . do herself in. That wasn't in the cards. Even James wasn't that cruel and vicious."

"So," I said, "the idea was to pretend you were dead, and then you'd light out for parts unknown. What led you to come here?"

"Several things," he said. "First, I thought it best to actually get out of the country. Europe was too far away, and Canada was not my cup of tea. I don't care for winter, Scintilla, and the climate here suits me a lot better. So do the women." He cracked a crooked grin that showed me he was still just a mischievous little boy. "But I needed to be near the border for various reasons. I keep my money in a bank in Presidio and just draw out whatever I need. I figure you know I keep having to hound Mother for money. I can't help feeling that, for her, out of sight is out of mind. I have a very strong feeling she's pretending I don't really exist, and I keep having to remind her that I do. Frankly, I don't ask for much. . . ."

"Forty thousand a year isn't much?" I asked.

"Not to her!" he shot back. "The company makes that much in about a week. I may not have a head for business, Scintilla, but I know the Crawford clan ain't hurtin' for dough. There's plenty to go around."

He was getting agitated again, so I tried to calm him down. "OK, OK, I'm sure you're right. So why don't we get to . . .?"

"Get to what happened that day in 1924?" he said. "Yeah, I figured you'd wonder when I'd get to that. Well, let me just say—things didn't go quite according to plan."

He took a deep breath. "That doctor guy . . . Granger...had to be involved. Said he would give me something that would simulate death—or as close to it as anyone could tell—and then later some other drug that would revive me. So we had to contrive for him to come over . . . and all we could think of was a dinner party. In all honesty, we really didn't want so many people there—those Bislands were there by accident—but time was getting on, and James (and Mother too, for that matter) wanted this taken care of sooner rather than later. Maybe it was tactless of me to invite Eva over . . . I really didn't want to put her through that . . . but James enthusiastically endorsed the plan, because he said it would prove to her that I was definitely out of the picture.

"That evening really was one of the strangest of my whole life. There I was, eating, drinking, and talking as if I didn't have a care in the world, knowing that in a few minutes the whole house would be thrown into a tizzy because I had died. I won't deny that the idea of playing a corpse tickled me—not that I could possibly be aware of what was going on.

"Anyway, after dinner James and I slipped into the study, and after about half an hour we knocked over a chair to create the impression that I'd keeled over. James ran out of the room, shouting that I'd taken ill and begging Granger to come over. He came by, shot something into my arm, and that's all I remember."

"It turns out someone saw him," I commented.

"Oh, yeah? Well, I'm not surprised. He was petrified at having to be involved in this whole business—said it would be the end of him if it ever got out. But I figure James or Mother had paid him well for his services. Paid off that bonehead police chief too—Myron Franklin, or whatever his name was. I knew he'd be shaking in his boots at even stepping foot into the palatial Crawford estate, and there was no chance he'd make a ruckus, if enough dough was thrown in his direction to shut his trap."

"So James's wife, Florence, wasn't in the know?"

"Not a chance," Frank said. "No need to involve people who didn't need to be involved. As it is, we told Mother only because we were afraid she'd have hysterics if she thought I was dead. She may not have thought much of me, but I was still a Crawford, and she'd already gone through the death of one of her sons. So we had to let her in on it. But no one else if we could help it."

"Obviously not Eva Dailey."

"Well, obviously," Crawford snapped—his look of irritation immediately giving way to a stab of pain. "We knew *she'd* have hysterics, and she did; but that couldn't be helped. We were in a bind . . . at least, James convinced us that we were."

Frank Crawford took a deep breath and went on.

"So the next thing I know is . . . *I'm in a coffin in the undertaker's back room, with Nathan Granger standing over me with a needle.* He was looking a bit apprehensive, as if the shot he'd given me, whatever it was, wasn't working. He knew he'd catch hell if I didn't come out of the induced coma or whatever it was that that first injection had done to me.

"The rest I learned later, of course—mostly from Granger and Mother. Days had passed, and we'd gone through the whole mummery of a service and everything. Man, I'd like to hear what my grieving relatives said about me then! A lot of bull about what a loving brother I was, what a credit to the family, blah, blah, blah. Hah! Those goddamn hypocrites. I was glad I was going to leave them in the dust. Let them have Thornleigh—I was, as you said, lighting out for parts unknown."

Crawford wallowed in self-pity before resuming.

"We had to go through the whole service because we had to

convince absolutely everyone concerned that I was dead. God knows, maybe Granger had to keep shooting me with whatever it was that had knocked me out the first time. And that undertaker—Harold Knowles, I think his name was; had been working for our family for years—was of course bought off. It was an open casket service—couldn't hide anything at that stage.

"So that was that. Granger woke me up, I walked out of my coffin, and hid in the house for a couple of days—Gawd knows there's enough vacant space in that cavern of gloom that even the servants don't go into much—before I headed out of town and out of the country. Mother tried to buy me off cheap, with a few thousand dollars for immediate expenses, but I knew she'd cough up more dough when the time came. I had her—and James—over a barrel, and they'd keep shelling out the loot so long as I didn't, as it were, come back from the dead."

Crawford looked at me with a sudden intensity.

"But look here, Scintilla: *I was as bowled over as anyone when I heard that James had turned himself in as my killer.* That wasn't in the plan! Why should it have been? I harbored no hostility to him—I just wanted out. The idea was just to say I'd died of natural causes—'heart failure,' as I recall Granger chuckling. An all-purpose cause of death, which means nothing and explains nothing. But it would do. And who was there to question it? *Why would anyone want to confess to a killing he didn't commit?"*

"That's what I'm still trying to figure out," I said. "You know, he said that you were fooling around with his wife."

Crawford burst out in a guffaw. "What a bunch of bull! I may like the skirts, Scintilla, but I do draw the line somewhere. I don't say Florence wasn't nice to look at, but to go after your own sister-in-law is beyond the pale of even my questionable morals. Anyway," he added a bit sheepishly, "she really wasn't my type."

"Any chance Granger had something to do with James's confession?"

"I can't see how," Crawford said, face screwed up in bafflement. "I could swear he was as dumbfounded as I was when he told me the news. And as for Mother, I couldn't get a word out of her. It's almost as if she *wanted* him in jail—for what possible reason, I can't say. He was supposed to be the savior of the family—and now he was going to rot in jail for decades, maybe forever. What gives? It makes no sense."

"So you think your mother knows something?" I asked.

"She has to. She took all these events too calmly, as if this was exactly what she wanted to happen. She's a tough old bird, Scintilla—a kind of spider whose web has caught us all. She hates it that I have something over her—the mere fact of my existence—and I wouldn't be surprised if she had some hit-man come after me if she thought my gouging her for money got to be too much. . . . In fact—"

He looked at me a bit sheepishly.

"In fact," I picked up, "you thought I was the hit-man."

"Well, yeah," he said with that crooked grin of his. "At first I thought you might be a copper, but what kind of copper would go to this much trouble to prove that someone *wasn't* dead? So the next thing that occurred to me was that you were here to . . . get me out of the picture. Eliminate me. Erase me from the map. Get rid of this fly in my mother's ointment."

"A not unreasonable conjecture," I admitted.

"Yeah, you're telling me. It was something I had to live with for twelve years. Who knows but that one day some guy would come along, knock on my door, and say 'Are you Frank Crawford?' I'd almost forgotten my real name in all that time. As the years passed and nothing happened, I figured I was in the clear . . . but I could never sit comfortably. In the back of my mind there was always the thought: 'Someday, somebody's going to come after me. And then—look out!'"

He looked up at me with the closest thing to an apology he could manage.

"Sorry for trying to blow you away. But you gotta understand my situation. I was happy down here, and didn't want anything to spoil that."

"Don't worry about that," I said offhandedly.

"So"—nervously—"what happens now?"

"That's up to you," I said shortly.

"Oh, c'mon, Scintilla, don't give me that bull. All you gotta do is go back and turn me in and the whole jig is up."

Once again, his face collapsed in defeat and self-pity as he envisioned the demise of his cushy life south of the border. No more free money, no more señoritas—or, for all I knew, señoras—willing to share his bed, no more of whatever else he did to fill the gaping days and months and years out here in this microscopic village on the rump of the United States of America.

"Crawford, I can keep my mouth shut," I said. "There's no reason for me to spill the beans to anyone but to my client. She has to know—she's paying me to find out what's going on here. What she does with that information is her business. I'm sure she likes you well enough, but her main concern is to get her dad out of jail."

"But"—and Crawford turned fiery again, almost unhealthily so—"James doesn't *want* to get out of jail! Don't you see? *He went there of his own free will.* He *wants* to be there."

"Why?" I said simply.

That brought him up short. "How do I know? I've never understood what made him tick. Why don't you ask him?"

"Oh, I intend to," I said.

CHAPTER FOURTEEN

But first things first.

There's no point dwelling on the long, tedious drive back to El Paso, or the long, tedious flight back to Bennett Field. I needed at least a night to get the dust of Texas out of my mouth—and also to brace myself for what would no doubt be a couple of tense days shaking the truth out of people who had flatly lied to me or, at the very least, been a bit frugal in the "whole truth and nothing but the truth" schtick.

And then there was Lizbeth to deal with. I should have guessed her reaction when I told her the upshot of my trip south of the border.

She quite literally danced a jig.

Then she threw her arms around my neck and planted a wet kiss on my mouth.

She continued to cling to me as she peered into my face with an appraising smile, as I tried to get the scent of her perfume out of my nose.

"Why, Joe Scintilla," she chirped, "I do believe you're blushing."

"I don't blush, lady," I said gruffly.

Of course, I didn't tell her the whole story—especially the part about Frank Crawford trying to blow my head off, or the Mexican babe he must have had holed up in his place when I came knocking on his door. But the mere fact that he was alive and kicking was enough to send Lizbeth into a tizzy of delight.

"I *knew* I was right!" she kept saying over and over again. "I just knew it!"

"How did you know?" I asked quietly.

She stood stock still and looked at me with wide eyes.

"Oh, I don't mean I knew about this whole business of faking Uncle Frank's death and sending him down to Mexico," she replied hastily. "Up till the time you . . . um . . . dug up Frank's grave, it never occurred to me to think that he was alive. I thought he'd just died of natural causes . . . but even then, talking with my father year after year in prison, I felt that he was covering up something.

"You see, Joe"—she looked at me intensely—"I was the only one who ever *cared* about my father. Everyone else"—she choked up suddenly—"seemed content to let him rot in prison. It's like it was a penance for something . . . but for what? Whatever it was, it was *not* for killing Frank—that seemed to me so obviously a put-up job that I just couldn't swallow it. And then, when you found that grave empty, I knew Frank must be alive somewhere. And now you've found him!"

She gave me a broad smile, as if I were now her favorite uncle.

"OK, Lizbeth," I said, "but we . . . I still have some work to do. This case isn't solved until we figure out *why* your father took responsibility for a murder he didn't commit . . . for a murder that didn't even happen. That part still makes no sense."

Her euphoria quickly turned to pensiveness.

"I know," she said reluctantly. "I don't understand that either." She looked up into my face. "You're going to have to talk to him again, aren't you?"

"Sure I am," I said. "But there's someone else I need to talk to first."

"You better get Dr. Granger out here right away," I said briskly to the secretary.

She looked at me, first with outrage, then with alarm, then with something akin to fear. Without a word, she stumbled out of her chair and retreated into the inner office without a backward glance.

In a few moments Granger walked out, obviously irked.

"Scintilla," he said, "you'd better have a good reason for bothering me again. I'm a professional man, and I have many patients relying on my expertise."

His bluster wasn't going to get him anywhere this time. In any case, his waiting room was, at this particular moment, entirely empty.

"Granger," I said heavily, "I think I have a pretty good reason for being here. Let's go back to that night of March 19, 1924. Are you aware that someone saw you giving a hypodermic injection to the prostrate body of Frank Crawford?"

It was as if I'd electrocuted him. He staggered back against door of his office; if the door hadn't been closed, he would have tumbled into it.

"Wha-what did you say?" he almost whispered.

"You heard me."

I'll give him credit: he recovered quickly. "What of it?" he barked out. "I thought he'd suffered cardiac arrest. I gave him a shot of adrenalin to try to restore his heart action." By this time, he was fully in command, once again the high-class medical professional. "Obviously I failed, but that's because Frank Crawford was beyond the point of recovery."

"Oh," I said blandly, "I wouldn't say that. I had a nice chat with him a few days ago in Mexico. He seems to be doing just fine."

Maybe it was a low blow, but I had to break him down. And I did.

If he hadn't clung to the doorknob, he would have collapsed to the floor. Gruffly saying to me, "Get in here," he opened the door and almost shoved me into his office, slamming the door almost in the face of his startled secretary.

He staggered to his padded chair behind the desk and almost fell into it. Then he covered his hands with his face.

I sat calmly in the chair opposite the desk and waited.

Finally he looked up at me. All the blood had drained from

his face. At that moment he probably looked more like a corpse than Frank Crawford had done in that charade of a funeral service.

"Scintilla," he said hoarsely, "what do you want from me?"

"Just the truth, Granger."

"The truth?" he almost wailed. "What *is* the truth? I still don't know what that whole business was about. . . . I was just obeying orders, Scintilla. OK, maybe that's not much of an excuse, but it didn't seem harmful at the time. After all, no one was really dead . . ."

"But Eva Dailey died a little later," I reminded him.

"Hey, I had nothing to do with that!" he snapped. "Her death is not on *my* conscience! It may be on Frank's or James's, but not mine. You can't pin that on me!"

"I'm not trying to pin anything on you," I said a bit wearily. "Just tell me what happened."

"I tell you," he said almost in a whine, "I *don't know* what happened. That is, I don't really know why this whole business had to be arranged the way it was. All I was asked to do—and believe me, Scintilla, I didn't take a dime of the Crawfords' money; I didn't need it and I didn't want it—was to give Frank a heavy dose of morphia to immobilize him, and make sure that the police didn't do their own examination. That was the easy part. After that, we carted Frank off to the undertaker—whose palms, I'm sure, were liberally greased—and the whole farce was perpetuated. The fact is, I kept having to give Frank additional doses of morphia over the next several days . . . and so when I came to revive him with adrenalin, I was a bit alarmed that he didn't seem to respond immediately. But finally he came out of it, and he just walked out of his coffin and lit out for Mexico.

"But to this day, Scintilla, I don't know why it had to be done that way. It was all James's idea, and he somehow managed to convince us it was the best way."

"Is that so?" I said. "What about the mother?"

"Helen?" he said with a puzzled look. "Well, yes, I think she knew about it . . . but James came up with the plan."

"Why?"

Again he looked at me with a face almost twisted in bafflement. "What do you mean, why? He just wanted Frank out of the way. I guess both he and Helen had determined that Frank would really never be a Crawford in the fullest sense of the term, and now with this trouble with Eva, they must have figured that the best way was to make him vanish."

"But why not just have him leave for parts unknown? Why go through this cumbesome fake-death scenario? That's what makes no sense to me."

Granger paused before speaking. "Well, Scintilla, I'll be honest and say it didn't make all that much sense to me either. But somehow James and Helen convinced us this was the way it had to be.

"But you gotta understand, Scintilla . . . the plan was *not* to have James pretend to have *killed* Frank! That was really a shot out of the blue. . . . You could have knocked me over with a feather when James came out with that line to the police. But I could tell he was dead serious—he wanted to confess, and he wanted to go to jail. And of course I couldn't do anything: if I said that Frank wasn't dead and that the whole thing was just a trick, a con, a put-up job, then all kinds of bad things would have happened. I would have lost my license, my practice, everything!"

He looked at me pleadingly, as if he was in my power.

"How did Helen react," I said, "when James made that confession?"

"It's pretty hard to know what's going through her head," Granger said. "She's a tough woman—been through a lot, and worked like a demon to keep that family together. To be honest, I don't recall any reaction at all from her at all. She just took it in stride.

"She isn't a lovable woman, Scintilla. She may be rich, but the family she'd married into has been a constant trial to her. I don't think she ever got over the death of her eldest son, Bill.

He was always her favorite. Ever since then, she seemed to go around with a look of anger and grief on her face. I wonder if she ever smiled after that . . . ." He trailed off.

"So she might have known that James was going to make that confession?" I asked.

He shrugged. "Yes, I suppose she could have."

"Could she even have put him up to it?"

"Why would she have done that?" he said in puzzlement.

"That's what I'm trying to figure out," I said.

He considered for a moment. "I suppose she could have. But I just don't see what purpose that would serve. He was now the eldest son, running the company, or at least in charge of the family's finances and standing in the community . . . and you better believe this incident caused the Crawfords a pretty serious blow to their social life. I don't think they were invited to parties or dinners for years thereafter. Of course, people gave way in the end . . . money does that. But to this day, people think there must be something wrong with that clan."

"Well," I said, "I don't doubt that there *is* something wrong with that clan. And I need to find out what it is."

There was nothing for me to do but to go to the source. I began planning for another trip to Rahway.

I would have gone the next day if I didn't learn that Lizbeth had been kidnapped.

CHAPTER FIFTEEN

It was pure luck that I got the notice as early as I did. That morning I trudged to my office to take care of some paperwork relating to another job; without that work to occupy me, I would have headed out for Rahway at the crack of dawn. Instead, I found, in the morning mail, the following letter—if it could be called that—enclosed in an unmarked sheet of paper:

**DROP THIS CASE IF YOU WANT
TO SEE LIZBETH ALIVE**

The writing was in plain block letters; the writer had used a blue fountain pen in a hand that seemed to shake slightly.

The first thing I did was to pick up the phone and call Thornleigh.

The phone was answered by Joseph, whose voice was almost shrill with consternation and worry. It didn't take me long to find out the essentials of what had happened.

"Is Lizbeth missing?" I barked.

"Y-yes, sir," Joseph stammered. "Taken in the night. . . . The whole household is in an uproar . . . ."

"Have you called the police?"

"Yes. They're here now."

"Good. Keep 'em there. I'm coming right away."

Stuffing the note and its envelope into my pocket, I flew out the door and into my Ford. I had no choice but to take the Miller Elevated Highway, the western backbone of Manhattan, up to the still new George Washington Bridge, which had opened only five years before. Across the bridge, I roared through Englewood, Teaneck, Hackensack, and what seemed like dozens of other deceptively placid communities until I finally came to the southern outskirts of Pompton Lakes. At this point I floored the pedal until I skidded recklessly into the interminable drive up to the front door of Thornleigh.

Police cars were littered like untidy children's blocks near the entrance, and I nearly rammed one of them in the back in my haste to pull up and get out in one motion. My pounding on the door raised a thunderous din within, but in seconds Joseph had opened the door and let me in.

What I found was pandemonium. Servants seemed to be running around to no apparent purpose; Florence Crawford was collapsed on a sofa with her head in her hands, weeping loudly; police were everywhere, hardly less confused than the servants; and, to my surprise, Dr. Nathan Granger was on the scene.

So was Frederick Taber, the Pompton Lakes police chief. I went up to him.

"What can you tell me, Taber?" I snapped.

He looked me up and down for a second and was on the verge of saying something he might regret; but he settled for: "What's it to you, Scintilla?"

"Lizbeth Crawford is my client, Taber. I need to know what's going on."

He relented grudgingly. "I don't know much more than what I've been told. Miss Crawford was apparently seized in her bedroom a little past one in the morning. Some of the servants heard a scuffle and maybe a scream, but this house is so huge that no one could immediately figure out where the disturbance was coming from. By the time they realized it was from Miss Crawford's room, she was long gone."

"Have you been to that room?" I asked.

"Yes, of course," Taber replied with some asperity.

"Let's go there."

I waited for him to move. Once again he looked me over;

then, with ill-concealed irritation, he led me off to the west wing.

To my surprise, Lizbeth's bedroom was on the ground floor. It was a spacious room, and every object in it spoke powerfully of her presence, not least the faint trace of her usual perfume. The furniture was slightly disarranged, but somewhat less than I had expected; the bedcovers had been pulled violently back and were partially on the floor, and a chair seemed to be knocked over, but otherwise the place seemed to be in good order.

A window was yawning wide open. Through it you could almost make out—if you knew where to look—the clearing where the Crawford family gravesite lay.

I went to the window at once.

"No one has touched anything?" It was more a statement than a question.

"That's right," Taber said.

"I assume you've noticed that there's no sign of forced entry," I said. "The latch is open. All someone had to do was pull up the window and they'd be in."

I peered out the window to the ground a few feet below. The garden bed there had been violently disturbed, with flowers crushed and upturned and with what seemed like dozens of footprints in the wet earth.

"There's no doubt she was taken through the window?" I said.

"That's how I see it," Taber replied.

"Anyone hear a car drive off, or anything like that?"

"No. It isn't likely someone would pull up to the front door, go around to the side of the house, drag Miss Crawford out, and drive off. They must have taken her through the woods there"— he pointed in the direction of the cemetery, beyond which was the road that Gene Merriwether and I had driven along on that night we dug up Frank Crawford's grave—"and had their car over there. That road isn't used much, and no one would notice a car parked there for an hour or more."

"Yeah, you're right," I said. After a pause: "So what do you make of this?"

Taber looked me in the face and said: "What do *you* make of it, shamus?"

Suddenly I got steamed. "What do I make of it, Taber? I'll tell you what I make of it! *This* is what I make of it!"

And I pulled out of my pocket the note I'd received that morning and stuck it under Taber's nose.

He read it in seconds, then turned to me with both alarm and suspicion in his face.

"What's the meaning of this?" he said gruffly. "What's been going on here? Whose business have you been poking your nose in?"

"Lay off me, Taber," I snapped back. "I was hired by Lizbeth . . . Miss Crawford to do a job. I've been doing it. Someone obviously doesn't like some of the things I've found." I held my hand up in his face before he could interrupt me. "You know I'm not going to tell you what those things are—they're my affair and they don't concern you.

"What *does* concern you is finding Miss Crawford. And you'd better start by looking at that window."

"What about the window?" Taber queried petulantly.

"You moron, look at that latch. *It's unlocked.* What chance was there that Miss Crawford would have left it like that on a cold November night? Clearly it had been unlocked at some point yesterday when she was not here, precisely to make the job of snatching her easier.

"In other words, Taber, this was an inside job. I'll tell you this much: what I've found has a pretty direct bearing on several members of this family, and it's as sure as anything that one of them had something to do with this. They're obviously trying to scare me off, and they're holding Lizbeth hostage until I walk away and promise to keep my mouth shut."

Taber peered at me closely, as if I were some baffling specimen he was gazing at through a microscope. "You're accusing a member of the Crawford family for kidnapping one of their own?"

"It doesn't have to be one of them," I said. "It could be any number of others. But someone had to have had access to Lizbeth's room sometime yesterday, and that points very strongly to someone living here. They would have the opportunity, and I suspect they would have the motive."

I paused while I fished the envelope out of my pocket.

"And look at this, Taber," I resumed. "Take a look at that postmark: Pompton Lakes, 10:30 P.M. yesterday. *This letter was mailed before Lizbeth Crawford was seized.* Whoever wrote and mailed it was awfully certain he was going to succeed in this little kidnapping gig."

Taber just shook his head. "This is getting way too weird for me, Scintilla." He took a deep breath. "I can't risk my job arresting a member of the Crawford family unless I have pretty strong evidence. They'll hang me out to dry if I make a mistake."

"No one's asking you to arrest anybody. Our first priority is to find Lizbeth. After that, you can arrest the man on the moon for all I care."

"But Scintilla," Taber warned, "you know you're endangering Miss Crawford's life by pursuing this case. For her sake, you gotta drop it. If someone's so desperate to stop you, they're not going to be shy about knocking her off. You better be careful."

"Don't worry about me, Taber," I said. "I want Lizbeth alive a lot more than you do." I wasn't going to say how much more— because I was trying not to think about that myself. "I have a plan, anyway."

We marched back into the parlor, where a certain semblance of order had returned.

The first thing I did was to walk up to Dr. Granger and pull him aside.

"Just out of curiosity," I said with what I will admit was a certain snide tone of voice, "exactly what are you doing here?"

In spite of the hint of fear that lurked in the back of his eyes, he wasn't about to be intimidated.

"Don't try to bully me, Scintilla. I'm the family doctor, remember? Joseph called me because Florence Crawford was in a state of near-collapse. She's still pretty worked up, but the sedative I administered has helped. I knew nothing about this until I came over here a few hours ago."

I looked into his face pretty much the way Taber had looked into mine a few minutes before.

"So you have no idea what could have happened to Lizbeth?" I said.

"How could I?" Granger replied in mingled confusion and outrage. "Surely you don't think *I* had anything to do with this!"

"No, I don't think that," I said honestly.

As I began walking away, he grabbed me by the arm.

"Scintilla," he said nervously. "Listen . . . there's no reason to . . . to spill the beans about Frank Crawford, is there? It could be the end of my career . . . I'm not made of money, Scintilla—my work is all I have . . ." He trailed off indecisively.

"Calm yourself, Granger," I said. "I'll not blab about anything . . . yet. I gotta find Lizbeth. She knows most of the story, but not quite all of it. We'll let her decide what to cough up and what not to—if she comes back alive."

I walked away without a backward glance.

Making my way to the couch where Florence Crawford was still sitting, huddled in a ball and weeping quietly, I said:

"Ma'am, I know this is rough on you, but I wonder if I could have a few words."

After a few seconds, she looked up at me, her tear-stained face the very picture of crestfallen despair.

"Mr. Scintilla," she almost wailed, "I just want my baby back. She's all I have in the whole world. I have no reason to live if she's . . . gone."

Either she was the greatest actress in the world or she was telling the plain truth. At least provisionally, I crossed her off the list of suspects.

"Mrs. Crawford, I'll do whatever I can to get your daughter back. I don't think there's any immediate danger of anything serious happening. I'm sorry to say this, but she seems to be a pawn in a larger game."

Maybe my choice of words was unfortunate, for Florence snapped back: "And what 'game' might that be, Mr. Scintilla?"

"I think you have a pretty good idea," I said. "It's the case that Lizbeth had me investigate. As you know, it's upset a lot of people."

I felt it was the better part of valor not to mention that note I'd received this morning: it would only unnerve her further and make her demand that I give up the hunt. I wasn't quite ready to do that, if I could do so without harming Lizbeth.

Florence Crawford just looked at me pleadingly and said: "I just want to see my daughter alive and well. I don't care what happens to anyone after that."

I felt dismissed, and I doubted that she had anything of value to say anyway, so I walked away without a word.

My mind was, in any event, working furiously. A number of scenarios had to be considered, each more unsavory than the last.

In spite of his protestations, I wasn't ready to clear Granger. If his piteous pleas to me reflected his real feelings, then he in many ways had the most to lose if the truth about Frank Crawford came out. As he said, he could lose his license and his practice—and then where would he be?

Florence Crawford was probably off the list, for I couldn't see what motive she might have had in having her own daughter kidnapped. Why should she have cared if the fake "death" of Frank Crawford were exposed? I will confess that a suspicion lurked in my mind about her relatives, Daniel and Norma Bisland. Could they have wanted Lizbeth out of the way as a means of gaining the Crawford fortune? In the absence of any descendants, who else would the money go to except the Bisland clan? And yet, the overriding problem with this conjecture was opportunity: how could either Daniel or Norma have gotten into the house to unlock that window latch in Lizbeth's bedroom? They would have to have persuaded Florence to do the job, and I couldn't see her agreeing to that.

And then there was James Crawford himself. He was still

the mystery man in this whole case, deliberately confining himself to decades of prison for reasons no one could fathom. I wouldn't be surprised if he had somehow heard of my findings and sought to nip them in the bud. Maybe it was a mistake for me to have seen him at all and thereby to have tipped him off to my investigation of the case that had led to his incarceration. I wouldn't be surprised if he had various confederates whom he would persuade or pressure to do his bidding for him, no matter how unsavory that bidding might be.

There was another prospect that I thought so fantastic that I refused to think of it—yet.

But my first order of business was to settle one simple point. I came up to Joseph, who was hovering ineffectually in the parlor, face contorted with anxiety and hands wringing in a nervous tic. His devotion to Lizbeth was unquestioned, and I saw him as just about the only true ally in this whole twisted household.

"Joseph," I said, grabbing him by the arm and pulling him away to a far corner of the room, "let me ask you something."

"Yes, sir," he breathed, looking at me as if I could somehow conjure Lizbeth back with a few passes of my hand.

"Did any member of the household leave the house last night for any reason?"

He looked me deeply in the face, his eyes bulging in fear. "Why do you want to know?"

"Just tell me, Joseph. It could be of immense help."

Something was preventing him from speaking—terror, apprehension, concern for Lizbeth, concern for his own standing in the family, or something altogether different.

Finally he said: "Yes, someone did go."

"Who?"

It took Joseph what seemed to be an eternity to say: "Mrs. Crawford, sir."

"Florence Crawford!" I nearly shouted. "Are you sure?"

"No, sir," Joseph almost whispered. "Not her. The elder Mrs. Crawford."

I closed my eyes in wearied disbelief. It was my worst fear. Lizbeth had been kidnapped by her own grandmother.

CHAPTER SIXTEEN

The information Joseph provided seemed to make it pretty clear what was going on. Helen Ward Crawford had taken one of the family's fleet of automobiles—she had driven it herself, without the use of the chauffeur, one Perkins—around 8:30 yesterday evening. She was gone for more than an hour. I had little doubt that she did more than mail that little greeting card to me at the nearest mailbox in town; and I had a fairly good idea where she had gone.

For I was under no delusions that Helen had done the job of kidnapping Lizbeth herself—that would be beyond her powers and beneath her dignity. The footprints under the window of Lizbeth's room made it clear that at least two people—at least one of them a man of sizeable bulk—were involved. But to my mind, there was no question that Helen was the one pulling the strings here—for what possible motive, I couldn't even begin to fathom. It was obvious from the beginning that she was hostile to Lizbeth's poking around in this whole matter; but would she have gone to the length of snatching up her own granddaughter just to shut her—and me—up?

What, really, had I discovered? Only that James Allen Crawford had *not* killed his brother Frank, and that Frank was alive and kicking and seemingly content being out of the family. How was that a threat to Helen? What did she stand to gain by this incredibly desperate and foolhardy measure?

The overriding question, therefore, was nothing more than this: *Why did Helen Ward Crawford want to keep her own son James in prison?* It was not as if she had someone else—at least, someone within the Crawford clan—lined up to take over the family business. The idea that Lizbeth could run the show after Helen's passing seemed fantastic—not that Lizbeth wasn't a smart, headstrong, dynamic person, but there wasn't the slightest indication that she was being groomed to take on such a responsibility.

Well, all that was a secondary consideration now. My prime concern was to get Lizbeth back—and get her back alive. Nothing else mattered, and nothing was going to stop me.

I wasn't quite so confident of my own ability—or quite so confident of Helen's sanity—to think that Helen (if indeed she were the mastermind of the kidnapping) wouldn't take drastic action, up to and including killing her own granddaughter, if I pursued my inquiries too boldly. So I made a show of announcing to all and sundry that I was suspending my investigation pending the release of Lizbeth Crawford.

I did so as Helen Ward Crawford, who had drifted into the parlor like a kind of evil spirit, stared stonily at me from a dim corner. Her gorgon face revealed nothing except rage and malevolence. It quickly became clear to me that she was the toughest of tough nuts to crack, so my only option was to do a sort of end run around her.

And for my ally in that undertaking, I chose Joseph the butler.

Pulling him aside, I muttered a few comments and questions to him. Getting a satisfactory reply, I made my exit.

I won't say that I wasn't glad to see the back of Thornleigh—for now.

But I was back on the scene at around midnight.

The most discreet of knocks at the front door brought an immediate response. Joseph opened the door hastily and silently. He was standing in front of me, dressed all in black—and I'm not referring to his usual monkey suit—and topped with a beret that made him look like some kind of cat burglar. I admired his diligence, but couldn't resist cracking a grin.

But this was no time for frivolity. Earlier I had asked him:

"Can you handle a gun?"

He had snapped: "Yes, sir, Mr. Scintilla."

"I'm not referring to that shotgun you like to carry around"— at this, he'd turned crimson at the recollection of how he'd (perhaps justifiably) tried to blow my head off during my unearthing of Frank Crawford's grave—"I mean an automatic. Know how to use it?"

"I do, sir."

"Good. That's all I need to know."

Now, as he closed the door without the faintest hint of sound, we proceed to make our way through the forest to that deserted road where, I suspected, Lizbeth's kidnappers had themselves stashed their vehicle to make off with her. A cold, steady rain had begun about an hour before, and my own Fedora was quickly ruined. The walk through the woods was dismal and cheerless, and we made no small talk to enliven the occasion. Only when we were well beyond the confines of the house did I feel safe enough to light the same kerosene lamp that I'd brought here for a very different purpose only a few days before.

We reached my car in good time, although we were by this time soaked to the skin and shivering with cold. The drive into Pompton Lakes was also short, for I had a very specific goal in mind.

We pulled up a block or so from the home of Myron Franklin, ex-police chief.

It was, I admit, only a conjecture that he was involved, but I thought it a good guess. Who else could Helen Ward Crawford have manipulated to commit such a deed? Over whom did she have any kind of power or influence? Who else would feel pressured to commit an actual crime that could easily send them to jail? Lying about a fake death was one thing; kidnapping a young woman was something else altogether. None of Helen's society friends was remotely ripe for this kind of seedy operation; but it may well have been right up Myron Franklin's alley.

Leaving the car and shielding ourselves from the omnipresent rain as best we could, we trudged in the direction of

Franklin's decrepit shack. How likely it was that Lizbeth was actually there, I was by no means certain. From my recollection of the place, it had only a couple of rooms on the one and only floor, and I don't believe there was a basement.

As we approached the house, I made it my task to confirm that last conjecture. I was right: the house consisted of nothing but a living room, bedroom, and kitchen. Peering through the windows, between the small gaps left by the tattered curtains, I could see nothing unusual. Franklin's fancy and well-used Packard was parked crookedly on the street, and I had little doubt he was snoring his head off in his untidy bed.

I'd already given Joseph one of my two automatics. I muttered a few more instructions to him.

On my command, we both kicked in the front door.

It made a thunderous noise as it crashed against the inner wall of the house. At nearly the same time, a hoarse shout emanated from the bedroom. Plunging into the house, Joseph and I took refuge behind what few sticks of furniture there were in the living room as I shouted:

"Franklin! It's Joe Scintilla! I know what you've done with Lizbeth Crawford, so give her up right now!"

Franklin's only response was to fire a gun in my direction. The bullet came surprisingly close, nearly grazing my ear. Franklin may have been out of the force for a decade or more, but he was a good shot.

I had told Joseph that it was essential we take him alive. As I suspected, Lizbeth was not here, so there must be even more people involved in this kidnapping conspiracy. With Franklin dead, we'd have no chance of finding her. But Franklin clearly wasn't going down without a struggle.

In the pitch darkness, it was nearly impossible to make out what was going on in that grimy bedroom of his. It appeared he had flopped behind the bed so that it was between us and him. From my vantage point behind a Morris chair, I could barely make out the top of his head. Joseph was behind a couch, eyes goggling with adrenalin. It was a standoff.

I shouted: "There are two of us, Franklin! You'll never make it!"

"What the hell are you doing, Scintilla!" he screamed. "Are you insane, breaking into my house? Get the fuck out of here! I don't know nothin'!"

"Don't give me that bull!" I shot back. "We know you were put up to kidnap Lizbeth, so if you know what's good for you—"

"You're crazy!" he said, aiming another shot in my direction.

In reply, I shot a hole into the wall near his head. But the last thing I wanted to do was to make a direct hit. So one more time I hissed some instructions to Joseph. Giving him some cover by aiming several shots in Franklin's general direction, I saw him dart out of the house.

In a matter of seconds, the glass of one of the bedroom windows crashed inward, showering Franklin with shards and making him shriek with terror. At that moment I moved rapidly forward so that I was just to the right of the open door leading into the bedroom. With Joseph now pointing his weapon directly at Franklin's back, I shouted:

"Give it up, man! We have you covered! Throw down your weapon—we just want to talk."

For a few moments Franklin sat cowering on the floor near his bed, irresolute. Then, with something of a whine, he threw his gun on to the bed and raised his arms.

"Get up—slowly," I said in a quieter voice.

He lumbered to his feet. He was wearing nothing but his underwear. In spite of the cold, his face was covered with sweat, and his large frame shook all over.

"OK, shamus," he said in wearied defeat. "Go ahead and kill me if you want to. I don't care anymore."

"Come off it, Franklin," I said. "Just sit down and let's talk."

I snapped up his gun from the bed, and he sat down on one corner of it. Not long thereafter, Joseph came back in the house, standing in the doorway of the bedroom with his automatic extended somewhat awkwardly. I told him to put it down, and he did so grudgingly.

"Franklin," I said, turning back to the ex-cop, "we know what's gone down. Helen Ward Crawford has had her grand-daughter kidnapped, for reasons I don't quite understand. We know you were involved. Better spill the beans."

I was fully aware that all this was a conjecture, but I had to put on a guise of certainty to get Franklin to cough up what he knew—if anything.

Franklin peered at me for a moment as if he were trying to read my mind. After a time, he collapsed within himself and said:

"OK, you win."

I had to smile a bit to myself, because if I'd been wrong, I suspect I'd have had to look for another line of work.

"But she's not here, Scintilla," Franklin went on hastily.

"Where is she?"

"I tell you, I didn't even do the job myself. . . . There's a couple nearby . . . they owed me big-time . . . I saved them from the chair after a robbery that went wrong . . . he was an old high school pal of mine . . . he got off with just eight years . . ."

Franklin seemed to be lapsing into some kind of reminiscence of his past life, but I put a quick end to that:

"Enough of that, Franklin. Just tell me where Lizbeth Crawford is."

Franklin looked at me pleadingly. "I don't know for certain, shamus. . . . I guess she must still be in their house somewhere— but maybe they moved her . . ."

"Well, we're going to find out," I said with resolution.

He didn't quite understand what that "we" signified, for he sat there on the bed, gaping up at me.

"Get up," I said, "and get some clothes on. We're going for a ride."

The address Franklin had given was about half a mile from his house—in a section of town even worse, if possible, than his own. Every other house seemed either boarded up or about to tumble down upon the ears of its sorry denizens; all kinds of paraphernalia—from kids' toys to a kitchen sink to a bicycle without wheels—littered the yards, and the cars on the streets or driveways seemed about as dilapidated as the houses. If there was any area that could pass as the very symbol and image of the Depression, this was it.

Before we left Franklin's own unsavory abode, we tied him up with some twine from his kitchen and bundled him into the car. Joseph looked at me in surprise as I started binding Franklin's arms and legs, but I quickly explained that I wasn't taking any chances on his tipping off his pals—a couple named Jake and Effie Nolan—before we showed up; and if he was lying altogether about Lizbeth's whereabouts, then I wanted him right under our nose so I could use various methods of persuasion to make him cough up the truth.

This whole business of Lizbeth's kidnapping had produced a slow burn in me. I wanted to knock someone's head off, and was rapidly ceasing to care whose it was. I knew I had to get a grip on myself.

We again parked more than a block away from the Nolans' house. The rain had mercifully let up a bit, but the cold still penetrated into our bones, making even the least motion a source of pain. As we approached the house, we saw a rattletrap of a jalopy—an ancient 1925 Nash—in the gravel driveway. I hated the thought of Lizbeth being crammed into that odoriferous vehicle even for a moment. As Joseph and I exited our own vehicle, we had no choice but to leave Franklin tied up in the back seat. Making sure that his bonds were secure, we got out and approached the house.

It was larger than Franklin's, but not by much. However, there was a back door, which Franklin's own house lacked.

There was also a basement, as I could see from two very narrow windows placed at ground level in the back of the house.

The house was pitch dark and dead quiet. If anyone was in there, they weren't publicizing the fact.

Those basement windows were so grimy, on both sides, that it was nearly impossible to look through them. I moistened my hand on the wet grass and tried to clean the central pane of one of the windows. The effect was still like looking through gauze, but I saw enough.

In a tiny clearing amidst a vast and confused mass of clutter, a woman in her nightgown was tied up to a straight-backed wooden chair. She was slumped over, either asleep or unconscious.

Once again I had to get a grip on my emotions. It would be insanity just to burst in there, pistols firing, before I knew exactly where the Nolans were. If one or both of them were in the basement somewhere, standing guard, any sudden hostile act could spell the end of Lizbeth Crawford. The Nolans weren't going to go down easy, and I didn't want to prod them into taking desperate measures.

Taking a few deep breaths, I surveyed the back of the house. I couldn't tell where the stairs to the basement were, but the back door was only a few feet away. A quick check showed not only that it was locked, but that a deadbolt was in place.

I was, however, prepared for that.

Out of a bag I got my suction-cup device and quickly—and silently—began cutting a circular hole into the glass pane of the door nearest the deadbolt. As Joseph looked on in amazement, I completed the circuit, pulled out the suction-cup with the glass now attached to it, reached my hand in, silently unlocked the deadbolt, and then turned the doorknob from the inside. The door began to yawn open, but a slight creak caused me to halt abruptly. However slowly I opened that door, the creak continued to sound. At this point I whispered some instructions to Joseph, who stayed just outside the door, automatic ready for use, while I pulled the door open just enough to let myself in.

I was in the kitchen, which was ferociously untidy and stank of stale cooking and alcohol. Luckily, the basement stairs directly faced the back door, so that it was the work of seconds for me to begin my descent. So far as I could tell, my entry was undetected.

The basement stairs, inevitably, creaked also, no matter how lightly I trod on them. It seemed a century before I descended those thirteen steps to the basement floor, after which I had to navigate a baffling maze of cartons, old toys, decrepit furniture, and other objects of a less comprehensible sort. The basement was sizeable, but seemed smaller because of all the debris cluttering it.

It wasn't long, however, before I made my way to Lizbeth Crawford.

She was tied firmly with thick twine to the chair—her hands and ankles tied together, and a rope that wrapped around her midsection and proceeded to the back of the chair. There was also a dirty red bandana gagging her mouth. Her hair was mussed, her nightgown was torn and rumpled, and dried tears had streaked her face. She made no movement as I approached.

I gently lifted her head, which had slumped over to one shoulder. With a penknife I rapidly sliced through the bandana, which fell to the floor. Taking precautions, I covered her mouth with my hand.

That was a smart move, for my actions had caused her eyes to pop open, and a shrill moan or scream began working its way out of her throat.

I tightened my grip on her mouth and hissed into her ear, "*Shhhh!* Be quiet. I'm going to get you out of here."

Her entire frame, which had clenched in shock and fear, relaxed abruptly, almost as if she were a balloon that someone had let the air out of. She looked at me with such a mixture of relief and gratitude that it wrenched my heart.

But I had work to do.

I quickly cut the ropes tying her to the chair. I gestured to her not to try to get up too quickly, as I suspected that she would need to restore blood circulation to her legs and arms before she could become ambulatory. She had nothing but slippers on, and they—and her thin, wispy nightgown—would have to do to protect her from the elements until we got to my car.

If we made it that far.

It seemed inconceivable that the Nolans had not been aroused by this invasion of their wretched abode. Could they really be such heavy sleepers? Could they be so careless of their prize after committing a serious felony? Was it possible they weren't even in the house?

I got the answers to all my silent queries when a gunshot exploded out of the dark and whizzed past my ear.

At once I flung Lizbeth to the ground and fell directly on top of her, to shield her from any more bullets. In spite of the clutter in the basement, there was nothing substantial behind which we could take refuge, so all I could do was fire blindly in the direction where that gunshot had lit up the area for a fraction of a second. The only thing that happened in response was a ferocious volley of shots that lit up the basement like freakish little pellets of lightning. Most of them went wildly astray.

But one got me in the left shoulder. It seemed to go all the way through, for only a few seconds after my own grunt of pain, I heard Lizbeth emit a little squeal. My right arm was, however, unaffected, and I returned fire as best I could, firing upward toward the top of the stairs.

Without warning, a heavy body tumbled down those stairs and landed violently on the floor. After an initial groan, it was motionless and silent.

Suddenly the lights blazed on, and I took in the scene quickly: The body on the floor must be Jake Nolan, although in overall girth he looked not unlike Franklin. At the top of the stairs was Joseph, beaming with pride and holding his automatic out in front of him like Wyatt Earp after a showdown.

But he celebrated a bit too soon. Out of nowhere behind him, a middle-aged woman, shrieking like a banshee, barreled into him with her arms extended. Before he had a chance to turn around, she had thrust him violently down the stairs. If he hadn't reached spasmodically for the rickety banister, he would have tumbled to the floor. As it was, he was forced to let go of his weapon, which clattered on to the floor of the kitchen above. Seizing the opportunity, the woman snatched up the weapon and leveled it at Joseph, teetering on the stairs while clutching the banister for dear life.

Before she could fire the weapon, I went into action. Forcing myself into a roughly sitting position in spite of the pain in my shoulder, I aimed my own automatic—not at her, but at the gun in her hand. I hit it squarely, and it flew out of her hand and tumbled down the stairs, landing not two feet from the recumbent form of her partner in crime.

She shrieked with pain and turned tail. I hastily crawled over the basement floor, picked up Joseph's weapon, and pocketed it. Nolan seemed unconscious, maybe dead, but I wasn't taking any chances. Only a few seconds later, I heard a car door open, then slam shut. There was a grinding of gears, a shriek of brakes, and then a motor revved up to full speed. In less time than it takes to tell, the sound of a speeding car receded into the distance.

The fleeing Effie Nolan was the least of my worries. A little weak-kneed, I made my way back to Lizbeth. I saw the back of her nightgown covered with blood and was momentarily alarmed; but her expression, while fearful and apprehensive, had little of pain in it. I began to realize that most of that blood was probably my own. As I looked down at my shoulder, I both saw and felt more than a trickle of blood emerging from the entry and the exit of the bullet.

I staggered to the very chair that Lizbeth had been tied up in. As she rose to her feet, she cried out in alarm, "Joe! You've been hit!" and stumbled over to me. There was little she could do except pass a hand gently over my face. There was nothing within easy reach to stanch the flow of blood—that dirty red bandana would not have served the purpose—so all she could do was coo at me.

Meanwhile, Joseph had staggered to his feet and made his way down the stairs. He stood looking at the body of Jake Nolan, now almost petrified that he had been the cause of someone's injury or death.

"How is he, Joseph?" I managed to breathe.

"I . . . I don't know, sir," he stammered. "I think he may be dead."

I saw a gunshot wound in his lower back, and a small pool of blood emerging from under his belly.

"Turn him over," I said. "Let's see what gives with him."

With extreme reluctance, Joseph took Nolan by the shoulder and tried to roll him over. His size—and Joseph's distaste—made the task difficult, but he managed it in the end.

We were rewarded by a low groan from deep within Nolan's throat. The front of his shirt was doused in blood, and he could do little but moan in pain.

"Better call the police, Joseph," I managed to say, "and an ambulance."

Then I passed out.

CHAPTER SEVENTEEN

I awoke to find myself in a room in the only hospital in Pompton Lakes. As I opened my eyes, I found Lizbeth slouched half-asleep in an uncomfortable chair near my bed. I was propped up in a half-sitting position, and my left shoulder was heavily bandaged. Aside from that, I seemed fine.

But as I shifted my body to get into a more comfortable position, a shooting pain went through my shoulder and down my back. I groaned heavily and fell back on to the bed.

My cry startled Lizbeth awake, and she sat up sharply, half surprised and half fearful. Then, as if suddenly remembering where she was, she sat back, exhausted. She looked all in. I hated to think that she had spent the entire night—or what was left of it after our escapade—in that dreadful chair.

"Can you tell me what's going on?" I managed to croak.

Lizbeth was hardly capable of speaking herself.

"There's so much to tell," she said wearily. "After you . . . um . . . fainted, Joseph managed to get to an all-night drugstore and call the police. I stood guard over you"—she smiled at the memory—"holding your gun. . . . The police came and took both you and that horrible man—"

She shuddered at the memory.

"Nolan?" I said. "Jake Nolan?"

"Yes, I suppose that's his name," she went on. "Anyway, they brought us all here. It seems Mr. Nolan just got a flesh wound... but I guess he'll go to jail. They're still looking for that wife of his."

"What about Myron Franklin?"

"Joseph said he was still in your car—he was slouched over on the back seat, all tied up, and sleeping. The police have him too. I think he spilled the beans about the whole business. . . ."

"What do you mean, exactly?" I said sharply.

"Well . . ." she seemed reluctant to speak further. Finally, in a rush:

"They've arrested Grandma."

"Have they now?" I said with a grim smile. "So Franklin squealed on her?'"

"I guess so," she said in a small voice.

"Well, that makes things a little easier," I said. "Where's Joseph now?"

"He went back to Thornleigh after the police finished questioning him."

"What about you? Don't tell me you've been sitting here all night?"

"Yes," she said softly. "I had to be here. I wanted to make sure you were OK."

"So what's the prognosis on me?"

"I think they said you'd be all right. The bullet went all the way through you, but no bones were broken. I think it grazed me a bit . . . they put a little bandage on me also."

She seemed proud to have endured her share of suffering during our rescue of her.

"So what happens now?" she went on.

"What happens now," I said heavily, as I struggled to get up out of the bed, "is that I have it out with your father. Maybe not today—I need to rest up a bit. But I have to get him to tell me what he knows about all this."

"You're just going to get up and leave?" she said in alarm. "But you're wounded! You have to wait till the doctors say it's OK to go . . ."

"I don't have to wait for anyone," I said gruffly, finding my clothes hung up in a closet. "Do you mind leaving while I get dressed?"

Lizbeth continued to flutter around me like a mother hen. "Joe, please, you have to rest. . . . Anyway, I think the police want to talk to you. They have a guard outside, I think. You'll have to meet with that police chief first."

"Yeah, OK, I can do that. But I'll see him—he doesn't have to come here and see me. Now out you get."

I shoved her out the door, closed it, and put my clothes on.

The policeman outside the door was startled to see me up and about, but I told him bluntly that if Police Chief Taber wanted to see me, somebody'd better take me to the station. Lizbeth had mentioned that Joseph had had to take my own car back to Thornleigh, and she called him to bring it to the station.

My talk with Taber confirmed what Joseph had told him earlier. Nolan had confessed that Franklin had pressured him and his wife Effie to do the actual kidnapping; Franklin had then pointed the finger at Helen Ward Crawford. Joseph had admitted that Mrs. Crawford had taken a drive into town the night before the kidnapping. That was enough for Taber, who had roused the household at Thornleigh at something like two in the morning and taken an outraged and fuming grandmother in handcuffs to jail.

I suspected, however, that it wouldn't be long before some expensive and high-powered attorney got her out on bail. So I said to Lizbeth:

"You're staying with me tonight."

Her eyes opened wide at this. "Joe, but I couldn't . . . ."

"You can and you will. I can't risk having you stay at Thornleigh until this matter is settled. Don't worry," I went on. "My girl Marge will be there."

She looked down at her feet. "I wasn't worried about anything like that."

"Good. Then it's settled."

Joseph brought my car over. He was grinning from ear to ear—whether from the recollection of his thrilling feats of the night before, or because the gorgon matriarch of the clan had been clapped in jail, or both, I couldn't say. I grinned back at him and gave him the thumbs up.

Then I drove Lizbeth to my crummy little flat on West 14th Street in Manhattan. By this time it was mid-afternoon, and I'd given Marge a call to tell her to come by after work. After that, I collapsed in my bed.

I awoke to find *two* mother hens clucking over me.

One of them was fixing up some kind of witches' brew—which turned it to be a pretty good beef stew—in my primitive kitchen, and the other was pulling up the blankets over me as if I was some little boy with the mumps. I was so exhausted I didn't know who was doing what.

Sleeping arrangements that night had to be improvised. Both girls refused to let me sleep anywhere except in my own bed, saying I needed to recover my strength. I hate being babied by women, but there wasn't much I could do about it. Marge would share my bed, while Lizbeth professed herself to be happy on the couch in the living room. I didn't relish the thought of her spending two uncomfortable nights in a row, but I guess we all had to rough it.

I was propped up on the left side of the bed, since lying flat still sent shooting pains all down my shoulder and back. The latest issue of *Black Mask* should have held my attention, as a new guy named Chandler was doing good work; but the pain-killers I was still regularly taking made me feel woozy and confused. I was thinking of just calling it an early night when Marge sidled into her side of the bed. She had a file folder in her hand.

"This afternoon I looked through the files for anything relating to the Crawfords," she said. "You'd asked me to look up the Bislands, but I thought maybe the Crawford file might be useful too."

I tended to doubt it, but I took the file from her and began leafing through it. It was surprisingly ample, but at a superficial glance it seemed to be anything but promising. The usual society column fluff—parties at Thornleigh where the New Jersey *haut ton* gathered like a herd of zebas at a watering-hole; the redoubtable Helen Ward Crawford making a name for herself by donating to local charities; even a brief notice, on November 8, 1918, of the birth the previous day of a little girl named Lizbeth Allen Crawford.

Nothing here that I didn't know already.

Then a clipping fell out of the folder and fluttered to the ground. I tried to snatch it out of the air with my right hand, but even that motion caused jolting pains all up and down my left side. Slowly and gingerly, as Marge looked on with a mask of concern on her face, I reached to the floor and picked up the clipping.

"What do you have there, Joe?" she said.

"I don't know," I said. "Maybe it's nothing."

But it was something.

It was a short, simple notice of the wedding of James Allen Crawford and Florence Bisland, which occurred—if the hand-written date scribbled on the top of the clipping was accurate—on March 6, 1918. That itself was unremarkable, but a single sentence in the notice caused me almost to fall out of the bed.

". . . the celebrations were festive in spite of the cloud of gloom that hung over the family from the death of James's elder brother, William, at Thornleigh only a month before."

The death of James's elder brother *at Thornleigh*.

If this clipping was right, then something was seriously wrong. Everyone had told me that Bill had died *in the war*. But according to the notice, he *hadn't* died in the war. He may have died *during* the war, but not *in* it.

He had died at Thornleigh.

The next morning, as soon as I was able, I got dressed and made plans to head back to Pompton Lakes.

Marge, leaving for work early, did her best to get me to promise not to overstrain myself. I didn't even reply to that, and she left in a bit of a huff, complaining about the pigheaded-ness of the male sex. Lizbeth, for her part, continued to flutter around me, trying to help me do things that no self-respecting man would let anyone help him with. Finally I had to speak to her a bit sharply, after which she flushed, backed off, and just looked at her toes.

When she said she wanted to accompany me back to New Jersey, I said:

"Not a chance, Lizbeth. There are things I gotta do alone. You'll have to stay here."

"But Joe, please," she pleaded, "maybe I can help . . . ."

"Maybe you can," I said, as gently as I could, "but it's really best if I do this by myself. Please take my word for it."

By this time I had taken her by the shoulders and was looking right into her eyes. She tried to match my gaze, but eventually she gave up. Choking back tears, she slumped down on the couch and said:

"OK, Joe. Do what you have to do."

I can't remember what I said to that. It wasn't much. But I got out of there as quickly as I could.

That police station in Pompton Lakes was beginning to feel like a home away from home.

Taber and others looked at me in surprise as I marched in.

"What's up, Joe?" Taber said with the faintest whiff of apprehension.

"I need to look at your records again."

"I thought you already saw everything pertaining to the Crawfords."

"I saw the file for *Frank* Crawford. Now I need to see the file for *William* Crawford."

Taber wrinkled his forehead in puzzlement. He was obviously unaware that there even was such a file. But I had to believe there was.

And, sure enough, there it was.

Why hadn't I seen it before? Even though everyone called him Bill, his given name was of course William. It had been placed, properly enough, directly behind the file for Frank. But a stray sheet of paper had protruded above the file and covered over the tab that had William's name on it.

OK, call me careless. But at the time I was looking at Frank's file, I had no reason to believe there even was a file for William. So that fraction of an inch of paper had sent me on something of a wild goose chase.

Anyway, the file contained much of interest. William Allen Crawford had indeed died at Thornleigh, on February 8, 1918. He was on furlough and had been home for close to two weeks. I saw that he hadn't even gone overseas to the war zone; instead, he had spent his entire military career stationed as a reserve officer at Fort Standish in Boston. I didn't doubt that his mother's influence had kept him out of harm's way. She may have had to give up at least one of her sons to the war effort, but she could at least contrive it so that he came back in one piece.

But it hadn't worked out the way she wanted.

The police report was ambiguous in some particulars, but from what I could piece together, it seemed that William had, on that morning of February 8th, fallen into the lake that abuts the rear of Thornleigh and drowned. There was some little mystery about this, because William had been known to be a reasonably good swimmer. A wound to the back of the head had been assumed to have been the result of his hitting a submerged rock.

The death had been reported by William's brother, James Allen Crawford.

So James Allen Crawford may or may not have killed his brother.

But it wasn't his brother Frank.

It was his brother William.

CHAPTER EIGHTEEN

"So why did you kill your brother William?"

I was sitting across a tale from James Allen Crawford in the interrogation room at Rahway State Prison.

Maybe I shouldn't have been so blunt. His response was explosive.

He shot up violently from the chair, sending it hurtling back against the wall. He himself, after making an initial move in my direction, backed himself into a corner like an animal at bay. His eyes blazed, and a curious choking sound emerged from deep in his throat.

The tumult roused the guard, who was standing outside the door. He made a move to enter, but I stopped him with a gesture of my hand.

I turned back to the prisoner.

"I know the whole story, Mr. Crawford," I said. I didn't, but I had to claim that I did to get Crawford to cough up what had actually happened.

Still cowering in the corner, but seeming ready to leap in my direction at any moment, Crawford said: "What do you know? How could you know anything?"

I closed my eyes for a moment and let out an exhausted sigh.

"I have the goods on you, Crawford. I dug up your brother Frank's empty grave—and I found Frank himself, alive and kicking, in Mexico. And I now know that it wasn't him you killed, but William. The sainted William whom everyone said died in the war.

"The only thing I don't know, Crawford, is *why*.

"Why did you weasel out of a murder you *did* commit and confess to a murder that you *didn't* commit?

"What gives with you, Mr. James Allen Crawford?"

For a time, Crawford just looked at me, his expression mutating from outrage to a kind of crestfallen self-pity. His face crumpled in wretchedness, and his slipped to the floor, burying his head in his hands.

I just stood there looking down at him.

After a long time he peered up in my direction. He seemed to want to plow himself as deep into the corner of this stark little room as he could, as if he could somehow vanish from my sight, and from the sight of the world.

Finally he said very softly: "Scintilla, can you even begin to imagine what kind of hell my whole life has been?"

"Oh, come off it, Crawford," I snapped. "You mean to tell me you can't buy happiness with all that money you and your family have?"

I didn't mean that, of course: I was beginning to have some inkling of the truth of what he had just said. But I needed to prod him into spilling the beans.

My tart comment may have done the trick.

Now enraged again, he sprung up from the floor and seemed intent on throttling me with his bare hands—just the kind of throttling he pretended to have given his own brother a dozen years ago.

I stood motionless, and some innate restraint held him in check. Trembling from head to foot, he quietly picked up the fallen chair, carefully restored it to its position by the table, and sat down in it.

"You want to know the score, Scintilla?" he almost whispered. "OK, I'll tell you. If you want to be my father confessor, then you'll get the whole story. God knows I've kept it locked inside me long enough. Maybe that's why I've become what I've become . . ."

Those last few sentences seemed to have been spoken to

himself, and he wasn't even looking at me anymore.

I quietly sat down in my chair as Crawford resumed.

"Do you know what it's like to have a brother who over-shadows you in every way? 'The sainted William'—yes, that's exactly what he was. Bright, quick-witted, handsome, good in sports—and you better believe my parents made no secret of the fact. Bill was always being groomed as the head of the family and the natural successor to his dynamic father. And after Dad died, just before the war, Bill became the savior of the Crawford clan—the great white hope for the next generation.

"I don't know that Bill ever regarded me as anything but a joke. Everything came easy to him—the girls, the honors, the adulation of his peers. I had to fight tooth and nail for everything I got—and that wasn't much. I was only two years younger, but it could have been a century. He never wanted me hanging around him—he looked at me as if I were some kind of worm or insect; said I 'held him back.'"

Crawford looked at me with a kind of pleading look.

"Scintilla, do you know what it's like to look upon someone with this twisted mix of love, hate, envy, admiration, and longing? I wanted to *be* William more than anything in the world—and I wanted it all the more exactly because I knew I never could be.

"There was a time"—Crawford almost choked at the memory—"when, as teenagers, we were swimming in the lake behind our estate. Yes, yes, Bill was a great swimmer, and I was only average—dogged but mediocre. And for no reason at all but for the fun of it, he held me down—with one hand—under the water until I almost drowned. I can still hear that dreadful laughter of his as I was blubbering under the surface. Was this to be the end of me? Was I going to die hearing my own brother laugh at me while he killed me for sport?

"That's how it was, Scintilla. He got everything, I got nothing.

"And so the war came. My mother couldn't keep all of us out of it, but she still managed to pull enough strings to get Bill into a safe stint at Fort Standish, where there wasn't the slightest chance of his coming into harm's way. She said she needed me at home to help run the business, so I got exempted altogether. And even that was a humiliation: Bill could parade around in his shiny officer's uniform, while I was stuck being a glorified accountant.

"And then there's Florence . . . ."

At this point Crawford's expression turned from self-pity to blazing anger.

"That was in some ways the most humiliating thing of all.... Mother of course wanted to make sure that at least one of her boys produced offspring to carry on the family name. But the sainted Bill could never just be set up with a suitable female like a stud thrown into a field with a heifer: he was given the luxury of finding his true love—so long, of course, as it was one of our own class. But as for me . . . well, it was just fine for me to get paired up with Florence, a kind of consolation prize thrown into my lap as good breeding stock. We'd known the Bislands for years, but they were decidedly second-tier—almost like poor relations. . . .

"So there I was, working like a dog to keep the family business going while Bill was playing at being soldier. . . . And as for Frank—well, he dealt with things in his own way. He didn't seem to care that Mother thought him even more contemptible than me; he just wanted to have a good time. Was he a skirt-chaser? So what? He didn't care! As long as he had enough money to buy an endless parade of willing female flesh, he was happy."

Once again Crawford peered into my face with eyes slitted and blazing.

"So you want to know what went down that day in 1918, Scintilla? OK, here's the scene. . . .

"So my wedding had been set for March. I can't say I was looking forward to it; not that I disliked Florence—then—but I resented being some kind of pawn that my mother was moving around as if she owned the board. Nothing mattered to her save that everyone play the parts she had assigned to them; and woe betide anyone who struck out on their own! . . . Well, the joke of it is that, after all this careful planning, everything blew up in her face!"

He laughed mirthlessly at the memory.

"Florence was already ensconced in Thornleigh . . . God knows there was enough room for her in that cavern of a house, and she and Mother were planning the whole wedding themselves, no expense spared. Not that she cared one way or the other about our happiness; but she knew that a Crawford wedding at Thornleigh had to be a spectacle if it was to bring due credit to the family.

"And so Bill shows up on a furlough. And what does he proceed to do? He seduces my own fiancée under my nose.

"Oh, it was nothing so crude as what Frank would have done— and I can assure you that his advances were fully returned by their recipient. Florence had known Bill for years, of course, but I suppose something about that uniform he strutted around in turned her head. Or maybe it was just that she saw that he was in every way a new and improved version of me—money *plus* brains *plus* good looks, and now an army career to boot. Who wouldn't want that over a dull plodder like myself?"

I sat silent, letting Crawford wallow in self-pity for a few moments. If he was going to get things off his chest, he had to do it in his own way.

"So, yes," he resumed, "I could tell that Bill was getting pretty chummy with his future sister-in-law. He actually came up and told me that she had just the kind of delicate good looks that always appealed to him. I was on the verge of saying, 'Well, why don't *you* marry her, then?' but didn't have the guts. Anyway, I knew that, as far as Mother was concerned, Florence wasn't quite well-connected enough for her favorite son.

"But that didn't stop him from paying a visit to her bedroom one night in February.

"How do I know?" he snapped in reply to a phantom question from me. *"Because I saw him coming out of her room the next morning!"*

He was clutching the table with both hands in a vise-grip, eyes boggling, nostrils flaring, and mouth working.

"Is that so?" is all I could think of saying.

"Yeah, that's so, Scintilla," Crawford said snidely. "And Bill couldn't even be troubled to be ashamed of it. He just gave me this crooked smile as if he were saying, 'I'm just getting a little advance taste, little brother,' and walked off with a snicker.

"That did it, Scintilla. From that point I vowed that Bill wouldn't live to enjoy his cuckolding of me. I just didn't realize how quickly I'd get my chance.

"Later that morning I found myself near the lake, fuming with rage. What could I do? Call the whole wedding off? My mother wouldn't hear of it. Even if I told her what had happened, all she would do was say something like, 'Oh, get over it, Bill has a right to everything that's yours anyway.' But the idea of my having to spend the rest of my life with a wife and a brother who had betrayed me was too much. Something had to snap. And it did.

"So the next thing I know, Bill is standing right beside me. There was still a bit of a grin on his face, but at least he had the decency to look a bit chastened. Maybe he was going to apologize—I don't know. I didn't give him the chance.

"The moment he came near me, I lashed out at him, throwing a punch that didn't even connect. He backed off a bit—I don't think I'd ever hit him except in self-defense—but by this time I was pretty near insane with fury. I struck out at him in every way possible—with blows, kicks, scratches, everything I could think of that would inflict even a tiny fraction of the injury that his very existence had wreaked on me for twenty-five years.

"But it was useless. The army had trained him well, and he fought me off with ease on that cold February day. Finally he seemed to lose patience and dealt me a vicious blow to the chin with his fist.

"I went down in a heap. I think I may have passed out for a moment. I was quite literally lying prone at his feet. I looked up at him, and he gave me this look of mingled pity and contempt that I'll never forget.

"I felt like a cornered rat. I knew I could never beat him physically. So I had to use cunning.

"I moaned and groaned, writhing on the ground and holding my jaw as if it were broken. The trick worked. Bill bent down to see if I was OK, and at that moment I grabbed a rock that I'd seen before and dealt him a vicious hit to the side of the head.

"Now it was his turn to fall down in a heap. Scintilla, I don't think I've ever felt such a surge of pleasure as at that moment. Yes, I know it's reprehensible to fight with your own brother, but a lifetime of humiliation seemed wiped out with that one blow.

"He was only stunned, so I knew I had to act fast. He was a big man, but I managed to drag his body into the frigid lake. I knew that just a minute or two would be enough for the job. The moment his body felt the cold water around him, he roused himself a bit; but he was still so dazed and hurt that it wasn't hard to hold his head down under the water—just as he'd done to me a decade or more ago—until he stopped moving.

"That was it," Crawford said. "It proved surprisingly easy to kill someone. But I knew this was only the beginning. I also wanted to escape the consequences of my crime.

"So I ran back to the house, screaming that Bill had fallen into the lake and that I couldn't get him out. Everyone knew he was a good swimmer, but that water was freezing cold, and no one could blame me for not being able to rescue him. Everyone also knew that my own capacities as a swimmer were modest at best.

"Here again it was surprising how easily things went. And the funny thing is that Mother proved a big help. You know, Scintilla"—he peered at me sharply—"I'm convinced that woman has no morals at all. All she cares about is herself and the family. I'm sure she knew what I'd done; I caught her looking askance at me for months, maybe years afterward. Oh, she knew all right—but right from the beginning she was determined to take action to protect her interests.

"The easiest part was dealing with the police. That brainless ass Myron Franklin was no obstacle."

"Did you buy him off then, just as you did later with Frank's 'death'?" I said.

"Didn't have to," Crawford replied shortly. "Franklin knew he had to tread lightly when there was anything involving the Crawfords. He wasn't going to make waves unless he was forced to. And, as it happens, a case of 'accidental death' was the most plausible scenario anyway, and there were no witnesses who could have told a different tale.

"So that seemed to be the end of that," Crawford said with a kind of sigh. "But of course, it wasn't the end. . . ."

He looked down at his hands, uncertain how to proceed.

"Scintilla, maybe I haven't done a good job of telling you how I felt about my brother William. I did love him, you know, and I respected and admired him. He was my brother, for God's sake! You can't live with someone your whole life and not have feelings for him. No matter how he had treated me over the years—and, in fact, I guess he didn't treat me any different from what many other older brothers would have done—and no matter how much I may have resented him, not so much for his accomplishments, which he had earned, but for the shameless favoritism my parents had shown toward him, he was still my brother.

"And now I had caused his death.

"I'm not prepared to delve into the legal niceties of whether it might have been justifiable homicide or self-defense or any rubbish like that. The overriding fact is that I had engendered the death of another human being, and my own flesh and blood at that. It ate at me, Scintilla—it would eat at anyone who had any grain of decency in him. I was a murderer; I had committed fratricide. There are precious few crimes in the world worse than that.

"But what was I to do? I had to drag out my cheerless life with a wife who didn't love me—and who, I imagine, also had a strong suspicion of what I'd done—and a mother who secretly had contempt for me but who was now compelled to regard me as the head of the family instead of the other son she had been grooming for the role for his entire life.

"My only salvation was Lizbeth."

He looked at me with tears in his eyes.

"Yes, Scintilla, she was Bill's child. I knew that; Florence knew that; probably even Mother knew that. But that little bundle of flesh was my one and only link to my dead brother, and I vowed to cherish her as if she were my own. And I think I've done a fair job at that, Scintilla. She's the only one who's stayed loyal to me—maybe because she's never known anyone else. Her devotion to me has carried me on all these years. . . ."

I was surprised at his revelation of Lizbeth's true parentage and touched by his tenderness toward a child that wasn't even his. But he had only told half the story.

"But Crawford," I said, "what I don't get is this whole charade with Frank . . . ."

He again almost exploded with rage—although perhaps it was more at my denseness than at anything else.

"Don't you see, Scintilla? I had to make amends . . . I had to take responsibility for my actions. I was a murderer. With the passing of the years, I felt more and more consumed with guilt. I had committed a heinous crime and had escaped justice. To me, the mere fact that I was a free man was more galling to me than that I'd rubbed out my brother.

"So when Frank got into this mess with Eva Dailey, I sensed an opportunity to put things right. Maybe I'd dodged the law for one murder . . . but I wouldn't dodge it for another.

"Yes, of course it would have been a lot easier to have paid Eva Dailey off, or to have Frank just disappear somewhere. The whole farce of staging his death would have been preposterous—*except as a way for me to get my just desserts*. Perhaps that doesn't make sense to you, Scintilla—I know you deal with a lot of shady characters who'd do anything to stay out of jail...."

"You got me wrong, Crawford," I said heavily.

He stopped abruptly and looked me in the face. But he could

meet my gaze only for a moment.

"I'm sorry about that, Scintilla. I don't know you, and I have no warrant for accusing you of anything. But the point is that I had to serve the time I felt I deserved. That's why I'm here, and that's why I want to stay here.

"Once again, the whole thing proved surprisingly easy. I had to bring Dr. Granger into it, and of course Mother had to know. And this time, I suspected that Franklin would indeed have to be bought off. It was a bit of a task to convince them that this fake death was the way to go, but Mother helped in that. I had a feeling she wanted me out of the way as well: both I and Frank, in our different ways, had disappointed her, and she was glad to see the back of both of us. Things were helped by the fact that Florence had proved surprisingly adept at handling the family business, rendering me pretty much supernumerary.

"I won't lie, Scintilla. I didn't just want to make amends with the law and with my own conscience; I wanted to get out of Thornleigh. Life since Bill's death had become intolerable. There was no joy or cheer in that household—we were all just going through the motions of being a loving family. Tension was everywhere—between me and my slut of a wife, my *roué* of a younger brother, and especially my mother, who seemed increasingly to be some kind of witch who had cast a spell on us and was manipulating us to her own evil desires. Only little Lizbeth was oblivious to it all . . . but in the end, even she wasn't enough for me. I had to get out of there. Twenty years in prison would be better than twenty years in that loveless tomb of a house."

He stopped abruptly. Then he looked me in the face.

"So what happens now, Scintilla? Are you going to spill the beans to everyone?"

I looked back at him without expression. "That's not my call, Crawford. I'm not the police. I've been hired to do a job, and I've done it. What happens now is out of my hands."

I got up to leave, but Crawford grabbed me by the arm.

"Scintilla . . . you gotta understand something. I don't want

Lizbeth hurt . . . any more than she already has been. She thinks I'm her father, and she seems to think the world of me, God knows why. Don't take that away from her. She doesn't have to know."

I wasn't insensible to the pleading look he gave me.

"Crawford, I can keep a tight lip when I have to. And I think this is one of those times when I should."

It was, I think, the first and last time I saw him smile.

CHAPTER NINETEEN

There was one more conversation I had to have.

Thornleigh seemed a bit less funereal than usual, chiefly because of the continued absence of Helen Ward Crawford and because Joseph the butler still seemed in a state of ill-concealed euphoria after his feats of derring-do. He greeted me with an enormous grin and a bluff, "How's tricks, Mr. Scintilla?" when I showed up at the door.

I smiled at him and said things were going fine.

Then, with a little more concern: "How's Miss Lizbeth doing, sir?"

"She's very well," I assured him. "She's at my place, but probably it's safe enough for her to come back here later today. But right now," I went on, "I was hoping to see Mrs. Florence Crawford."

Joseph's eyes expanded a trifle at that, but he murmured something noncommittal and went off to look for her.

Florence drifted in after a few moments. She had always struck me as a kind of Pre-Raphaelite beauty, with her delicate countenance and a perpetually sad or pensive look. Today was no different, and she greeted me with something less than enthusiasm, even though she was well aware that I had had a big hand in the rescuing of her precious daughter.

"Joseph said you wished to speak to me," she said.

"Yes, ma'am," I replied. "Can we sit down?"

We both seated ourselves on the couch in the parlor, as far apart as possible. She looked at me square in the face, as if preparing herself for some kind of blow.

"Mrs. Crawford, I've spoken to your husband, and he's told me pretty much everything. I don't know how much you know about what's been going on here—"

"Not much," she interjected.

"I thought as much. But Mr. Crawford has made some remarks about you and his brother William . . . ."

Her expression didn't change much, except that perhaps her mouth got a little tighter. I was hoping she would pick up the conversation, but she refused to take the bait.

"Maybe," I said quietly, "it's none of my business . . . ."

"Maybe it isn't," she replied with unwonted tartness.

"But you know," I said a little more sharply, "that I have a responsibility to my client. Lizbeth Crawford is my client."

"What do you want me to say, Mr. Scintilla?" She had raised her voice only fractionally, but for her it was tantamount to a shout. "How much do you know, and how much are you going to tell Lizbeth?"

"That's up to you, I think."

"Is it, Mr. Scintilla?" She suddenly got up and began pacing the room. Splotches of red now mottled her usually pale face. "Do you really want to tell my daughter that the man she has worshipped all these years isn't her father?—that her real father was murdered by his own brother? Is that your idea of having a 'responsibility' to your client?"

"So you knew all that?" I said quietly.

"Of course I did," she said with some impatience. "Both Helen and I knew at once what had happened. *That* was the real cover-up. This whole business with Frank was just a ridiculous lark."

"So it's true that you and William . . . ."

"Yes, yes," Florence said wearily. "I daresay James has put the worst possible interpretation on what happened . . . I know what he says about me—that I'd . . . I'd make myself available to anyone in trousers—but you have no idea, Mr. Scintilla, what sort of a person James is. If there is anyone on this earth who is entirely undeserving of any woman's love, it's that man."

She sat down in exhaustion and, after a few moments, continued.

"Bill and James—what a contrast. . . . I'd known both of them for a long time, and saw how, with each passing year, James's resentment and envy of Bill grew to the level of some horrible obsession. And then to have me offered up like some sort of sacrificial lamb to James . . . Oh, I don't blame either my parents or Helen—they were just doing what they thought was best for both families . . . But my feelings for Bill were not some kind of girlish infatuation, much less a crude desire for . . . physical satisfaction."

She swung around to face me.

"I *loved* him, Mr. Scintilla—loved him in a way that James could never understand, and with a love that James could never inspire. And that's how it was."

"Not to be indelicate," I said, "but how can you be so sure that Lizbeth is William's child?"

Florence looked at me with an expression of amused pity, as if I were a slow-witted kindergartener.

"How can I be sure? I'll tell you how. James and I . . . have never had marital relations. Never. Not once. Is that good enough for you?"

"I imagine it is," I said.

"I won't pretend I've missed anything," she said with a harsh laugh that didn't suit her. "James of course thought I was polluted by Bill's embraces; and for my part, I was happy he refused to touch me. In that sense, it was a dream come true. I won't pretend we've had a happy marriage, but it would have been much worse if he'd . . . he'd forced himself on me."

She blushed a deep crimson and looked down at her hands.

"You don't need to say any more," I said.

But she quickly looked up at me with a frown of worry on her face.

"There's no need to tell Lizbeth any of this, is there?" she said in a tone that was strikingly similar to James's when he had made the same request.

"Look, ma'am," I said, "how you deal with the skeletons in your family closet are your affair. I've done what I've been hired to do—prove that James Allen Crawford is innocent of the murder of his brother Frank—and beyond that, it's not my place to say anything."

She reached out her hand to touch my own.

"Thank you, Mr. Scintilla. I'm not sure how we're going to handle things now, but we'll do our best. Lizbeth deserves that."

I had nothing more to say.

I brought Lizbeth back to her home later that day. I told her as much as I could about my meeting with her "father" without violating any of the promises I had made to both James and Florence. She was content with the fact that her father had been proven innocent of Frank's death, and she was still resolved to get him out of prison in spite of his own wish to stay there. I had to shrug off her persistent queries as to why James wanted to remain locked up, saying it was something she'd have to ask him about.

There was no neat resolution to this whole messy affair. I learned later of several developments:

Helen Ward Crawford was let out of jail and all charges were dropped, because Lizbeth refused to press kidnapping charges. Helen's flunkies, Myron Franklin and the Nolans, were also released. Helen seemed chastened by her few days in the hoosegow, and I could only hope she would be a little less of a gorgon than she had been.

James Allen Crawford was released from jail, although the Crawfords had to appeal to the governor for clemency. Frank Crawford made a flying visit to Pompton Lakes to prove that he was still above the earth, then fled back to his comfortable lair in Mexico. Lizbeth promised to visit him there, but he didn't seem keen on that prospect.

Lizbeth said that her parents were attempting to become reconciled, although it was going to be a long and slow business. Her own happiness at her father's release seemed to be helping matters. Maybe James felt that the time he had already served was sufficient penance for his various crimes and derelictions.

Lizbeth seemed to think of me as a kind of replacement for the uncle who had vanished south of the border. And that was fine with me.

"You really liked that kid, didn't you?" Marge asked me as she snuggled up to me.

I winced a little—my shoulder was still tender—but I liked her softness and warmth next to me.

"Yeah, sure, I liked her," I said. "Who wouldn't? But she's just a kid."

"A big, shapely, well-dressed, and wealthy kid," Marge said with a smile.

"And I'm sure she'll find a nice husband among the blue-bloods of New Jersey."

"Not your type?" she kept needling.

"Oh, I wouldn't say that," I replied blandly. "Any dame with curves like that is my type. But"—looking right in her face—"you got curves too, and something else besides."

"What?" Marge asked, wide-eyed. She couldn't imagine she had anything over the fetching Lizbeth.

"You've developed a tolerance for a guy named Joe Scintilla," I said, wrapping her in my arms as tightly as my bum shoulder would allow.

As I said, I ain't no monk.

And she ain't no nun.

ABOUT THE AUTHOR

S. T. JOSHI is a widely published critic and editor. He is the author of such critical studies as *The Weird Tale* (1990), *H. P. Lovecraft: The Decline of the West* (1990), and *The Modern Weird Tale* (2001). For Penguin Classics, he has prepared three annotated editions of Lovecraft's tales, as well as editions of the works of Lord Dunsany, Algernon Blackwood, and M. R. James, and the anthology *American Supernatural Tales* (2007). His exhaustive biography, *H. P. Lovecraft: A Life* (1996), won the British Fantasy Award and the Bram Stoker Award from the Horror Writers Association. He is coeditor of Ambrose Bierce's *Collected Short Fiction* (2006; 3 vols.), and has edited several editions of the work of H. L. Mencken. He is coeditor of *Supernatural Literature of the World: An Encyclopedia* (2005; 3 vols.) and the editor of *Documents of American Prejudice* (1999), *Atheism: A Reader* (2000), *In Her Place: A Documentary History of Prejudice against Women* (2006), *Icons of Horror and the Supernatural* (2006; 2 vols.), *The Agnostic Reader* (2007), and other volumes. Among his writings on politics and religion are *God's Defenders: What They Believe and Why They Are Wrong* (2003) and *The Angry Right* (2006). He has compiled bibliographies of H. P. Lovecraft (1981; rev. 2009), Ambrose Bierce (1999), Gore Vidal (2007), H. L. Mencken (2009), and other authors. He lives with his numerous cats in Seattle, Washington.

www.ingramcontent.com/pod-product-compliance
Lightning Source LLC
Chambersburg PA
CBHW020749250626
47155CB00003B/997

TRAGEDY AT SARSFIELD MANOR

Sarsfield Manor, a palatial home on the Eastern Shore of Maryland, has seen more than its share of horror and tragedy. It was built by four wealthy brothers in the eighteenth century, who abruptly committed suicide some years after it was constructed. Many years later, John Kenneth Sarsfield was carted away to an insane asylum for reasons no one can ascertain.

In 1937 the members of the Sarsfield family have been brought to the manor by the terms of the strange will of John Kenneth Sarsfield, who had set up a riddle that they must solve on the premises. Private investigator Joe Scintilla is brought in to investigate a bizarre murder seemingly committed by his school friend, Charles Jameson, who was found holding a dagger that had been plunged into the back of his aunt, Judith Kellar. But this crime is only the final act of a tragedy that reaches back centuries, making Sarsfield Manor a house haunted by deeds of unthinkable violence.

TRAGEDY AT SARSFIELD MANOR

A JOE SCINTILLA MYSTERY

S. T. JOSHI

THE BORGO PRESS

MMXI

TRAGEDY AT SARSFIELD MANOR

Copyright © 2011 by S. T. Joshi

FIRST EDITION

Published by Wildside Press LLC

www.wildsidebooks.com

TRAGEDY AT SARSFIELD MANOR

CONTENTS

CHAPTER ONE

I was racing down to the Eastern Shore of Maryland at breakneck speed to help my friend, Charles Jameson.

We were college buddies—Johns Hopkins, Class of '23—but I hadn't seen much of him in the fourteen intervening years. I knew he had become a professor of classics at the University of Maryland at College Park—the author of any number of immensely learned notes on textual problems in Juvenal and the like—but there was something about him that always disturbed me.

In short, Jameson was what one would call a "sad sack." He cultivated pessimism and a kind of brooding misanthropy as if it were a badge of honor. Being around him actually made you more cheerful—the "there but for the grace of God go I" idea. Many of his college friends felt he was just putting on an act, or that he had read too much of Swift and Byron and found it amusing to dwell on the futility of all effort, the kind of thing that Schopenhauer had summed up in the plangent utterance, "Human life must be some kind of mistake."

But I sensed that there was something more in Charles's low spirits than a callow reflection of fashionable philosophers. He had hinted of things in his past, or his family's past, that had permanently colored his perception of himself and of the world around him. No one could keep up a mere pretense of depression so faithfully or unremittingly.

And now he was in trouble. In short, he was in jail on a suspicion of murder.

It was not surprising to me that the case involved his family. The wild story he blurted out on the 'phone while locked up in the Chestertown police station was little short of fantastic— something to do with a bizarre contest or riddle that had to be solved at his ancestral home, Sarsfield Manor, well outside that centuried town. His incoherence was enough to persuade me that something serious was afoot, for Charles was ordinarily as cynically phlegmatic as the Sphinx.

The short version of the story was that he had gathered at Sarsfield Manor with a number of his other relatives; that his aunt Judith had been killed; and that he was found with his hand gripping an antique dagger that had been buried in her back.

It did not look good for him. His vehement denial of guilt seemed heartfelt, but I was not about to let an old friendship impel me to pervert justice, if he were indeed the culprit. But the case, from what little I knew so far, presented so many oddities that I felt obliged to pursue it. Where it would lead, I had no idea.

As I entered Maryland from the north, crossing from New Jersey to Pennsylvania north of Philadelphia, I had to resist the unconscious tendency to continue down to Baltimore, where I had spent several of the most rewarding and stimulating years of my life. I myself was not a little callow in those years as a wide-eyed student of philosophy, and couldn't then have imagined that my future career lay as a hardened private investigator. I wanted to look up Henry Mencken, holding forth as he had done for decades from his house on Hollins Street, but suspected that our political differences would dynamite any attempt at cordiality. I was a supporter of FDR, he an increasingly cantankerous opponent, writing screed after screed in an *American Mercury* that was already in the process of declining from an iconoclastic nose-thumber of the booboisie to a haven of cranky right-wingers.

We would, however, have seen eye-to-eye on one matter. Mencken had bravely spoken out against a lynching that had occurred on the Eastern Shore six years before, something that

shocked him and other Marylanders who felt that, in spite of their residence below the Mason-Dixon line, the vicious paranoia of Southern white trash was inconceivable in their blandly wholesome state. It had happened in Salisbury, and some of the details were chillingly gruesome—such as the fact that someone had cut off several toes of the wretched Negro and taken them away as souvenirs.

It was hard to imagine incidents of that sort occurring as I skirted the northern shore of the Chesapeake and headed down to Chestertown, an exquisite colonial village on the north bank of the Chester River and home to the venerable Washington College. It was as if a little corner of England had been uprooted and planted in the New World, where it blended with smiling farms and pleasant country roads to create a flawless picture of civilized placidity. As I entered the town I saw in the distance the imposing brick façade of Sarsfield Manor, which similarly boasted a history stretching to pre-Revolutionary days and was a testament to the wealth and taste of its builders, the four brothers Sarsfield.

During our college days Charles Jameson had once taken me to the village of Chestertown, but had perversely refused to show me the manor or lead me anywhere near it. I had taken offense, suggesting gruffly that there was no need for his pseudo-aristocratic family to look down their noses on a commoner; he had apologized profusely, stating that a certain adolescent trauma had made him regard the place as a kind of nexus of spiritual evil. How that baleful characterization could have harmonized with the stolid Georgian brick of Sarsfield Manor puzzled me at the time; in the years since then, I have learned not to judge books, houses, or people by their covers.

The Chestertown jail was not difficult to find, and the rotund police chief, Frank Powers, was not inclined to make a fuss about my seeing Jameson, even though I had no legal standing to do so. Of course, Charles had hired a lawyer, but, as he presently told me, it was painfully evident that that veteran jurist was inclined to think the worst of his client and to do little but

hope to save Charles's hide in the manner of Clarence Darrow's prestidigitation in the Leopold and Loeb case thirteen years before. It was for this reason, indeed, that Charles had frantically called me: the case presented such a number of anomalies that only a seasoned private investigator could, in his perhaps excessively optimistic judgment, plunge to the bottom of it.

I greeted Charles warily. He was sitting disconsolately in his cell, hardly aware that the police chief had allowed me entrance into the cell block. When I called out to him, he jumped up in alarm—almost in horror—before relaxing in relief. Through the bars he extended a hand, looking at me with a kind of harried desperation, as if I were some kind of personal savior.

"Joe . . . God, I can't tell you how glad I am to see you!"

As I shook his hand, I couldn't help thinking that this was presumably the same hand that had gripped a dagger that had killed his aunt.

He noticed my hesitation and dubiety, and after a brief shake withdrew the hand as if it were polluted. For a time we stared at each other without uttering. Then:

"Joe, I'm in a bit of a jam . . . ."

"I can see that," I said, trying to drain my voice of any suspicion of sarcasm.

"You have to believe I didn't do it," he said breathlessly, peering into my eyes as beads of sweat appeared on his brow. "I know what they say . . . I know my cousin saw me holding that weapon in Judith's back . . . but that was *afterwards!*" I didn't understand what that meant. "She was lying there dead, and I was only trying to help. . . . What possible reason could I have for killing her?—I hardly even knew her! They'll tell you it was because I wanted the money—the money from John Kenneth Sarsfield's will—that Judith had solved the riddle and that I was trying to shut her up . . . but it's all—"

I interrupted him sharply: "Charles, slow down. I can't follow you. You need to tell me the story from the beginning. What brought you and others of your family to Sarsfield Manor? I know you hated the place. Who is John Kenneth Sarsfield, and

what's the business about his will? What's the riddle you were trying to solve?"

Charles looked at me with an unutterable weariness that almost sent him to the floor of his cheerless cell. Passing a hand over his face, both to rub away the sweat and, it seemed, to brace himself for the long account he knew he would have to tell, he sat down heavily on his narrow bed and urged me to seat myself in a chair nearby.

For a time he did nothing but stare into his hands. At last he began his tale. And this is what he said:

CHAPTER TWO

The letter was dated July 16, 1937—God, it's hard to believe that was less than three months ago!—and bore the letterhead of a law firm, Parke, Gordon, and Parke, of which I had a dim but unplaceable recollection. It read something like this:

Professor Charles Jameson
Department of Classics
University of Maryland
College Park, Maryland

Dear Professor Jameson:

It is not likely that you will recall my identity. I am the administrator of the Estate of the late John Kenneth Sarsfield, who died in the Sheppard–Enoch Pratt Hospital in Towson on June 28. The matter which I must put before you is a bit strange—and a little tragic—and I trust that you will bear with me.

Your uncle John Kenneth Sarsfield left a somewhat curious will which may cause you and others some inconvenience for the next month or so. It would be too complicated for me to explain here what is involved; suffice it to say that you will be asked to dwell for a longer or shorter time in Sarsfield Manor outside of Chestertown. The will states that all the adult members of your line inhabit the manor until one of you finds

the solution to a riddle in the will. (I am aware of how silly this sounds, but since the will was made before your uncle was deemed mentally unbalanced in 1924, it would be highly cumbersome, and probably illegal, to evade its provisions.) The one who solves the riddle will gain the great majority of your uncle's assets, valued after death duties at approximately $3,000,000.

The other members of your family who are to be summoned are your aunt Judith Sarsfield Kellar (with her husband, Professor Edward Kellar); their son and your cousin, Jacob Kellar; your uncle George Sarsfield; and your cousin Winthrop Sarsfield (son of George), and his wife, Alice.

If you can meet me at my office in Baltimore at 2:00 on the 25th of this month, I shall explain to all of you the peculiar details of this whole affair.

Again begging your forgiveness for this inconvenience, I am

Cordially yours,
Wilbert Parke
Attorney-at-Law

I read this letter—particularly the second paragraph—twice before I began to understand it. The superficial eventlessness of my life—my routine as a college professor was rarely disrupted by anything more dramatic than an unruly student or a tiresome faculty meeting—made it hard for me to accept that anything like this could be happening to me. I had come to feel that I was not of the world—not, at any rate, of the world of business and law and external affairs. On the third reading of the letter I closed my eyes in weariness and felt a warm lump in my stomach, thinking not only of how much time that ought to be devoted to scholarship would be wasted, but how unpleasant it would be to deal with relatives whom I had, for the most part, not seen since I was a boy but who, as relatives, would expect an intimacy and cordiality I always found it hard to display.

But mingled with my irritation at the disturbance of my schedule was a tension—almost an apprehension—I could not quite diagnose. There was undoubtedly a taint in the Sarsfield line that no amount of wealth or prestige could disguise. I was a Jameson, but I was also a Sarsfield: my mother, Henrietta Sarsfield, had married Franklin Jameson at an early age—was it purely for love, or was it to escape the oppressive atmosphere of Sarsfield Manor? Henrietta, Judith, John Kenneth, and George—four siblings who, in their way, paralleled the earlier quartette of siblings (all brothers) who had built Sarsfield Manor in 1765. And the parallels extended not only to the financial acumen of each group of siblings but to a nameless tragedy whose details and ramifications remained maddeningly unclear.

Around the time of the Revolution, those four brothers Sarsfield—having acquired much wealth in the West Indies trade and settling down in their middle age to an English-style manor house built to their specifications—had all committed suicide one evening after having killed their only servant. The servant, it was said, could have told nasty things if he had been given the chance; but he was not. The brothers Sarsfield had taken to a mild form of occultism by which they had unearthed medieval tracts on the "Black Arts" and followed them with an assiduity that seemed to bespeak no more than a harmless fanaticism; but the rumors of the country people were always there, the more disturbing because they were unsubstantiated. The brothers had become absurdly penurious in their old age, being extravagant only in books and other predilections; hence the sum of money that had sifted down and accumulated to our day. John Kenneth Sarsfield was an antiquarian, and perhaps he had learned things better left unlearned. . . . Madness does not come of its own accord.

On the 25th of July I made the short trip from College Park to Baltimore. I was almost late in reaching the lawyer's office—largely because I dawdled in Monument Park and didn't leave enough time for the inevitable searching for his office—but as I arrived there I saw my cousin Winthrop and his wife Alice

alighting from their Silver Shadow. Their father, George, whom I only dimly remembered, had become the family patriarch and historian after John Kenneth's confinement, and Winthrop's own occupation as a banker ensured his living in the luxury to which he—and particularly his wife—had wished to become accustomed. He had, inevitably, grown a little stouter since I had seen him last.

He welcomed me without a smile; for although he grudgingly respected my achievements as a classical scholar, he could never repress the feeling that I was burrowing away at a dead end and was wasting the best years of my life. Philology, he felt, should be restricted to near-sighted pedants beyond the prime of life. His wife was a vivacious woman somewhat younger than he, whom he had married after a romance surprisingly brief considering his stolidity. I wondered how they got along, for they seemed to have little in common. She seemed to have little but charm, he little but money. Perhaps that was enough for them.

"What do you make of this business?" he asked me after mutual courtesies had been exchanged.

"I'm rather captivated by the idea," Alice burst out suddenly. "I've read a lot of mystery stories, you know . . . ."

I glanced at her blandly and replied to Winthrop as if she had not uttered. "I'm not excited at the prospect of spending a month or more in Sarsfield Manor, especially since no one has lived there for years."

"Well," he said, "it's certainly going to knock a hole in my schedule—I'll probably have to miss a meeting of the Maryland Bankers Association on August 12, unless we solve this 'riddle' by then. And then there's—"

"But Winthrop, dear," said his wife as if talking to a child, "don't forget the three million dollars."

He looked at her in high disdain. "Do you think that all I care about is money?"

She said nothing, but looked at me and smiled. We entered the lawyer's office.

We were apparently the last to arrive, for the other four were already seated in the spacious if reserved inner office of Wilbert Parke. I barely recognized old Uncle George, whom I had not seen since I was a teenager and who must have been approaching seventy. His face did not disguise his age, but his physique did; for he was as vigorous and lean as a man of forty, and made Winthrop look pudgy and unathletic indeed.

The other three occupants in the room I knew even less than George. Aunt Judith had not been a welcome guest at most of our family reunions (such, at any rate, as I attended), for rumor told that she was a positive virago. Her sharp-featured countenance suggested shrewdness and cleverness of a calculating sort—the hallmark of the successful businesswoman that she was. Her husband, Edward Kellar, looked like nothing but the typical absent-minded professor; he conformed almost parodically to the image in his snowy and disheveled hair, his pince-nez spectacles, his portly frame, and his look of perpetual confusion. I knew of him as a professor of music who had done some sound if mechanical work on Handel and some of the forgotten English composers of the eighteenth century (he had developed a curious fondness for the work of John Stanley, derivative and academic though it was); but I gathered even then that his studies were conducted less out of scholarly interest than as a tonic for his wretched life. He was doing little scholarship now, and was suffered to teach at Goucher College only out of gratitude for his long and faithful servitude there. They were just waiting for his death.

The son of Judith and Edward was a minor blot upon the family's escutcheon. Jacob Kellar was in his thirties yet still lived with his parents—it was thought he was somewhat soft in the head, but subsequent conversations with him convinced me that he was hardly lacking in intelligence. His troubles seemed more psychological than intellectual; and a certain wildness in his eyes led me to suspect that he had difficulty maintaining a grip on his emotions and actions. A nervous tic that caused him to tap the arm of his chair rapidly with his index finger was also

not encouraging.

Parke entered only moments after Winthrop, Alice, and I had been ushered into the room by some nameless assistant. He was a thin, gaunt, twisted man with abnormally large eyes and a crooked grin that made him look at once sinister and grotesque. He nodded aimlessly at us as he bustled to find the right papers, mumbling to himself in a monotonous drone that was almost soporific. Finally, with a cry, he discovered whatever he was looking for and sat down abruptly—almost more abruptly, it appeared, than he had expected.

"I'm afraid," he began, "that you are going to find this matter somewhat curious. This is really most irregular, but—as I must have explained to each of you in my letter—there is nothing we can do about it now. In any case, the business will certainly be harmless, if perhaps a bit bothersome. Let me read you the will."

And he did. It was a strange affair, written in an attemptedly satirical style that mingled ill with the legal and formulaic language in which it had to be couched. The gist of it was that we seven would venture to Sarsfield Manor—which, Parke assured us, would be cleaned and aired for our arrival—and there discover the solution to a jingle that my uncle had devised. The jingle was this, Parke reciting it in a pompous and pedantic manner that made the doggerel sound the more absurd:

"Four lights in a forest
    Shine brighter than day;
They laugh when it's windy,
    They laugh tho' they're clay."

It was obvious that this ridiculous quatrain made no pretensions to literary merit but was only fashioned laboriously and contrivedly to fit some preconceived plan. Indeed, its wretchedness made me query the lawyer whether the text was correct.

"That last couplet seems," I said, "to bear no relation to the first save the concluding rhyme. How can a light laugh?"

"That," Parke muttered, "is what you are apparently to find out."

"But why," Aunt Judith burst out shrilly, "must we go to Sarsfield Manor? What has it to do with this . . . this poem?" She uttered that last word as if it soiled her mouth.

"The solution," said Parke, "is somewhere on the estate, as the will states . . . ."

"Parke, do you know the solution to the riddle?" Winthrop asked bluntly.

"No, I do not. But it is written in this envelope." He produced a small white envelope that bore a sheet of paper inside; the paper seemed to have remarkably little written on it. "Your uncle wrote the solution here and asked that it not be opened until all of you have conveyed to me your answer to the riddle."

There was a silence for a time; then old Uncle George burst out: "Parke, how could you have let such a thing happen? Surely there is some law preventing such nonsense. It's the silliest thing I've ever heard of."

"My dear George," Parke whined pleadingly, "what could I do? It was an irregular will, but there seemed no harm in it— why, he was leaving all his money to his proper heirs, not to strangers or to a pet cat or something of the kind; and I thought there would be nothing wrong with humoring the fellow. I was young, George, and your uncle was a very important client." No one present had to gloss that adjective to its proper underlying meaning. "I didn't have any idea he'd go mad," Parke ended lamely.

"But what," Alice piped up, "if no one solves the riddle? What then?"

"Well, I suppose that if after a month none of you finds the answer, we may as well divide up the estate equally. The will curiously says nothing on that point . . . ." His voice was trailing off until it was almost inaudible; but suddenly he brightened. "But you should really enter into the spirit of the thing! Where's your sense of mystery? It might be a lot of fun . . . ."

He trailed off again as he saw no one sharing his enthusiasm.

His face bore a quizzical and pleading look something akin to a basset hound's.

But there was nothing we could do. For a moment I thought of abandoning the whole enterprise—there was no stipulation that any of us were obliged to attend; my late uncle had assumed (rightly) that the lure of three million dollars would be too much for most to resist—but at last decided that it might be a quaint diversion. I could always take a sufficient amount of work with me and do it there, I thought.

We discussed briefly with each other the most convenient time for departure. Uncle George was retired, so that the matter boiled down to Winthrop, Uncle Edward, and myself. I had to begin teaching only at the end of September, Edward a little later; and Winthrop said he could afford to miss his bankers' meeting and whatever other events of cosmic importance were on his agenda in the coming weeks. We decided that we would leave within the week. We would arrive at Sarsfield Manor on August 4.

CHAPTER THREE

The house was huge—it could, I suppose, have qualified as a mansion. It was so flawlessly Georgian that for a moment I forgot the dubious circumstances that were bringing me here and gave it a heartwarming gaze, half expecting to find a Walpole or a Gray writing in one of the studies. It was shaped like a T, the horizontal bar being rather longer than the vertical; the latter was, in fact, nothing more than a monumental foyer leading to the house proper. Above the portico, supported by elegant Corinthian columns, was a balcony leading from the second story, from which one could gain a panoramic view not only of the forest of dark slim elms that guarded the whole front and sides of the house but—as it was built on a modest acclivity— the countryside that spread in a luxurious green to the south. Behind the house, facing north, was one vast open space—the trees having been cleared so long ago that no traces of trunks or roots remained—that ceased only after about an acre, where it met another forest that loomed to the end of the northern horizon. Sarsfield Manor looked not in the least eerie, for even the gardens surrounding it had been attended to with care after its abandonment; it was disturbing only to those who knew.

We had decided to come each by ourselves, and I welcomed the chance to witness, even while driving, a breathtaking Maryland countryside that, in my scholarly sequestration, I was dangerously close to forgetting; but the hills and valleys and glens and streams and copses along the way revived me, and I was glad that I could still be moved by them.

As might have been expected, I was the last to arrive at Sarsfield Manor, for I saw three autos already parked on the gravel driveway at the side of the house. I removed my bags (one of them solely of books and papers) from the trunk and made my way slowly in. There was still a musty odor in the house that bespoke either an incomplete or a too perfunctory cleaning, but it was counteracted by the mellow wood that quietly proclaimed its incorruptible dignity. I heard a bustle on the second floor, hence made my way there; finding all the others in an unusual excitement—unpacking their things, exploring crannies, and acting in sum like children who had found a new toy to play with. Even archaic Uncle George and staid Winthrop had become enmeshed in the hubbub, and rushed about from room to room with a glow on their faces that was somehow ineffably pathetic. The entire second story seemed to consist of bedrooms—though later I discovered a gallery and a display room—and I entered an unoccupied chamber and dumped my bags unceremoniously on the floor. I was fatigued more by their bustle than by the trip, and did little but rest my eyes as I sat upright on the bed.

It was silence, curiously, that disturbed me. Of a sudden I heard my relatives' cries muffled and knew that someone had closed the door of my room. Opening my eyes, I saw Aunt Judith standing in my room, her back to the door and her hand still on the knob. Her smile—no, smirk—seemed to me a little too condescending.

"I hope," she said, "that I'm not disturbing you?"

"No, not at all." I had learned that the shortest way to deal with potentially annoying people is not to contradict them—especially in trifles.

"It's obvious, Charles, that you don't remember me very well; but you know, you *did* see me once. You were six, I believe, and I had come to celebrate your father's thirtieth birthday. You were such a sweet lad, I could tell. Now you've become a very serious scholar, and you don't smile much anymore."

I was going to say something nasty about the superficiality

of humor, but replied instead: "You commemorated my father's birth but not his death." She and Edward had not attended my parents' funeral.

Her countenance suddenly froze in an expression of affronted disgust, as if I were a beetle that had just entered her bedroom. Only her blazing eyes told of her anger. "Did no one tell you, Charles? You should have known that Edward was on the point of death from pneumonia, and I could hardly leave him. Really, Charles, your callousness offends me."

"The fault of youth," I said dolefully, trying not to smile at her nonplussed expression. She changed the subject.

"You don't seem to have gotten into the thrill of the chase, dear. Doesn't the thought of three million dollars mean anything to you?"

"Finding the sixteenth satire of Juvenal means more."

"Charles, don't be a pedant."

"Aunt Judith, don't be mercenary."

There was a silence.

We did not exchange many words more: when she found that I neither respected her nor was bothered by her transparent sarcasm—that poor relation to satire—she soon left. I unpacked my things slowly and with purposeful deliberation, trying to engross myself in the task so that the shadows of pessimism— always hovering close to my spirit—might be banished.

A bit later I came down to the main floor, asking one of the two servants—a young couple—to make me a cup of tea before dinner. Taking it upstairs, I was inclined merely to retreat back to my bedroom when I saw a door down the hall ajar, although it was dark within. On a sudden impulse I entered the room and switched on the light.

It was the portrait gallery, which I had passed by several times without particular notice. I could not but smile at the harmless affectation: the room bore even a portrait—labori- ously painted to match the Georgian style of the others—of my late uncle, John Kenneth Sarsfield. It was done, I noticed, in 1924, when he was sixty—the very year of his confinement. He

was an ordinary-looking fellow, rather larger in frame than the normal and tending toward portliness.

I must restrain a tendency to declare that any of the other portraits in the room—even the four brothers Sarsfield of ill rumor who had built this place—exuded an aura of strangeness. I will make the attempt—difficult though it now is—to envision my very first sensations on gazing at those visages; and if I felt any apprehension or perturbation, it may only have stemmed from the peculiarity of my present circumstances and the unpleasant encounter with Aunt Judith that had tainted my day. Actually, I was somewhat relieved when I saw those four thoroughly sane-looking, dignified colonial gentlemen; for they seemed to symbolize the propriety and elegance that was a natural and unaffected inheritance of their time and their culture. The latter scions were just as healthy: American Victorians gazing at me with a stuffiness that few of that time seem to have escaped; most of them men, but a few of them women with the luxurious gowns and the pristine and innocent faces—touched sweetly with red at the cheeks and one with a golden curl hanging almost seductively at her temple—that had become almost too representative of their era. I wondered how odd whisperings could have developed about any of these figures, undistinguished save for an elegance and dignity that, regrettably, has not carried over into our own age. But I admit that this very anomaly sent a shiver through my frame.

I had forgotten much of the history of the Sarsfield clan and suspected that Uncle George—who, since his retirement from schoolteaching, had become the family historian—would fill in the lacunae both for me and for the others. For a long time I stood there looking at the portraits, holding my long-finished teacup uselessly in my hand. My reverie lasted only when, seeing that it was nearly 5:30, I felt that I had to prepare for a dinner whose company I frankly did not welcome. I walked back to my room—only a short distance down the corridor and to my right—and shut the door. For some reason that I do not even now know, I turned and quietly bolted it.

CHAPTER FOUR

My desired history of Sarsfield Manor came rather sooner than I had expected; for Winthrop was as curious about the matter as I, and in the course of a not entirely unsatisfying dinner he asked Uncle George to tell what he knew of the house and its inhabitants. George agreed to do so after the completion of the meal; so that when it was over all seven of us moved to the spacious living room—with huge windows overlooking the dark forest that shrouded the whole front of the house—and sat down, oddly separated from one another, awaiting the tale.

George sat in an enormous armchair, quietly smiling to himself and thiking how to begin. He was remarkably swarthy, as if having spent long years in the tropics; and his large, lined face beamed with a quiet geniality such as might have been worn by Father Christmas. I was more fond of him than of any of my living relatives, for all that I had not seen him since a teenager: his mild friendliness, wholly lacking in condescension, was a fond memory that a mere twenty years could hardly efface. I remembered him as a born storyteller and always felt that he could have been a fine author had he given himself the practice. He was far more intelligent than his humble former occupation as an elementary schoolteacher—a job chosen through his wholly genuine love of children and the desire to see them gain that modicum of civilization which was becoming so rare in today's youth—betrayed; for he could, with some further specialization, have sat nobly on a professor's chair in almost any department of the humanities. A lifelong love of history—

the archaic ideal of history as artful narrative and incident, not the modern conception of complicated social and economic factors that stand inhumanly behind external affairs—had led him to take up genealogy upon his retirement five years previously. He had amassed a great deal of family papers—including much that related to the Sarsfields—and codified them with an assiduity that spoke well for the retention of his faculties. With his researches had come a family pride by which he scorned the bizarre rumors surrounding much of the Sarsfield line, doing so with the confident dogmatism of one who can defy traditional interpretation through the private possession of secret and revolutionary knowledge.

As he began his tale—his mellow voice, laced with charming archaisms, subtly but surely filling the room and making any sort of interruption unthinkable—I sat back in my chair, closing my eyes so that I could envision in my mind the eighteenth-century narrative that was being unfolded. Thackeray could have made a tremendous saga out of it, while its hints of the *outré* might have led a Hawthorne to produce a worthy companion to his own supernatural historical romances.

The four brothers Sarsfield had been born in the early years of the eighteenth century—Joseph in 1711, Richard in 1712, Jonathan in 1714, and Samuel in 1715—and had grown up in those buoyant years before the French and Indian Wars and the troubles with England would mar the later decades of the century. Being themselves antiquarians (to the point of not giving up, even after the emergence of Johnson's dictionary, some seventeenth-century forms that made their correspondence read like the screeds of Cotton Mather), they frowned upon the increasing commercialism of a society that was even then losing its ties to the rural landscape. Some of their letters burn with a withering contempt for tradesmen which Swift might have claimed for his own.

And yet they had, all four of them, jumped with both feet into the West Indies trade—surely the most commercial (and at times outrightly dishonest) occupation that could be imag-

ined. But—said Uncle George with a crafty expression that was the closest he ever came to cynicism—it was only their way of mocking the nation of shopkeepers that the colonies, following the English model, had already become. Establishing ties with their northern counterparts—the four Brown brothers of Providence—they made immense profits in the trading of tobacco, sugar, and slaves. By about 1760—when increasing tensions between the colonies and the mother country were causing disruptions in trade—they decided that it was time to retire and settle down to the squirarchy that they felt was the aim and end of existence, and for which they had toiled for twenty-five years among mercenary plebeians.

And while their antiquarianism had given them a taste for the Middle Ages that—well before the emergence of Radcliffe and Scott as symbols of the wretched death of Dr. Johnson's century—so rare in their time, they appreciated the classic soundness of Georgian architecture enough to cause the noble edifice called Sarsfield Manor to be erected. Here in the fifteen years given them before their lives would end so abruptly and mysteriously on June 16, 1780, they allowed their fancies to roam at will. Some wrote strange tales that, if they had survived, might have been a curious chapter in the history of Gothic fiction; others amassed hoary tomes from antiquity to their own day—even the shockingly modern *Castle of Otranto* by the Horace Walpole whose architectural tastes they had so wisely eschewed—which ultimately led to their being branded as lunatics and devils who performed nameless rites in their unhealthy solitude.

Whether it was conventional occultism or some new compendium of mystic lore that the brothers found of such consuming interest was not entirely clear, as documents from this late period were curiously absent or at best fragmentary. All that could be known was taken from the rumors and legends handed down by the country folk and ultimately gathered and codified by John Kenneth Sarsfield; and this body of data was hardly reliable, as the whisperings ran the gamut from standard demonology to

sexual perversity and sadism to an almost breathtaking fore-
shadowing of the cosmic myth-making of Lord Dunsany. Their
curious collecting habits—from occult bibliophily to Hellenistic
weaponry to West Indian cult objects—did not help to establish
their sanity or normalcy; and in the decade and a half of their
residence here every mysterious death or disapperance was laid
to their door.

As George was nearing the end of this portion of his narrative, his voice was gaining a bitterness that disturbed because
it was so foreign to his character. And at the last he burst forth
with a valiant defense of his unusual ancestors to which I did
not quite know how to react. He had studied, he declared, all
the existing documents—notably the correspondence exchange
with an equally odd gentleman in Carroll County that had been
collected by John Kenneth Sarsfield and given to him—and felt
that there was more here than met the eye. Under the superficial
occultism—which, as a German writer has recently written, is
nothing more than the "religion of the stupid"—he sensed that
there lurked dimly a fumbling attempt to probe the foundations
of human knowledge that might in time have been as significant as Newton's. The four brothers Sarsfield were no fools, and
knew Latin and Greek—along with several modern tongues
and even the rudiments of some Oriental languages—with a
thoroughness that was noteworthy even in their day. They were
not eccentrics, George held; they were only deemed so by rustic
buffoons who could not understand their unconventional bril-
liance. But when George uttered that all genius is misunderstood, I wondered whether he had ever reflected that what is
misunderstood is not always genius.

The subsequent history of the Sarsfield was tameness itself,
as the family settled into the grayness of nineteenth-century
American life. Although rumors about the four brothers went
comparatively undiminished, their scions were so ordinary—
perhaps deliberately so—that they were hardly held with the
fear and loathing that was their ancestors' fate. None of the later
Sarsfields ever tried to explore the circumstances surrounding

the sudden deaths of the four brothers and their servant: either because, as George had discovered to his perplexity, virtually all clues as to the details of the affair had been expunged from existing records, or because the subsequent residents of Sarsfield Manor—cousins of the unmarried brothers from the major branch of the family in Baltimore—had little interest in investigating such unsavory occurrences in a line that had almost been disowned but for their impressive assets. The later Sarsfields resided peacefully and with a remarkable dearth of incident in the manor; carrying out their role of squire with a repugnance and hesitancy that, in a line already tainted (so the brothers would have declared) with mercenary bankers and petty tradesmen, was at once ludicrous and pathetic. One wondered why anyone lived in the manor at all; but perhaps the age of Emerson and Whitman had not entirely crushed their love of Georgian elegance.

Interest in the family arose again only with the generation preceding my own—and specifically with the John Kenneth Sarsfield who had posthumously conveyed us hither. Born in 1864, he had early cultivated a taste for the past through youthful readings of the well-stocked shelves in the library, filled with volumes in which the "long s" was the rule rather than the exception. Though his siblings—my mother, Aunt Judith, and Uncle George—had chosen to leave the manor soon after attaining adulthood, John Kenneth remained. A portentous event in his adolescence was the discovery—in a hidden compartment of a desk in the second-story study—of a substantial horde of documents relating to his ill-famed ancestors. Most of these apparently consisted of notebooks in which were scribbled over the years the rambling thoughts and schemes of the four brothers. The great majority of these documents, regrettably, had not survived; indeed, John Kenneth's own diary in which he recorded these events suddenly stopped here, leaving one baffled as to the contents of the notebooks—no doubt filled with the massed learning of the brothers' last two decades— and as to their influence upon John Kenneth's subsequent life.

It is clear, however, that his decision not to attend Johns Hopkins was the direct result of the examination of these documents, for he had declared—as letters from his disheartened parents told—that he had far more important studies to undertake than could be gained at college. The family's financial security had alone granted his wish, along with the really keen intellect that made his parents ultimately conclude that his decision was probably not frivolous. Their death when he was thirty-three—their carriage overturning while on a visit to friends—seemed to cause him singularly little grief; and when George told us this fact (gained through servants' whispers and neighborhood gossip), I noticed that, while all the others were shocked by their relative's callousness, I myself could readily understand—if not wholly sympathize with—the sentiment of one who seemed from youth to have devoted his entire life to almost fanatical scholarship.

The years immediately prior to John Kenneth's confinement at Sheppard are almost wholly blank. We know that he codified the rumors anent his dubious ancestors only through the fact that a notebook containing them is extant; we are thus in a position we encounter all too often among the authors of classical antiquity—we must infer their lives solely from their literary remains. In this way we know that John Kenneth began studying the arcane tomes that had lain untouched for generations, and may even have begun conducting experiments of some sort (the evidence here was cloudy) upon the estate. He kept up to date on the latest mystical findings and pored over the works of Blavatsky, Summers, Donnelly, and others as soon as they were off the press. In a way I regretted the trend of his readings, for I knew that much of this work was charlatanry perpetrated by weak minds who had chosen this path in reaction to the horror of contemporary life, with its wars, its mechanization, its alienation; yet I was heartened by indications that John Kenneth did not swallow their maunderings uncritically but seemed to weigh them in a true scholarly spirit, correlating them with the arcane secrets handed down from Ramses to Friar Bacon.

The reason for his confinement was as mysterious as that quintuple tragedy of a century and a half before which we all sensed was in some inscrutable way related to it. Officials at the sanitarium had refused to reveal their documents even to the family, and police records were also curiously lacking. We could only rely, as before, on whispers; and these inevitably took the same tone as those uttered by the neighborhood gossips a hundred and fifty years before. Was John Kenneth too an unrecognized genius whose doom had come through ignorance and small-mindednes? George was convinced of it, although a visit to his brother ten years ago—virtually the only visit the man would receive in his thirteen years of confinement—had not done much to confirm this belief. John Kenneth had been very silent, muttering innocuously but creating the impression of vast stores of knowledge held in reserve.

Thus the history of Sarsfield Manor and its tenants ended as ambiguously as it had begun. We all felt that an enormous wealth of detail and significance lay behind and beneath even this laboriously collated narrative; but the hints were too few, and our mind's eye looked only into an undissolving mist. And when George told us—in a rhetorical flourish whose contrivedness was so apparent that I smiled—that the four brothers Sarsfield were actually buried on the estate (for their remains had not been allowed to pollute healthier churchyards), in a dark corner at the rear, we could not but march out in a body and examine the anomalous site. Standing silently there, I could not help feeling that their remains and the half-obliterated inscriptions of their crumbling markers symbolized a barred mystery whose unlocking should be sedulously avoided.

CHAPTER FIVE

The next day, after breakfast, I quickly made my way up-stairs before anyone could detain me. A sense of overwhelming mental exhaustion had come over me, and I wanted nothing but solitude. I had made up my mind not even to attempt the solution of the absurd riddle of the will, since I knew either that someone else would solve it in due course of time or that after at most a month of incarceration I would be released and could settle again into my scholarly routine.

As I ascended the stairs, I glanced out of the windows and over the parklike rear of the estate. I was tempted to take a stroll in the warm and invigorating sunshine, but changed my mind when I saw Alice there leading her husband about in quest of the lucrative puzzle. They must, I thought, be going to the graves to see if those slabs harbored any clues. I merely winced and decided to retire to my room.

As I advanced along the second-story corridor, however, I heard an anomalous muttering that made me stop in my tracks and gaze inquisitively about. At the very end of the hall and to the left, a door was ajar. To this I advanced; and, entering the room, uttered a wide-eyed gasp.

The causes of my astonishment were twofold. The first was the contents of the room. Displayed on every wall of the roughly square room was the most remarkable collection of arms— scimitars, javelins, hand-knives, and countless other types— that I had ever seen. The weapons room at the Philadelphia Art Museum would have only barely surpassed this impressive array

of killing devices. A brief glance told me that these items—as well as those in a huge glass display-case that filled the center of the room—represented the collection of Hellenistic weaponry that, as Uncle George had related, the four brothers Sarsfield had amassed over the decades. While I had been mildly intrigued at discovering this classical predilection of my ancestors, I had assumed that their collection had at some point during the past two centuries been turned over to a university or museum for proper display and study. Instead, I saw here the most extensive conglomeration of arms—from Macedonia, Asia Minor, Syria, Persia, and even as far away as Bactria—that I had ever seen in private hands. I was amazed—almost appalled—at the discovery, and made a firm mental note to report the find to my university's department of classical art and archaeology.

But the othe cause of my astonishment was far more mundane; for it was merely the presence of my cousin Jacob in the room.

Not having noticed my entrance, he was still mumbling incoherently to himself as he pored over the rectangular display-case. But when I cleared my throat to make my presence known, he wheeled around with a gasp, eyes grotesquely flashing.

"You oughtn't to sneak up on a fellow like that," he said almost breathlessly. "It's not nice, you know, it's not nice." He grinned luridly.

From my few contacts with Jacob, I was felt uneasy, even a bit alarmed, in his presence. He was one of those people about whom you are ever in doubt as to their ability to control their actions and lead a normal, socially responsible life. He was not by any means mentally deficient—indeed, he was attempting to be a writer of lurid fiction, and may perhaps have even landed a story or two in some of the cheaper pulp magazines—but one always felt that the customary inhibitions that restrain most people from flaring out and committing unthinkable acts of violence were, in him, reduced to the vanishing point. I knew little of his family life with his ill-matched parents, but their obvious disappointment at his inability or unwillingness to develop into a mature, stable adult could not have been condu-

cive to his own mental stability.

"I just wondered," I noted quietly, "what you were doing and saying, Jacob."

"As to that," he replied tartly, "I was looking at these weapons—for you're not the only classicist here—and I was making plans for a story. What if I mutter?" His face donned a philosophical expression that was as malapropos as it would have been on Frankenstein's monster. "Don't you think that talking to oneself, far from being a sign of a feeble mind, suggests that one can't keep one's mental wheels from turning?"

I actually agreed with him on the point, but wondered of its validity in his case. I felt, however, that I had best not antagonize him, so I merely said:

"It's quite a collection here, isn't it? It ought to be in a museum."

But even this was not innocuous enough for him.

"Museum?" he flared. "What rubbish! This is our family's collection, and it should remain here where we can appreciate it and make use of it."

I looked at him sharply. "Make use of it? What do you mean by that?"

To my surprise, his anger wilted away into embarrassment or confusion. "Nothing, nothing," he said rapidly, waving a hand at me as if I were a servant he was dismissing. "There's much to study here, and I'd like to get to it."

I gave him a cold stare. I knew when my presence was not wanted, and I had no intention of extending my own acquaintance with him longer than was necessary, so I hastily exited the room. Turning around, I saw him continue to stare intently at several pieces in the display-case. *He's welcome to them,* I muttered almost aloud.

I idled till dinner, attempting to do some work but largely failing to summon up sufficient concentration to make any significant headway. Accordingly, I was almost glad of the diversion of a meal, for all that I would have to associate with relations who were becoming more and more irksome to me. I

was, when I reached the dining room, one of the first to arrive; the others apparently were in the thick of the chase, poking over the whole house and grounds for clues to the ludicrous death-riddle. I found only Edward and George in the room: apparently they felt themselves too aged to engage in such frivolous if profitable activity. We waited a full fifteen minutes before all the others arrived, the last being an irritated Alice and an exhausted Winthrop who had probably never gotten so much exercise in the entirety of his previous life. Regrettably, they had found nothing—or at least nothing that seemed to have any bearing on the mystery.

I quietly addressed Edward, remarking that he didn't seem much interested in the riddle, to which he quickly nodded. But before he could speak, his wife spoke up sharply.

"Well," Judith said, "while you old men"—evidently she included me in that designation—"have been accomplishing nothing, *I* have not been so idle."

"Aunt Judith," Alice said slyly, "what you have you been up to? Have you found the solution?"

The response that Judith made could have been predicted. "That, my dear, is for me to know and you to find out." Her expression suddenly became petulant. "And yet, I really cannot fit it into the riddle. It's very curious."

There was an awkward silence: no one wished to press Judith, who was obviously intent on keeping her cards close to her chest, nor could anyone think of a new topic of conversation. We were all so relatively unused to one another's presence, and had been thrown together so anomalously, that we could well have been strangers gathered from the street.

Finally Winthrop spoke, addressing George. "Father, what have *you* been up to?"

The old man looked up quickly, as if in a daze and hardly expecting anyone to bother him. "Oh, I've just been scanning the shelves. An astonishing library they had . . . ." He did not have to mention who his subjects were.

"George," said Judith half-reproachfully, "don't tell me

you've been puttering about those occult books?"

"No, no, no, not at all, Judith. Why in the world would I be doing that?" His puzzlement was genuine. "No, they have some excellent classical texts; Charles"—looking at me—"you ought to examine them." The idea had not occurred to me, and I resolved to follow his advice soon. "And they have some lovely editions of the Metaphysical Poets." He spoke with the admiration of a pronounced bibliophile.

"Books and books!" said Alice sharply. "Don't you people ever think of anything but books? I daresay those books are going to help precious little in solving the riddle."

"But what does that matter, dear?" said George mildly.

Alice was left speechless. I may have grinned.

And so the dinner—admirably, if stodgily, American—passed. With the meal concluded, I quickly withdrew to the library; catching a glance, as I went, of Alice dragging poor Winthrop on some new expedition, Judith summoning George for some private conversation, Edward retiring to the drawing room, and Jacob going rather too rapidly upstairs again.

The library was indeed as George had said: the standard classics through the nineteenth century (the recenter ones obviously added by later scions), the amazingly large collection of occult volumes—including such things as Remigius, Reginald Scot, King James's treatise on witchcraft, and even such curiosities as some of Ainsworth's and Bulwer-Lytton's novels, which apparently represented some descendant's valiant if misguided attempt to keep the collection up to date—and, of course, a classical collection that included several mouth-watering incunabula.

I picked only one volume—Hennenius's great 1685 edition of Juvenal—and took it away with me to my room. Somehow I thought it might impel me to do some work, but it failed to light the spark of inspiration in me. I felt the same spiritual weariness that had come over me last evening, but this time it was intensified; and it was worse because I could pinpoint no single cause. True, my relations were getting on my nerves more and more,

and the inconvenience of staying here, away from my library (more than once I cursed myself for not bringing some particular volume or paper whose absence created irritating lacunae in my work), was becoming increasingly pronounced; yet there was something more.

George's history of the Sarsfields had bothered me more than I could account for, considering its sketchy inconclusiveness; yet the implications were the more horrific for their being ungraspable. Nameless things had happened here, and I felt that their inevitable revelation would be no less cataclysmic for their occurrence in a now distant age. Behind even the absurd riddle of John Kenneth Sarsfield peered leering chimeras of grotesqueness that were far more hideous than any realized. I began actually to ponder the solution of the ghastly mystery—not because of the ultimate monetary prize but through an unaccountable realization that its decipherment was a necessity of the most terrific sort. I mumbled over and over to myself the puerile jingle to which each new utterance added a layer of the sinister:

> Four lights in a forest
>   Shine brighter than day;
> They laugh when it's windy,
>   They laugh tho' they're clay.

The first line could refer to nothing but the four brothers themselves, while the last obviously referred to the fact of their death; but, even assuming an extreme use of metaphor, there remained the difficulty of reconciling "lights" with "laugh." In what nameless fashion could lights laugh? And what was the significance of "windy"? And on top of the intrinsic obscurity of this quatrain was the further mystery of why we were all transported here in order to solve it. What possible landmark could exist in this thoroughly normal-looking estate that could have any possible connection with the riddle? Even my cursory examination of rooms and grounds told me that there was little overt strangeness in these surroundings; while the more

arduous investigations of my relatives had—but for some apparently uninterpretable evidence unearthed by Judith—been of hardly greater moment. Perhaps the answer was staring us in the face; perhaps John Kenneth Sarsfield had not been remiss in reading his Poe.

But I tried to shake off my somber reflections and pay attention to my studies. When I was no longer in the spirit to work, I did not know what to do; for I did not wish to encounter Uncle Edward in the drawing room, nor wished to meet any of my other relatives in their canvassing of the house and grounds. I thus made a quiet way to the uninhabited library and attempted to immerse myself in the lightest reading—I think it was Thackeray—I could find. I became, to my surprise, quite engrossed and charmed by his effortless urbanity and wit, and may have passed several hours in this fashion. I was only interrupted once, when old George poked his head in and was almost startled by my presence. My first sight of him shocked me enough to give him a second glance, for his face was more haggard and pale than I had ever seen it; but, glancing at my watch and noting the late hour, I assumed that fatigue from the trip down and the previous evening's long narrative had overcome him.

Finally, tiring of the volume, I decided to attempt more work and ascended the stairs. I heard some voices in a room I could not identify; it appeared to be the sharp but muffled voices of women arguing behind closed doors. A few moments later I knew that Alice and Judith were wrangling on some point or other—probably more trivial than not. I ought to have expected it from knowledge of their characters, but could not stifle a wince of disgust that virtually nullified the benefits gained from hours with Thackeray. I quickly retired to my room to avoid any further such experiences, nearly slamming the door behind me. Although I sat down at my desk with the thought of doing some work, a sudden sense of exhaustion overwhelmed me; I may even have dozed off for a time, perhaps from the delayed effects of traveling and subsequent exertion.

What disturbed me next was the scream.

That scream was such as could only have been uttered by a man encountering the stupefyingly horrific: it was not a normal sound, hence was doubly hideous because it was so inapposite. The walls of the entire house seemed to shake; and the echoes rang louder because of the preceding silence.

But I was more wearied than shocked: my initial shiver of fear quickly gave way to an overwhelming sense of fatigue. It was the only possible culmination, I thought, of all the previous events that had occurred in this house during the past two days: it was a knife twisted further into the wound.

Finally I got up from the desk and decided to investigate. Opening my bedroom door, I almost immediately saw something whose bizarrerie I had difficulty absorbing.

Over the threshold of a bedroom across the hall from mine lay the body of my Aunt Judith, the blade of a dagger—with a wickedly thin blade—protruding from her back, but with remarkably little blood flowing from the wound. There was no question that that dagger had come from the weapons room down the hall, although I did not specifically recognize the object from my previous examination of that room.

But this was not the worst. I saw all this so clearly because the blazing overhead light in her room cast a lurid shimmer over the room itself and poured itself out almost as a sentient entity into the otherwise darkened hallway. From the partially opened door I could see on the bed, his hands spasmodically clutching the sheets, my Uncle Edward—the obvious utterer of the scream—his eyes open in horror, mouth frozen askew. He was apparently dead of a heart attack.

Not knowing what to do first, I approached Judith in some vain hope that the injury she had suffered was not fatal. I gripped the dagger handle and was attempting to remove it from her body when several other doors opened nearly simultaneously.

Nearly all the other occupants—Uncle George, his face still ashen, whether from sleep or alarm or some other cause I could not tell; Winthrop and Alice, the latter looking apprehensively

over the shoulder of the former as if his mere bulk could protect her; and Jacob, whose face registered a kind of baffled incomprehension as if he too could not mentally digest the image of his parents lying dead before him—were looking me square in the face.

For a time no one uttered a word.

Then Jacob, almost hysterically, and in a high-pitched voice that again rang through that narrow space, shrieked:

"You killed her! You killed both of them! You bastard, you murdered my parents! What did they ever do to you . . .?"

My jaw dropped; in spite of my obviously compromising position, I did not conceive that anyone could have thought me to be guilty of such an act. I looked from one to the other, speechlessly attempting to convey my innocence. But I met no one's eyes; their expressions ranged from sorrow to horror, but none doubted that I was the culprit.

The police were not long in coming.

CHAPTER SIX

Charles Jameson's long and somewhat orotund narrative had tried my patience in more ways than one—but it had also presented numerous points of interest that needed to be examined. Quite frankly, the outlandish tale of how the Sarsfield clan had been summoned to the manor by way of a dead man's will seemed the stuff of cheap pulp fiction, while the older history of the four brothers Sarsfield of the eighteenth century had more than a few touches of the sinister. I suspected that Charles was right in thinking that, at least indirectly, the probing of that centuries-old mystery would play a role in the solution of the double murder of a few days before. I was not yet prepared to accept on faith the entirety—or, indeed, any—of Charles's narrative; in several places it seemed self-serving at best, outrightly deceptive at worst. But it was, for now, all I had to go on.

I got up heavily and looked sharply at Charles Jameson. His long narrative had apparently fatigued him, and he was leaning back against the cement wall of his cell, eyes closed. Suddenly, as if something had startled him, he opened his eyes wide and stared at me blankly, as if he didn't know who I was. Presently a curious expression—part apprehension, part an almost hopeless plea for succor—passed over his face. His mouth opened, but he did not utter.

I spoke for him. "Charles, there are a number of things in your account that are of interest, and I'll follow up on them as best I can. I'll be honest with you and say that some parts of it are . . . a bit hard to swallow."

"I recognize that," he said, now looking down at his hands.

"I need some more information," I said shortly. "First, where are all the other people who had come to Sarsfield Manor? Are they still there?"

"Yes," Charles said quietly. "The police thought it best to keep them on the premises. Of course, the . . . bodies have been taken away—to the morgue, I gather."

"How is your cousin Jacob reacting to the death of his parents?"

Charles shrugged. "It's never been clear to me how Jacob reacts to anything. He's a pretty unstable individual. I'm not sure he fully realizes what has happened."

I let the matter pass.

"What about your lawyer? You've hired one, I take it?"

"Yes," he said. "A local man named Samuel Parker. But quite frankly he hasn't been of much help. I hired him only because he appears to be on good terms with the police chief and knows how things work here. You know," he went on with the faintest tinge of irritation and petulance in his voice, "things are not done here quite as they are in Baltimore. The people on the Eastern Shore resent Baltimore—its power, its wealth, its status. Ask your friend Mencken—he'll tell you that the country legislators all over the state routinely gang up on Baltimore and pass all kinds of laws making it a liability to live there. I'm not a Baltimorean anymore, but they know of my ties to that place, and they'd be more than happy to take me down."

I didn't know what to make of that tirade. "Who are you referring to? The police? Surely you're not saying they're trying to railroad you into jail . . . or the chair."

That last phrase was probably a cheap shot, but I had to get Charles to realize the seriousness of his situation. He seemed to be living in some kind of fantasy world. Sure enough, those three words jerked him up out of his lethargy, so that he almost leaped in my direction, clinging to the bars of his cell.

"You're not saying they'd . . . do that?" he breathed in a whisper.

"If you're guilty, they will," I said flatly.

He looked at me with incomprehension. "Joe, you can't possibly believe . . . I just told you . . ." He stopped, almost choking on his words. "I didn't do anything! I'm not guilty! There's been some sort of set-up . . ."

"You mean to say," I said blandly, "that someone else killed Judith Kellar and enticed you to clutch that dagger in her back?"

"No, no, no," he said, shaking his head vigorously. "I didn't mean that. But I didn't commit this crime. I was only trying to help. Good God, Joe, when you see someone almost murdered before your eyes, you're not exactly in full control of your faculties!"

He had a point. But something he said triggered a new query.

"Charles, did you hear anyone's footsteps before that scream? Surely you would at least have heard Judith herself coming down that hallway. How about anyone else?"

He gazed at me as if I had presented to him the solution of a particularly difficult problem in differential equations. "You know . . .," he began haltingly, "come to think of it, *I didn't hear a thing!* That is to say, I *think* I heard Judith's footsteps—or at least *someone's* footsteps—coming down that hallway...but that was it! There was no *second* set of footsteps—but shouldn't there have been? How could someone have snuck up on her without making a sound? All right, maybe I wasn't really paying attention, but I could swear there was no second set of footsteps."

"How about a door closing?" I said. "If someone else committed the crime, they would presumably have retreated to their own bedroom after stabbing Judith. Do you remember anything like that?"

He again looked at me with a kind of awe and wonder. "I don't remember anything like that at all. . . . But someone *must* have fled in a hurry after doing the deed—I was out in that hallway only a few seconds after I heard that horrible scream from Edward. Where could they have gone? What could this mean?"

What, indeed. I had to add that to the puzzle.

I said little more to him, then left. For now, I doubted that he could help me much more than he had; I had to pursue my own investigation. And my first order of business was to talk with the police chief.

This man, Frank Powers, was sitting placidly at his desk in a private room in the spacious police station. In all honesty, he didn't seem very busy—I figured that, especially now that Prohibition was a thing of the past, there wasn't much in this placid community that required his services. He was a heavy man and seemed to like to chomp down on cheap cigars—but there are worse vices in the world.

As I approached him, he looked up blankly. "So what's the story with your client?" he said with an entire absence of interest.

"I wouldn't exactly say he's my client," I replied. "Just an old college friend. I may want to do some investigation of this business at Sarsfield Manor, if you don't mind."

Powers shrugged. "Be my guest. We're still on the case, of course," he added a little defensively.

"So you're not sure that Charles Jameson is the murderer?"

"I didn't say that," Powers said quickly. "Right now he's the logical suspect, based on what the others have told my men."

"How is that?" I said. "Merely because he was seen with his hand on the murder weapon? That proves nothing, and he's given his explanation of that."

"Well," Powers said, looking at me with a tinge of hostility, "it doesn't help him. He was the first at the scene of the crime, and all the others showed up very soon afterwards. They all saw him with his hand on the weapon."

"What was his motive?"

Again Powers shrugged. "Could be any number of things. Maybe his victim had solved that ridiculous riddle that had brought them all there, and he wanted to shut her up."

"Charles claims he wasn't interested in solving the riddle."

Powers almost chortled at me. "He may say any number of things, but who knows what was going on in his mind? Anyway,

there could be all kinds of other factors. Maybe he just didn't like her, and wanted to get rid of her."

"You can't believe that," I said incredulously.

"I don't know what to believe," Powers said gruffly. "But right now, he's the best suspect I got. And in this business, more often than not your first suspect turns out to be the culprit. Don't think, Scintilla, that you can pull someone out of a hat like some fancy-ass detective. Things like that don't happen. Police work is a tough, gritty business—not pretty and not glamorous. I really don't have time for amateur sleuths . . . ."

"I'm not an amateur. I'm a professional," I said with a glint in my eye.

He knew he'd overstepped the line, and he backed down. "Yeah, O.K., Scintilla. Sorry about that. I know something of your work—you're good, and you play straight. But if you think you can get your friend off with some jack-in-the-box trick, you'd better think again."

"I don't plan to do that," I said. "And, for your information, I'm not entirely sure he's in the clear. I just want to investigate this case and see where it leads. If he's the one, I'll give him to you on a silver platter."

Powers gave me a crooked smile. "I'm getting to like you, Scintilla."

I wasn't interested in buttering up Frank Powers. So I asked to look at the police report, after which I said I'd get out of his way and leave him to his work. He summoned a secretary to get me the file, and I sat down to it. It said little that I didn't already know or assume: Judith Kellar had died of internal bleeding after being stabbed in the back, and through the heart, with an antique dagger. The photographs of the deceased showed remarkably little blood exiting from the wound. Her husband, Edward Kellar, had died of a heart attack—presumably from seeing his wife dead before him. Testimony from each of the occupants of Sarsfield Manor pretty much confirmed what Charles himself had said: he was indeed first on the scene, and the others had emerged only a few seconds later. If someone

other than Charles himself really had committed the crime, that person had been awfully quick—and silent—in returning to his or her room before re-emerging into the hallway.

I went back to ask Powers if I could see the murder weapon, which I figured he must have somewhere. He glanced up at me a little suspiciously; then, with a grunt of effort, got up from his desk and went to a locked room where physical evidence was kept. It didn't take him long to find what I wanted.

The weapon was a grim piece of work—the blade incredibly thin and sharp, and the handle almost needlessly overornamented. Running my thumb over the blade, I quickly saw that, even if this thing was more than two thousand years old, it was still fully up to the task for which it was designed.

I handed it carefully back to Powers and left.

CHAPTER SEVEN

It was early evening by the time I finished my work at the police station, so I grabbed a quick and unappetizing meal at a one-arm diner nearby and then headed out to Sarsfield Manor.

The drive was short, but it was nonetheless jarring. In a matter of moments it seemed as if I had gone from the bland-ness of post-Prohibition America to a kind of fantasy-world England where butlers still functioned and afternoon tea was still served. Up and down the East Coast, wealthy colonials of the eighteenth century had maintained their ties to England in spite of the political disputes that tainted the latter quarter of the century—and those who did not actually become Loyalists and flee to Canada managed to ride out the Revolution and preserve their wealth and their devotion to England even when a new flag and a new Congress had emerged. The original brothers Sarsfield had clearly been of that sort; and I suspected that any number of their descendants, right down to the present day, followed in their footsteps.

My enthusiasm for investigating this case—or, perhaps more precisely, for interviewing the parties in this case—was not high. I may have been unduly influenced by Charles Jameson's tart words about several of them, and I had to guard against the tendency to see things through his eyes—especially since a fair amount of what he had said was likely to have been self-serving. The convenience of their all still being in the castle, as if they were all involuntary patients consigned to a mental hospital for their own good, made my life somewhat easier; but I also

sensed that their continued proximity might create a hothouse atmosphere of pent-up emotions where anything could occur.

There was in fact no butler, unless the young man who greeted me—half of the couple who appeared to serve as combined cook, housekeeper, and jack-of-all-trades—could qualify. But his apprehension and nervousness were as different from the bland sobriety of the classic butler as anything could have been. He did not live on the premises, but I don't doubt his discomfiture at having to work in a house of murder.

It did not take me long to introduce myself to the assembled guests; few of them were doing much of anything, although Alice Sarsfield's former enthusiasm for solving the riddle of the will now seemed metamorphosed into a different kind of excitement. Various policemen were still canvassing the place, and their presence did not conduce to normal behavior—assuming there was anything normal in the manner in which they had been brought here by a dead man and the subsequent killings that had taken place right under their noses.

My first point of business was to familiarize myself with the layout of the house. The ground level—foyer, drawing room, dining room, kitchen, and any number of other rooms—did not seem at the moment of any direct relevance. As I made my way upstairs, I noted the fact that the hallway was not carpeted, and that its bewildering plethora of rooms on either side of the hall must either have been bedrooms or the portrait gallery that Charles had told me about or—more significantly—the weapons room. That room was locked, but I didn't trouble myself to have a policeman open it for me; I suspected that the case where that Hellenistic dagger reposed was unlocked, so that anyone who knew of its existence could easily have snatched it unobserved.

For now, I needed to learn more about the personalities in this case. I suspected that old George Sarsfield might be the best source for certain initial inquiries, and I was glad to see he made no fuss about being interviewed by a person who had no vital or official connection with the case.

Retreating to the drawing room for privacy, I asked him

bluntly what he could recall of the few minutes before the crime had occurred.

"Not much, Mr. Scintilla," he said. I almost felt sorry questioning him, for his ashen complexion made me worry about his ability to carry on in this difficult time.

"You were in your room, I take it, when Edward Kellar's scream roused everyone?"

"That's right."

"Did you by chance hear anything before that? There's no carpeting in that hallway upstairs, is there? If Judith was walking down that hallway, then someone must have come up behind her to . . . er, kill her. So there must have been two sets of footsteps just before that scream. And whoever the killer was must have retreated to his or her room right after . . . unless, of course, you think that Charles Jameson is the perpetrator."

My flurry of questions seemed to disconcert him, and he just shook his head in combined weariness and perplexity. "I don't know what to think, Mr. Scintilla. I would hate to think of my own nephew as a . . . a murderer. What possible reason would he have for killing Judith? People say he was trying to stop her from revealing the solution of the riddle—but, in the first place, we don't even know that she had solved the riddle, and in the second place, I'm certain Charles really didn't care one way or the other . . . just as I don't."

He paused, then looked me right in the face.

"As for footsteps . . . I had retired early—I wasn't feeling well, am feeling worse now—and I'm sure I heard all manner of footsteps coming and going . . . no telling whose they were. But I'm reasonably sure I heard just one set of footsteps—I guess they must have been Judith's—before that . . . that scream." He shuddered visibly.

"Only one? How can that be?" I pursued.

"I have no idea." He gazed at me blankly, as if suggesting—rightly—that that was a problem I had to solve.

I shifted to another tack. "What can you tell me about your sister Judith? What sort of a person was she?"

George heaved a sigh. "Mr. Scintilla, I will be frank with you . . . Judith was not the easiest person in the world to be around, or live with. John Kenneth was the oldest of the four of us, followed by myself, Judith, and Henrietta. I must have more than thirty years on you, sir . . . we were all raised in a century very different from the one we now find ourselves in." I couldn't help feeling that George wished this century had somehow never come into existence. "Girls . . . women were treated differently then. They were sheltered, protected, shielded from the grim rigors of life. Little Henrietta didn't mind, but Judith rebelled at that treatment, even though it was meant for her own good.

"So she became a bit hard, a bit ruthless, even a bit cruel. I think she came to believe that the world was against her—she was smart and dynamic, so why wasn't she getting ahead? Our parents refused to let her get a job—it would have been unthinkable for a Sarsfield woman to be a . . . a tradesman"—the scorn with which he said that word could only have been managed by a scion of the nineteenth century—"and so all she could do was to marry advantageously. And she didn't even do that. She was, physically, not what one would call attractive, and so the best she could do—and it was far from the worst—was Edward.

"I liked Edward"—George said that frankly and ingenuously—"but I think he was not a good match for Judith. Even as a young man he was shy and unworldly—I think Judith largely bullied him into marrying her, chiefly because he was just about the only one to show any real interest in her. And somehow she got it into her head that he would become distinguished in his field, and thereby reflect distinction on her; but her constant prodding him to do more work and be more determined and aggressive—qualities he had in very short supply—must have been very trying for him. And then there's Jacob . . . ."

"What about him?" I added, sensing that George was not inclined to speak on the subject.

George eyed at me with a sort of quizzical expression. "I don't know what to say about Jacob. I've never understood him. He's . . . odd. One never knows where one stands with him.

Erratic, freakish, unstable . . . ."

"Mr. Sarsfield," I said quietly, "do you think there's any chance that . . . ."

"That what?" George said, almost daring me to finish the thought.

"I think you know what I'm saying."

"That Jacob killed his parents?" he whispered with a kind of venom.

I said nothing, but looked at him squarely.

He could not meet my gaze.

"I really don't know, Mr. Scintilla," he said after a long pause. "I really don't know. It seems that anything is possible with someone like him."

I paused, giving him time to recover his composure.

"Mr. Sarsfield, I believe you were talking to Judith the evening of her . . . death. Can you tell me the substance of that conversation?"

If possible, George blanched even more than before. For several moments his mouth worked; then he finally said:

"Nothing, nothing . . . it was nothing at all. She was just telling me . . . about some of her explorations. She'd found nothing about the riddle—in fact, she was trying to pump *me* about whatever I knew, even though she must have realized that I wasn't making the slightest attempt to solve that damfool puzzle. I really have no idea what she wanted . . ." He trailed off.

I peered at him sharply for what seemed like minutes. When I became aware that he was not going to say more, I let him go.

Winthrop and Alice Sarsfield insisted on being interviewed together, even though I would have preferred to see them individually. Winthrop was pretty much what Charles had led me to expect—stout, full of self-importance, and with a persistent sense of outrage that he was compelled to remain here when he clearly had more important work to do. Relatively youthful though he was, he seemed older than his years. His wife, on the other hand, was as sprightly as he was stolid. Attractive in a fleshy, doll-like way, she still found it difficult to repress a kind

of childlike thrill at being here under such peculiar circumstances—and that thrill was seemingly enhanced by the double tragedy that had just occurred. I didn't wish to be unkind to her, but I was more than a little inclined to believe that she lived in a world of her own imagination.

I opened by asking them the same questions I had put to George, regarding those few moments before the scream that must have signaled the death of Judith Kellar. Neither of them had anything to add to previous accounts. I was not yet ready to put any great significance in this—the absence of a double set of footsteps, the failure of anyone to hear a door closing before that scream (assuming, for the time being, that Charles himself was not the killer)—because I was well aware how inobservant most people are and how little they can remember of even traumatic events that would presumably sharpen their memories.

But one thing Winthrop said did stir my interest.

"You know, Mr. Scintilla," he said hesitantly, almost with a sort of perplexed embarrassment, "I did see something that may be relevant . . . ."

"And what is that?" I said sharply.

He was almost reluctant to speak, at least in the presence of his wife—he gave her a quick and harried glance before turning back to me.

"I . . . er . . . saw Aunt Judith perhaps two or three minutes before that horrible scream."

There was nothing like that in the police report.

"You what?" I said quietly.

Winthrop was so agitated that he suddenly jumped up from the sofa where he had been sitting. "It's not what you think! I didn't kill her . . . why would I have? And anyway, when I say I saw her, it wasn't as if I saw her face to face . . . ." He stopped in momentary confusion.

"Why don't you just tell me what you saw?" I said.

He made a move to sit back down, but his agitation led him to pace the floor back and forth in front of me.

"It's like this. . . . My—our bedroom has a window that looks

out on the balcony above the entrance. Well, it was very dark and I couldn't see very well, but I couldn't sleep and was going to go out for a stroll. Then I saw a figure there and she was looking over the railing. Suddenly she started and took a step backward, and then disappeared inside. Moments later—the scream . . . ."

I was thinking furiously. "Mr. Sarsfield, are you sure it was Judith?"

He uttered a mirthless grin. "Who else could it have been? That servant couple don't sleep here, and the only other woman in the house at the time was my wife, and I could see that she was lying in bed sleeping."

"Why didn't you tell this to the police?"

Winthrop reddened almost comically. "I . . . I . . . I didn't want to make trouble for anyone . . . ." Meaning, of course, for himself.

"Do you realize that it is a felony to withhold evidence of a crime?"

At this Winthrop turned almost apoplectic. "Mr. Scintilla, it wasn't like that at all! . . . I'm not trying to hide anything! Anyway, what could it possibly have to do with the . . . the crime? It wasn't as if anyone stabbed her while she was on that balcony . . . ."

I had to agree with him on that point. "But what could she have seen? Why did she give a start?"

It was Alice's turn to jump up. "Don't you see?" she cried, looking at us as if we were slow-witted children. "It's so obvious! *She had solved the riddle!*"

I looked alternately at the two of them. Winthrop, in turn, turned to his wife with a slack-jawed expression.

"You can't think . . . ," he began.

"Of course I can! What else could it be? We have to go there right now!"

And with that, she turned on her heel and almost ran up the stairs. For a few moments we were stunned into stony inactivity; then we darted after her as if she were a fox and we were

hounds at her tail. She was quicker than I had given her credit for, and she found herself on that balcony a good half-minute before we trudged up to her.

"Darling," Winthrop began, "what could we possibly see now? It's almost pitch dark . . . ."

Alice again looked at him as if he were a mentally deficient toddler. "Winthrop, you little fool, whatever Aunt Judith saw, she saw that night—so whatever it is must be visible only at night. What else makes sense?"

The balcony was rimmed on the three sides with urns that held luxurious and almost tropical foliage. I asked Winthrop to show me exactly where the dark figure of Judith had stood. I then went to the point he indicated, peering into the forest and the down-sloping fields beyond. After some moments:

"I can't see anything. What about you?"

I was addressing Winthrop, but Alice took it upon herself to reply. "Nothing," she said petulantly.

I continued to stare at that overgrown forest, not even conceiving what I could possibly be looking for. Then something caught the corner of my eye, and a chill of apprehensive disbelief went through me.

"Take a look at that," I said softly to the both of them, pointing high up in the trees to my right.

What I—and, soon, they—saw were four skulls, apparently tied together by string, wreathed from the neighboring branches of two trees; shining with a lurid pallor that could not have been natural, and hanging at such a height that I wondered how anyone could possibly have placed them there.

Whose four skulls they were I did not have to ask. They may have been imitations, they may have been the real thing. I was not about to undertake any more unauthorized digging in graves—I'd had my fill of that in New Jersey on another case—and it hardly seemed necessary. I had, of course, a sinking feeling that the skulls were all too real.

Imagine a man who digs up the graves of his ancestors, covers the skulls with phosphorus, drapes them—somehow—

across the branches of two trees like grisly Christmas decorations, so that they "laugh" eternally with the charnel laugh of the dead, and howl when the wind blew through their empty craniums—and then makes a riddle will that will plague his relatives with a macabre horror that he himself must have felt in some fashion in order to contrive this morbid joke. Such a man was John Kenneth Sarsfield.

And it seemed that the probing of his diseased psyche—the psyche of a man who had spent the last dozen years of his life in a sanitarium for reasons no one knew—would have some bearing on solving the tragedy at Sarsfield Manor.

CHAPTER EIGHT

I was not expecting, nor did I want, a share of the three million dollars that was the "reward" for solving the riddle of John Kenneth Sarsfield's will. I had more important things to consider. One chief difficulty was a simple matter of chronology. If it was really the case that Judith Kellar had seen the four skulls shining in the forest on her late-night venture on that balcony, and if Winthrop Sarsfield was telling the truth that her visit occurred only minutes before she was found dead on the threshold of her own bedroom, then the chief motive—a motive that I had frankly applied to Alice Sarsfield, Winthrop himself, and even to my old friend Charles Jameson, for all his denials—that someone had killed Judith to prevent her from "winning" the riddle was severely jeopardized:

For who, beyond Winthrop himself, was there to have seen her at the balcony, and who, even if they had seen her, could have so quickly concluded that she had solved the riddle and, in what seemed like bewildering haste, snatched that dagger from the weapons room and stabbed Judith as she made her way back to the bedroom?

The timetable was simply too compressed. Winthrop himself would never have admitted to me that he had seen Judith so soon before that dreadful scream, for it rendered him an immediate suspect; and I sensed that he was genuinely puzzled as to what Judith could have been doing on that balcony, until his wife, considerably more eager to solve the puzzle than he, had clarified the matter for him.

It is true that there were two other suspects—old George and young Jacob—whose exact whereabouts during these critical minutes was unknown. It did not take me long to ascertain that Jacob, at any rate, occupied a bedroom that also looked out onto the balcony. Could he have taken the occasion to kill his own mother simply in order to gain the prize? Or was that merely an excuse to dispense with her for other reasons entirely?

Little as I relished it, the time had come to confront Jacob.

I was prepared to meet an unstable, potentially violent person, but as I found him puttering in the library I appeared to startle him by the simple utterance, "Mr. Jacob Sarsfield, I wonder if I could have a talk with you."

The moment the words came from my mouth, he dropped a pile of books that he had been carrying—collected from the section of the library devoted to the old brothers Sarsfield's impressive holdings of occult titles—and turned on his heel to look at me as if I myself were a supernatural creature. As he saw who I was, he attempted to regain his composure, but his eyes still betrayed his wariness and alarm.

"I wish you wouldn't do that, Mr. Scintilla. I don't want to go the way of . . . of my father."

His face crumpled at the mention of his parent, and at once I sensed a turmoil of emotions in him that he was striving furiously to repress. Realizing that I may have misjudged him, I softened my tone.

"Jacob, why don't we just sit down and talk? There's no harm in that, is there?"

He continued to eye me with suspicion, but sat down with immense caution onto an overstuffed chair.

I sat in a chair facing him. For a time we both said nothing.

"Jacob," I began at last, "I'm sorry that I have to question you at what must be a difficult time for you—"

He cut me off abruptly. "Don't try to curry favor with me by false sympathy, Scintilla!" he lashed out. "You don't give a damn about my parents, and you and I both know it! All you care about is getting your client, the learned Charles Jameson, off the

hook and out of the chair! Well, let me tell you something, Mr. Private Investigator"—his voice dripped with sarcasm—"I'm going to see him fry if it's the last thing I do!"

I was not expecting such an outburst. Even in the depths of grief—if indeed he felt that—his bitterness and hatred of Charles took me aback.

I said quietly, "Why are you so convinced that he is the culprit?"

His sneer only deepened. "Oh, come now, don't be so dense! His hand was right on the murder weapon—we all saw him bending down over my mother with that knife in her back! Explain that away if you can!"

"Anyone could have stabbed her," I continued softly, "and anyone could have been found with a hand on that dagger. Perhaps he was trying to help."

"Perhaps not," Jacob parried, turning away from me with disdain.

I needed to steer the conversation in a different direction.

"Can you tell me something about your family life?"

That may have been even more of a mistake. He wheeled around to look at me and barked:

"Oh, no, you don't! You're not going to turn the tables on me! I know what they're saying . . . that I hated my parents and wanted to do away with them . . . ." For just an instant his face again collapsed in pain before resuming its sneer. "If I hated them so much, why was I living there with them all this time? My father"—his voice choked with emotion—"my father was a wonderful man . . . no one better . . . God, what he endured from my mother! But I didn't hate her either—her goddamn family had made her what she was!

"This whole family is cursed, Scintilla!" Jacob almost shouted. "Every one of them has some kind of taint! I must have it too, God help me, but I'm not a murderer! You can't pin this on me!"

Again not raising my voice, I said, "That dagger came from the weapons room, didn't it?"

"Of course it did!" he scoffed. "Where else? But don't try to tell me I was the only one who knew about it, or could have taken it. That bloody case was unlocked—and everyone knew it. I'm sure every bloody Sarsfield in this house poked their nose into that room at one time or other . . . particularly that little tart Alice, who's so intent on solving the riddle . . . she'll do *anything* to get that money!"

The thought seemed to lead him into a different line of argument. "Come to think of it, why the hell isn't *she* a suspect? God, if my mother was on the verge of solving the riddle, who but Alice had more reason to stop her? Have you thought of that, Mr. Detective?"

"Have you," I said, "thought of the fact that she was sleeping in a room she shared with her husband Winthrop when Judith must have been . . . struck?"

Jacob almost collapsed in crestfallen disappointment. But he revived quickly:

"Maybe they were *both* in on it!" He made the utterance as if he had discovered the theory of relativity. "Of course . . . how diabolically clever! Each providing the other with an alibi! Think of that, Scintilla, think of that!"

"I'll keep that in mind," I said dryly . . . but wondered if in fact he was on to something.

I talked a little more with him, but didn't seem to get anywhere. So after a time I got up, preparing to leave and let him go back to his books. But Jacob himself, once he knew the conversation was over, abruptly exited the room, as if my mere presence were a taint that he was desperate to avoid.

The library was, indeed, an impressive collection, both of general literature and of the books on magic, witchcraft, and less explicable subjects that the old brothers Sarsfield had found of such consuming interest. I doubted that there was anything here that would materially assist the inquiry, but I couldn't help scanning the shelves and wondering what kind of resources it would take to assemble such a collection today.

It was by the luckiest of accidents that I stumbled upon the

secret.

I had picked up a crumbling edition of Sidney's *Arcadia* and thumbed through it idly. The archaic typeface was difficult to read, so I quickly tired of the book and put it back on the shelf.

As I did so, a curious resonance in the wood made me look up sharply and ponder deeply. I was at the extreme right of the shelf, and I began to check the edges and top of the shelf—which occupied the entire wall—for anything unusual.

For the sound made by that book falling back into place suggested a hollow area directly behind the shelf.

It was not long before I found it. I had rested my hand casually at the right edge of the shelf, somewhat above my knees. There, I encountered an all but imperceptible circle, about the size of my thumbprint, raised above the wood. Pressing it gently, I found that the entire shelf simply slid away to the left, revealing a shallow pit with a metal ladder attached to one side; this led to an underground tunnel that appeared to run under the foundations of the entire house.

I quickly wheeled and closed the library door. There was no lock in the key, so I had to hope that the lateness of the hour and the apparent lack of interest in the library by the other occupants—except, perhaps, the inscrutable Jacob—would prevent any disturbance. There was no better time to get to the bottom of this matter than now, so I began my descent on that rusty metal ladder.

I had a small flashlight with me—luckily so, since the tunnel in front of me at the foot of the ladder was pitch dark. As I began walking down the tunnel, I observed a single set of footprints heading down the tunnel and back again—and the small, pointed shoes that made those prints could, I suspected, have only been made by Judith Kellar. She had done more, it seems, than merely solve the riddle of John Kenneth Sarsfield's will.

The way seemed phenomenally long, and after a time I began to walk more slowly. Looking behind, I could barely make out the thin pinhead of light from the single lamp I had left lit in the library. As the tunnel did not seem to bend or veer, I assumed

that we were heading due east—to the right of the estate, as the library was situated on the right or east side of the house. As I progressed I began to detect a fetid odor whose source—in a tunnel lined on all sides by neutral gray stone and littered only with dust and cobwebs—was more than a little disturbing.

I sensed the end of the tunnel only when its walls, illuminated by my flickering flashlight, suddenly gave way to a larger expanse. I had noticed a slight but unmistakable declivity in the path of the tunnel, suggesting that it was leading inexorably downward to an area—presumably a room of some kind—somewhat farther underground. The tunnel had to end in a room, as there seemed no reason to construct such a channel merely to provide an exit to another part of the Sarsfields' own estate.

I at last reached the threshold of the room, casting my flashlight quickly around it.

Oddly, the first thing I did was to count how many skeletons were hung upon the walls of the room, some by very curious clamps that caused the figures to be in highly peculiar positions. I thought there were sixteen of them—but then I realized that I had forgotten two more lying on a large oblong table of stone, one upon the other. The worst was the one figure on the wall that was not entirely a skeleton.

Only after that did I notice various metal utensils whose use required no explanation. Aside from these there were some old books lying around—one of them a battered *Malleus Maleficarum,* another a copy of Sade's *Juliette* that bore John Kenneth Sarsfield's inscription on the flyleaf. There was also a kind of leather notebook or ledger that, upon my brief examination of it in the near-dark, seemed to be a diary of some kind—relatively recent, if the clarity of the ink were any indication.

I would have explored it, and the room with its grisly trophies, more carefully if the world hadn't suddenly exploded in a galaxy of stars.

CHAPTER NINE

The gargantuan pain in my head was augmented by what seemed to be a beacon shining directly into my eyes, and which I eventually figured out was a kerosene lamp being held aloft a few feet above my face. The glare, in the midst of the surrounding darkness, made it difficult to ascertain who the holder of the lamp was. Gradually, as my eyes adjusted, they were able to focus in on my presumed assailant.

It was old George Sarsfield.

He was glaring at me with something approaching maniacal hatred. His breathing was stertorous, his eyes blazing, and his mouth muttering nameless obscenities to himself.

Groaning heavily, I sought to reach my hand up to my head to massage the area where I had been struck. But my hand moved only a few inches before its motion was abruptly halted.

I quickly realized that my hands and my feet were locked within four manacles at the corners of the long table in the center of the room. The rotting remains of the two bodies that had been there before had been unceremoniously dumped on the floor nearby. In a note of abstract wonder, I found myself impressed with George's strength in lifting me bodily onto this torture platform during my lapse of consciousness. I had no idea how long I had been out, nor how long George had been standing over me glaring and seething.

It was only after some moments that I saw that he had a dagger—curiously similar to the weapon that had dispatched Judith Kellar—clutched spasmodically in his hand.

George had seen my eyes open, but failed to address any words in my direction—all he did was continue to mumble incoherently to himself. Groggy and nauseous, I nevertheless made the attempt to speak.

"George, what do you think you're doing?"

For several moments he merely breathed heavily. Then:

"Mr. Joe Scintilla, you'll pay for your inquisitiveness. Do you hear me?" His voice was suddenly to a booming resonance. "You've chosen the wrong family to meddle with."

"What's your idea, George?" I said quietly. "You want to slit my throat? to torture me the way your ancestors did? to cut out my tongue so that I can't tell the world of the horrors in your family line?"

My taunt brought George—and, more pertinently—his weapon—dangerously close to my throat. "I warn you, Scintilla . . ." he hissed venomously.

"So these are your Sarsfields," I went on with muted venom of my own, "these your misunderstood geniuses. No: they were only sadists who chose this way to signify a rebellion against a society that had left them behind. They were too smart to believe in the occult—that was only another symbol of their defiance. Perhaps they found it too tame, too weak; so they resorted to...other means. It wasn't their cruelty, George, that was tragic; it was their puerility. They hated being ignored, and chose this way to assert their power."

It was more than reckless to talk this way to a man who was manifestly on the brink of losing total control of himself, but I felt I had little to lose. My life was hanging by a thread, but I had no inclination to descend into the humiliation of begging for it. George Sarsfield had devoted his life, and a large part of his sense of self, to championing his family line; and now he was brought face to face with the worst nightmare he could imagine. His ancestors were not shining beacons of civilization, but merely childish hoodlums.

My speech had a predictable effect.

"Shut up!" George barked in a voice raw with emotion. "Who

are you to speak of my family that way?"

I paid him little heed in resuming.

"So what happened, George? Why had they had all killed themselves so many years ago? Was it because their servant found out, or they themselves had had enough of this horror? Then the later Sarsfields settled into their Victorian mediocrity, and all this"—I took in the loathsome scene with my eyes, as that was all I could do—"would have been forgotten but for that antiquarian, John Kenneth Sarsfield—your own brother. Perhaps he was horrified at first; but the more he thought about it, and the more he studied the Sarsfields' journals, which must have gone into great detail about their picturesque rituals, the more he may have realized that what was done in the eighteenth century could as well be done in the twentieth.

"And so he had begun the horrors anew—only to be caught when he was sixty. They locked him up and destroyed all the papers they could readily find. But John Kenneth Sarsfield would have a posthumous jest if nothing else: he had dreamed up the riddle-will, and perhaps even expected one of you to stumble across these atrocities. And it happened just as he thought— Judith was here before you. Isn't that why she dragged you away after dinner the night of her death? Isn't that what she told you?"

My voice had grown stronger and stronger with each sentence I spoke, until it resounded against these stone walls that had borne so much horror.

George had mutated from rage to an overwhelming sadness. He began to weep quietly, muttering more to himself than to me:

"Stop it, damn you, stop it! . . . They *were* geniuses . . . they were . . . ."

"So is Hitler."

That remark was unwise, for it suddenly unleashed a torrent of anger that led George to brandish the knife in my face.

"You hold your tongue, Scintilla . . . I'll cut you! I swear I will!"

"Will you, George?" I said softly and evenly. "Is this how

you pay your respects to your ancestors? By mimicking the worst of their behavior?"

George seemed racked by a conflicting medley of emotions—anger, horror, loathing, confusion, disillusion. Almost without being aware of it, he brought the weapon close to my eyes and mouth, as if yearning to wipe the vision of this torture chamber from my sight and still the tongue that had shattered his dreams. Almost without realizing it, he sliced a long swath of red down my shoulder and forearm.

The curious thing was that I hardly felt the incision. It bled freely, but I was more surprised than pained by the injury.

"George," I said, "what are you going to do? Do you really want to follow in your ancestors'—and your brother's—footsteps? Am I going to be your next victim? Haven't you done enough harm by killing your own sister and thereby causing the death of your brother-in-law?"

He looked at me with genuine puzzlement.

"Wh-what are you saying?" he said, in a tone that suggested I had accused him of snatching the Lindbergh baby. Then a look of almost awed comprehension swept over him, and he whispered plangently:

"You think *I* killed Judith? Is that what you think? You... you believe that, just because she told me about this horrible place, I wanted to shut her up, and murdered her using one of the Sarsfields' own weapons? You must be insane . . . ."

There could be legitimate debate as to which one of us was more in control of his faculties at the moment, but I didn't raise the point. His befuddlement seemed so genuine that I was momentarily silenced.

"But if not you, then who?" I said, almost to myself.

"Mr. Scintilla, I'm no murderer. . . . Yes, I caught sight of you descending that ladder, and I knew that you would be making your way here . . . Judith had told me the whole story, and I was dreading anyone else finding this . . . this place. . . . I refused to set foot here until I saw you going there. I had to stop you! I had to!"

His eyes were developing that maniacal glare again.

"George," I said as soothingly as I could, "you've got to let me go. I'm only doing my job here. You don't have to become what your ancestors and your brother became. You have it in yourself to be better than they. . . . There is no taint in your family—there is no such thing. If some people have turned out badly, it doesn't mean everyone will. There has been enough horror and tragedy at Sarsfield Manor without you contributing to it. Let me go, and we'll see that this place is never heard of again."

He looked down at me, kerosene lamp in one hand and the now reddened dagger in the other. He looked at the latter with something akin to loathing before dropping it precipitately; its resounding clang on the stone floor startled the both of us. Turning ashen as he saw the wound in my shoulder, he dug deep into a pocket and got out a small key. With shaking hands he unlocked the manacles on my hands and feet.

I did not stand up immediately, as my head continued to throb. Slowly sliding my legs over the side of the grisly table, I rose gingerly to a sitting position. A wave of nausea nearly overwhelmed me, and the blood from my cut flowed down my arm.

To my momentary alarm, George bent down to pick up the dagger on the floor—but his only purpose was to rip some cloth off his own shirt to produce a makeshift bandage for me. I nodded to him in gratitude as he bound the wound crudely. When he finished, he flung the dagger as far from him as the narrow room would allow.

In silence, we trudged in unison down the long hallway back to the library. It was my fervent hope that we would be the last occupants of this chamber of horrors.

CHAPTER TEN

The cut in my shoulder required more stitches than I had ever had in me at one time, but the doctor who bound me up the next morning knew his business, and the wound was in any case not particularly deep; so I managed to get along without too much trouble. I wasn't expecting any more gunplay or swordplay, so I figured a bum arm wouldn't hold me back. The difficulties in this case were not physical but intellectual. I seemed to have all the pieces, but they weren't fitting together. Something was out of place; I sensed that I had failed to understand the significance of the most basic facts of the case.

I had no option, therefore, but to return to the police station. I wanted to look over the report one more time. What's more, there was one thing I had found that I needed to talk to Charles Jameson about, and urgently.

Before leaving the underground torture chamber at Sarsfield Manor, I had pocketed the notebook or diary of John Kenneth Sarsfield. George had momentarily looked askance at me, but said nothing and made no objection. So far, I had only had a chance to give it a cursory examination—but that was enough, at least on one point.

I once again sat down in front of Charles's cell, the notebook in my hand. Charles initially seemed happy to see me, but as soon as he caught sight of the notebook he froze and backed away in alarm.

"Wh-what do you have there, Joe?" he asked in a trembling voice.

"You seem to know what it is," I said mildly.

Rubbing a hand over his several-day-old stubble, he laughed nervously. "Looks . . . looks like some old ledger."

"Not as old as all that," I said.

Abruptly, he wheeled around so that his back was to me. It was as if I would disappear if he could not see me.

I was getting tired—tired of him, tired of this case, tired of the horror and madness of Sarsfield Manor and its clan. "Charles, why don't you face up to it?"

That made him spin around once more.

"What do you want me to say?" he almost shouted at me. Looking down quickly and harriedly at the notebook, he went on: "All right, I know what that is . . . of course I know. The question is: *What do you know?*"

"I know a lot of things," I said wearily, "but not everything. I know about the tunnel from the library. I know about the room where both the old brothers Sarsfields and John Kenneth Sarsfield carried out their atrocities.

"And I know you were there."

Strictly speaking, I didn't know that. But I realized I had hit home.

"Are you . . . are you thinking that *I* . . . that I had anything to do with that business?" he said in a frenetic whisper. "Yes, I stumbled upon that secret passage . . . yes, I saw the horrors in that room . . . the horrors that my ancestors, and the horrors that my own uncle, committed. But that was the extent of it! I never let *anyone* know what I'd seen . . . not even John Kenneth Sarsfield himself . . . although I gather he suspected . . . ." He trailed off.

"It says here," I said, tapping the notebook with my index finger, "that you were there in 1918 . . . just a year before you— and I—entered Johns Hopkins. Sarsfield says he thought you had found the passageway. No, of course you didn't tell him . . . but he could sense it by your altered behavior. You were shocked, appalled, traumatized . . . you were humiliated by what your family had done . . . what your own uncle had done....

Is that why you think the world is an evil place?—why you feel you are uniquely victimized by fate?—why you are perennially on the threshold of lapsing into depression and madness?"

My voice had unwittingly risen to a thundering boom, and my words did not fail to rouse the cheerless prisoner.

"What can you expect, Scintilla?" Charles Jameson spat back, with a sneer. "Think of yourself as an impressionable teenager, always taught to revere your family line . . . and then coming upon horrors that no human being ought ever to see! God, I thought I'd fallen into some horror out of the French Revolution!—something that Sade or Robespierre had crafted out of their perverse minds and souls . . . or something that Tiberius or Caligula had done for their amusement! Is it any wonder that I thought my entire universe had collapsed around me?

"I don't know what my uncle had written . . . but yes, I did stumble upon that horrible chamber. I remember knocking against that bookshelf by accident—I must have activated that hidden switch without intending to. . . . It was a bright summer day in 1918, but I plunged into that abyss of moral and spiritual darkness without a thought . . . tramped to that grisly stone room with those skeletons hanging in the most bizarre postures"—he rubbed his eyes as if to wipe out the memory from his sight and mind—"and a dreadful *fresh* one on that long table . . . the work of my own uncle. Who knows if it was the first, or the last? I have no idea what you saw there, but it couldn't have been any worse than what I glimpsed in that cataclysmic moment. . . .

"And the worst part of it was that I had to remain at Sarsfield Manor for weeks thereafter. I myself had insisted on spending the summer there . . . I wanted, God help me, to know my uncle better! . . . Well, I got to know him all too well! And the hideous part is that I had come to *like* him . . . and he liked me.

"Of course he knew something was up . . . I could hardly look him in the face, almost screamed when he touched me, could hardly eat or sleep . . . I saw him peer at me out of the corner of his eye . . . . He was thinking: *What does that boy*

know? And who will he tell? But he must have known I wouldn't tell anyone—it was too shameful and revolting. . . .

"Why did I even agree to go to Sarsfield Manor now, knowing what I knew? I dawdled in that library precisely to steer others away from the appalling secret . . . the secret that would reveal my family as a race of sadists and murderers . . . the secret that would bring shame and degradation upon everyone associated with that clan . . . ."

"But someone did find out," I said quietly.

"Yes, of course someone found out," he snapped. "That Judith . . . a shrew, but a smart, clever, resourceful woman. She didn't tell me, but I could tell from her smirk of triumph, and the way she bearded Uncle George that evening . . . . She may have been a Sarsfield, but she always scorned the line—always wished she were rid of the taint of her own heritage. . . ."

"And so you killed her," I concluded heavily.

Charles's reaction was nothing like what I expected.

He had been speaking more to the circumambient air than to me; but at my remark, he turned sharply to face me.

"I did . . . *what?*" he said in utter incredulity.

"Oh, come on, Charles," I said in exasperation. "You must have killed her to shut her up. You knew she would spill the beans about the horrors at Sarsfield Manor, and you thought you could keep the matter quiet by silencing her permanently."

He looked at me with a kind of wonder as if I were an alien from another planet who had just appeared out of nowhere in front of him.

"You . . . you think I killed her?" he whispered in a tone of awe. "Are you insane? I knew the secret would come out eventually . . . whether from her or from someone else. Why, I could have predicted that *you* would have found it—and I sure as hell wasn't going to kill *you!* No, Joe, the damage—for me—had already been done. I was already scarred . . . and shutting someone else up wouldn't have done a thing for me."

"Then, if not you . . . ," I said, more to myself than to him, "then who?"

Charles gazed down at me with an expression that could almost pass for wry humor.

"So, Mister Detective, you're stumped!" He snorted in mirthless humor. "You've solved so much . . . but you still haven't solved the case you were brought in to solve! Back to the drawing board, eh?"

I rubbed my face hard with my hands.

"Wait, Charles," I said, a bit harriedly. "There's something I don't understand . . . a number of things I don't understand. Let's go back to the scene of the crime. I'll give you the benefit of the doubt that you didn't kill Judith—"

"Thanks," he said dryly.

"But who did? Who *could* have? . . . Tell me again what you did. You heard footsteps—Judith's, I figure. You heard a scream. Then what?"

"Then," said Charles, as if speaking to a slow-witted toddler, "I went out into the hallway, saw the light streaming from Judith and Edward's bedroom, saw Judith lying on the floor with that dagger—"

"Hold it right there," I interrupted harshly. "Say that again: *You saw the light streaming from Judith and Edward's bedroom.* Are you absolutely sure of that?"

Charles gazed at me with puzzlement, as if I were trying to trip him up by some logical sleight-of-hand. "Of course the light was on. How else could I have seen anything? The hallway itself was pitch dark, and if the light hadn't been on in their bedroom, it would have been next to impossible to make out anything. Yes, there were large French windows at the end of the hall leading to the balcony, but there was not much of a moon that night—"

I waved him to silence.

"That's not important," I snapped. "There is only one thing that I need to know. *Where is the light switch in that bedroom?"*

Again that look of puzzlement and suspicion.

"I figure it must be right inside the door. The whole house was wired for electricity . . . had been done even before I'd

gotten there in 1918. I know my room's switch is there, so theirs must be also."

I again put my face in my hands. I sat there for what seemed like minutes before Charles, apparently alarmed at my reaction—I may also have been trembling—said tentatively:

"Joe, what is it? What have you found? What possible difference . . . ."

I raised my face to look up at him. My expression led him to trail off into silence.

"Charles, the murderer of Judith Kellar was her own husband, Edward Keller."

CHAPTER ELEVEN

Charles gave me a look that mingled incredulity, astonishment, and dubiety—a sense that I was pulling his leg and that my humor was in very poor taste.

"Joe, that's not possible. Edward was—"

I cut him off. "Charles, it is the only thing possible. He was the only one who had both motive and opportunity. It was just too horrible that the whole effort backfired on him . . . .

"Think of the motive, Charles. The idea that any of you— Alice, Winthrop, of you yourself—could have killed Judith to keep her from winning the three million dollars from the riddle-will was never plausible. People don't do things like that. It is evident that you all entered into the contest in a spirit of fun, and none of you were so desperate for money that you would kill one of your own relatives for it. Anyway, the *time* factor is all wrong. She discovered the secret of the riddle only moments before her death: who could have known about it in time to act upon it?

"And as for you or George silencing Judith because of what she had discovered about the Sarsfields . . . even that seems a stretch. George, the custodian of the family history, is an upright, decent man—he wasn't about to kill his own sister to prevent her from revealing what she knew. Like you, I suspect that George also realized that the secret would come out someday anyway. He may have tried to use persuasion, but he would never have stabbed his own sister in the back.

"No," I continued heavily, "it was only Edward . . . the long-

suffering Edward, who had endured decades of living with what everyone called a shrew . . . it was only he who could have developed enough hatred and rage to kill a wife he should never have married. Probably he had been seeking an opportunity for years . . . and this summons to Sarsfield Manor was a godsend to him, for he could, he thought, choose an opportunity where any one of you would be suspected of the crime, and it could never be pinned on him. It was a brilliant ploy—but it backfired."

"But Joe," Charles said, "listen to reason. Edward was lying in bed when Judith came in. Someone must have stabbed her then. It was the horror of seeing her dead that killed him."

"Charles," I replied, "you're wrong on nearly everything. Let me explain.

"Remember the nature of that wound. That dagger was razor-thin . . . there was almost no bleeding at the site of the wound—she died of internal bleeding. The blow was such that she must not even have felt it—especially if she was intent on other matters, as she obviously was. I well know"—I looked quickly down at my own shoulder, to Charles's puzzlement— "that a cut like that is scarcely noticeable."

I caught my breath for a moment.

"Let me tell you what must have happened. Edward had gone to bed early—or at least wished to create the illusion that he had. But Judith didn't turn in so soon: she was too concerned with what she had discovered earlier that afternoon. Edward saw a golden opportunity to commit the crime under everyone's nose . . . and he almost pulled it off.

"Imagine him listening in the dark for the approach of his wife. Perhaps he was planning to kill her as she entered; but when he heard her walk by his room, on the way to the balcony, he quietly opened the door—and stabbed her. *But she never felt it.*

"Judith walked right past his door—never knowing that she had been dealt a mortal injury. The rest is worse. Edward went back to bed, thinking he had finally rid himself of a hated wife; Judith kept right on walking. She went to the baclony, looked

into the forest, and saw the four skulls. *She had solved the riddle—with a dagger in her back.*

"Your cousin Winthrop saw her there—but it was dark, and he couldn't see the dagger sticking out of her back. And what did she do then? She quickly turned around, eager to tell her husband of the find. She opened the door of the room, turned on the light, and finally realized that she was dead.

"And Edward—poor Edward—do you wonder that he screamed like a madman? Do you wonder that he died of fright on the spot? You just said that the horror of seeing her dead killed him. *No—it was the horror of seeing her alive.*

"Think of the loathsomeness of it! Edward had killed his wife; he felt he was free. But no—several minutes later *she walks in and turns on the light.* She was the only one who could have done so: if anyone else had done the murder, that person would surely not have turned on the light so that Edward might wake up and see the perpetrator. No: Edward never knew what had happened to her—he had just stabbed her in the back, shut the door at once, and gone back to bed. But now—*here was his wife walking around as if nothing had happened.* Did he think her a ghost? an apparition? a vengeful corpse reanimated by hatred? Who knows? But it was too much for him—and he screamed his life away."

It was Charles's turn to collapse on the bed of his cell and cover his face in his hands.

"God, what an awful fate!" he said, his words muffled by his hands. "He didn't deserve it . . . . Yes, he may have been a murderer, but he didn't deserve to die that way. It was all a horrible tragedy . . . and somehow a weirdly fitting way to end the occupancy of Sarsfield Manor.

"That place ought to be torn down," Charles said grimly. "Or, at least, certain sections ought to be . . . sealed up for the good of the world. The taint, the curse, whatever it is, has gone far enough."

I didn't believe in taints or curses, but at the moment I wasn't about to dispute him.

I managed to persuade Police Chief Frank Powers that my reconstruction of the case was the only logical one. I was not entirely sure he believed me, but he was coming to recognize that the case against Charles Jameson was not as unshakeable as he had once thought, and that a clever defense attorney might easily secure an acquittal on the basis of reasonable doubt. Rather than face that humiliation, he released Charles and declared the case closed.

As for the riddle-will, it was determined to divide up John Kenneth Sarsfield's assets equally among the surviving heirs. I made it clear that I wanted no part of the legacy as the actual solver of the puzzle, and there was not the slightest hint that anything would come my way.

Charles's fleeting hope that Sarsfield Manor would be bull-dozed was wisely discarded. True, none of the remaining clan wished to occupy it, even though George and Charles did take quiet measures to seal up certain passages that ought to have been sealed up generations ago. It remains a monument to family pride and family tragedy, and perhaps one day the passage of time will have rendered it a harmless antique. But that time would be long in coming.

ABOUT THE AUTHOR

S. T. JOSHI is a widely published critic and editor. He is the author of such critical studies as *The Weird Tale* (1990), *H. P. Lovecraft: The Decline of the West* (1990), and *The Modern Weird Tale* (2001). For Penguin Classics, he has prepared three annotated editions of Lovecraft's tales, as well as editions of the works of Lord Dunsany, Algernon Blackwood, and M. R. James, and the anthology *American Supernatural Tales* (2007). His exhaustive biography, *H. P. Lovecraft: A Life* (1996), won the British Fantasy Award and the Bram Stoker Award from the Horror Writers Association. He is coeditor of Ambrose Bierce's *Collected Short Fiction* (2006; 3 vols.), and has edited several editions of the work of H. L. Mencken. He is coeditor of *Supernatural Literature of the World: An Encyclopedia* (2005; 3 vols.) and the editor of *Documents of American Prejudice* (1999), *Atheism: A Reader* (2000), *In Her Place: A Documentary History of Prejudice against Women* (2006), *Icons of Horror and the Supernatural* (2006; 2 vols.), *The Agnostic Reader* (2007), and other volumes. Among his writings on politics and religion are *God's Defenders: What They Believe and Why They Are Wrong* (2003) and *The Angry Right* (2006). He has compiled bibliographies of H. P. Lovecraft (1981; rev. 2009), Ambrose Bierce (1999), Gore Vidal (2007), H. L. Mencken (2009), and other authors. He lives with his numerous cats in Seattle, Washington.